The Swans of Harlem

Five Black Ballerinas,
a Legacy of Sisterhood,
and Their Reclamation of a
Groundbreaking History

The
Swans
of
Harlem

Adapted for Young Adults

KAREN VALBY

DELACORTE PRESS

Text copyright © 2025 by Karen Valby and 152nd Street Black Ballet Legacy Enterprises

All rights reserved. Published in the United States by Delacorte Press, an imprint of Random House Children's Books, a division of Penguin Random House LLC, New York.

This work is based on *The Swans of Harlem: Five Black Ballerinas, Fifty Years of Sisterhood, and Their Reclamation of a Groundbreaking History,* copyright © 2024 by Karen Valby and 152nd Street Black Ballet Legacy Enterprises. Published in the United States by Pantheon Books, a division of Penguin Random House LLC, New York, in 2024.

Delacorte Press is a registered trademark and the colophon is a trademark of Penguin Random House LLC.

Visit us on the Web! GetUnderlined.com

Educators and librarians, for a variety of teaching tools, visit us at RHTeachersLibrarians.com

Library of Congress Cataloging-in-Publication Data is available upon request.
ISBN 978-0-593-64356-3 (trade) — ISBN 978-0-593-64358-7 (ebook)

The text of this book is set in 11.3-point Warnock Pro Light.
Interior ballet slipper art by ID designer/stock.adobe.com
Front-of-jacket photographs: (clockwise, upper left) Sheila Rohan by Martha Swope © NYPL for the Performing Arts; Karlya Shelton, Courtesy of Colorado Ballet; Lydia Abarca by Martha Swope © NYPL for the Performing Arts; Marcia Sells by Sandy Underwood, Courtesy of Cincinnati Museum Center; and Gail McKinney-Griffith by Martha Swope © NYPL for the Performing Arts

Editor: Beverly Horowitz
Jacket Designer: Ray Shappell, based on design by Linda Huang
Interior Designer: Cathy Bobak
Copy Editor: Colleen Fellingham
Managing Editor: Tamar Schwartz
Production Manager: Tracy Heydweiller

Printed in the United States of America
10 9 8 7 6 5 4 3 2 1
First Edition

For Ava and Zinnia, always

Prologue

At the height of the civil rights movement, Lydia Abarca was a Black prima ballerina for a major international company, starring in iconic works like George Balanchine's *Agon* and *Swan Lake*, Jerome Robbins's *Afternoon of a Faun*, and William Dollar's *Le Combat*. Critics described her as "the dreaming soul of dance" and "a living ode to beauty, incapable of an ugly gesture or a false movement." She was the first Black company ballerina ever to grace the cover of *Dance Magazine*. She performed for queens and kings, in the movie production of *The Wiz*, and for Bob Fosse on Broadway. She was one of Revlon's original Charlie models. An *Essence* cover star. Roses collected at her feet around the globe.

Half a century later, during Black History Month, Abarca's thirty-two-year-old daughter, Daniella, wanted to brag about her mother to their friends and family. She went looking for evidence of all Abarca had done—all the barriers she had broken, all the history she had made—but in researching the history of Black ballet, she could only find stories about one young woman, Misty Copeland. Misty Copeland, Misty Copeland, Misty Copeland. The first Black ballerina, insisted the internet. And indeed, in 2015, Copeland became the first

African American woman to be promoted to principal dancer at American Ballet Theatre (ABT), breaking the company's seventy-five-year record of whiteness. Thank God for Copeland's talent and her perseverance, for the breaking of poisonous runs. But why, Daniella cried, had her own mother been so thoroughly disappeared from the telling of Copeland's accomplishments?

Just days later Abarca's only grandchild, Hannah, came home from preschool in the suburbs of Atlanta, her head flooded with stories about the singularity of Misty Copeland. Four girls in her class had chosen the ubiquitous ballerina as the subject of their Famous Black Americans project. Hannah had sat confused on the class rug, listening to how Copeland had been the first to kick down doors so that children like her could live more comfortably in their dreams.

"But what about Grandma?" Hannah blurted out at the dinner table that night.

Daniella was furious, unsure where even to direct her anger. "Where's your name?" she cried to her forgotten mother. "Where's your name?"

George Balanchine, long considered the father of American ballet, and the cofounder and artistic director of New York City Ballet, was famously said to prefer his ballerinas "the color of a peeled apple." (His apologists insist he was talking only about Suzanne Farrell, one of his most iconic muses.) To this day, City Ballet has yet to anoint a Black principal ballerina.

But it was also Balanchine, along with his City Ballet co-founder, Lincoln Kirstein, who recognized greatness in Harlem's own Arthur Mitchell and encouraged his rise to become the company's first Black principal dancer. Kirstein had been in the audience for Mitchell's high school graduation exercise at the School of the Performing Arts, when he performed a solo entitled *Wail*, choreographed to Béla Bartók's music. Mitchell had lacked formal dance training when he'd been accepted into the school. He relied instead on his exuberant sense of showmanship, auditioning in a rented white top hat and tails with a tap dance routine to Fred Astaire's "Steppin' Out with My Baby," taught to him by a vaudevillian performer he'd looked up in the phone book. Throughout his time there, Mitchell withstood pressure from the school's administration, which pushed him toward modern dance. They said "it was better for 'primitive peoples,'" he explained to a *People* reporter in 1975. "I said I wasn't raised speaking Swahili or doing native dances. Why not classical ballet?"

Upon Mitchell's graduation, Kirstein offered him a scholarship to the School of American Ballet, the preparatory school for New York City Ballet, telling the young dancer what so many successful Black people know to be true. "Lincoln put it to me with brutal frankness," Mitchell said. "He told me I would have to work twice as hard as anyone in my class."

Mitchell entered the company in 1955, the same year an exhausted Rosa Parks was told to give up her seat on a Montgomery, Alabama, bus. Some critics reduced a Black man in City Ballet to a "casting novelty" on Balanchine's part. Some said worse. Commercial television would hold out for years before it aired a performance of Mitchell partnering a white woman, but in 1968 he and Suzanne Farrell danced a pas de deux from Balanchine's *Slaughter on Tenth Avenue* on *The Tonight Show.* "And in living color, darling!" he cheekily told a reporter afterward.

Balanchine helped launch Mitchell into stardom by setting his 1957 abstract masterpiece, the central pas de deux in *Agon,* on his lone Black danseur and the white Southern ballerina Diana Adams. "My skin color against hers, it became part of the choreography," said Mitchell. His athleticism and technique were put to the highest test in a dance that was as sensual as it was intricate and austere. When a stagehand in the South balked at training the spotlight on a Black man, Balanchine told Mitchell to call upon the reserves of his own internal glow. Fellow City Ballet principal danseur Jacques d'Amboise remembered hearing Balanchine tell Mitchell, "You know, just make light brighter and don't worry."

Mitchell turned the lights up in every room he ever entered. Onstage and off, the force of his beauty and charisma hit like a wave. The man had key hooks for cheekbones and flashbulbs for teeth. He didn't smile; he shone. He didn't dance; he set a stage aflame. His herculean work ethic and his preternatural gifts as a performer, coupled with Balanchine's favor, earned him groundbreaking agency over his destiny. He became the first classical Black premier danseur in history, a beloved international star who performed on classical stages around the world, on Broadway, in the movies. Everywhere he went, critics hailed him as the exception to the rule that Black people had no place in ballet. But where some might have rested, fat on individual achievement, Mitchell only looked outside himself, wanting to do more.

In 1968, his career at City Ballet still going strong, news of Dr. Martin Luther King Jr.'s assassination shook the world. The trauma ignited within Mitchell a sense of spiritual purpose. He would build a ballet school in Harlem, the neighborhood that had raised him up. And because children deserve role models who show them what is possible, he would simultaneously establish the first permanent Black professional ballet company.

Art is activism. Let the gorgeous lines of his dancers' bodies serve as fists in the air.

When the school first started, in a church basement that doubled as a basketball gym, Lydia Abarca was a teenager living in the projects in Harlem with her parents and six younger siblings. She'd never had a Black dance teacher before. She'd performed only once in her life, as a fourth grader at St. Joseph's Catholic School, to a nun's choreography of "Waltz of the Flowers" from *The Nutcracker*. But as soon as she descended those basement stairs, Mitchell grabbed hold of her long, elegant feet and swept her into his tornado.

Abarca was a girl who loved to dance, who wanted to be a star. She wanted to be like her childhood heroes Ginger Rogers and Natalie Wood, emerging from limousines onto red carpets to snapping bulbs, the plot of her life playing out like one of the feel-good *Million Dollar Movie* films she loved to watch on her family's black-and-white television. And for a flash of time, a decade of her youth, she had a taste of all of that, as Mitchell's muse and Dance Theatre of Harlem's first prima ballerina.

But by the time her granddaughter came home confused and upset during Black History Month, all that was left of Abarca's legend were a few dusty plastic bins in the basement full of yellowing photographs, stacks of old programs, and an invitation for Abarca to perform for the queen. There were old profiles from *People* and the *Washington Post* that delighted in the star power of Mitchell's young ballerina. Her face beamed from magazine covers; reviews marveled over her beauty and talent. Her exquisite profile and flower-stem neck had been etched into a Revlon perfume box. Whatever remained of her spotlight years now lived in a couple of click-top bins and a shaky eleven-minute VHS recording of her breathtaking pas de deux in Balanchine's *Bugaku*.

Daniella knew the bones of her mother's past. But what she experienced in the day-to-day was a modest woman who took her administrative work in a doctor's office seriously, who'd taught ballet classes in Daniella's elementary school cafeteria and later helped her high school step team with their routines. She knew that her mother kept her figure to a strict size eight and that she booked extra work on local movie productions to make some cash on the side. And she also knew that in the evenings her mother drank too much rum. Daniella, a pastor and a single mother, had found the empty bottles hidden in her mother's trunk, behind her hair products under the bathroom sink. She understood that Abarca was lost or unhappy in ways her mother didn't yet have the language to express.

The gaslighting of one's own history can mess with a person's head. Abarca was losing grip of herself. The past and present had to converge if she was going to find any real way forward. She'd need the women who had been with her at the beginning of it all alongside her again. And they, it turned out, would need her too.

At the start of the Covid-19 pandemic, divorced from the normal rhythms and routines of their lives, five founding and first-generation Dance Theatre of Harlem ballerinas formed the 152nd Street Black Ballet Legacy Council, named for the street they helped make famous. Lydia Abarca-Mitchell (no relation to Arthur), Gayle McKinney-Griffith, Sheila Rohan, Marcia Sells, and Karlya Shelton-Benjamin had held each other up half a century earlier, and they would do so again through the dysregulating trudge of Covid-19. They all had been knocked off-balance by the anointing of Misty Copeland, by what felt like a deliberate scrubbing of their groundbreaking history. They would make peace with quarantine by gathering online every Tuesday afternoon, to throw out an anchor to one another from their scattered perches across the country. They would take advantage of this unexpected time to right a grievous wrong—they would take control of their own history. It didn't matter how daunting that task might have seemed. They had accomplished the impossible before.

These five intrepid girls had come together and made one of the most iconic childhood fantasies come true. Originally strangers, in so many ways the five had nothing in common, despite their being reduced in some early press reports to "black slum youngsters" and "high school dropouts." These young dancers were all unique human beings who came from specifically loving homes. Lydia Abarca was raised by working-class parents and had been bound for Fordham University on a partial academic scholarship when she first met Arthur Mitchell. Gayle McKinney-Griffith's father was a draftsman at a submarine engineer firm, and she was raised in a two-story colonial house on acres of land in Connecticut. Sheila Rohan's father died when she was a baby, and her immigrant West Indian mother cleaned houses on Staten Island to put food on the table for her eight daughters. Marcia Sells grew up on a Cincinnati cul-de-sac with a father who had his PhD and a mother who went back to school for her master's in her forties. And Karlya Shelton grew up in Denver in a working-class family that belonged to the local AME church and took elaborately planned road trips every summer to national landmarks in their Chevrolet station wagon.

What they shared, and what would forever bind them to each other, was a calling to the classical stage.

Misty Copeland, as she herself ardently insists, stands on the shoulders of all the early Dance Theatre of Harlem ballerinas, who in turn owe a debt to pioneers like Delores Browne, Janet Collins, Katherine Dunham, Sandra Fortune, Claire Haywood, Thelma Hill, Judith Jamison, Doris Jones, Carmen de Lavallade, Joan Myers Brown, Betty Nichols, Maria Tallchief, and Raven Wilkinson, and to women like Lauren Anderson, Aesha Ash, Debra Austin, and Cynthia Lochard, who carried the torch forward. Black excellence is not a one-off but a spectacular ongoing fact. The narrative of the successful Black woman as a lonely outlier, rather than part of a collective force, persists because we let it. No longer would the Legacy Council allow themselves, or the women who came before and after them, to be written out of history.

I started joining the ballerinas on Tuesday Zoom calls during the fall of 2020, the tape of George Floyd's murder playing on our screens in a loop. I wrote about the Legacy Council for the *New York Times* Arts and Leisure section, in a piece that mourned their erased legacies but barely scratched the surface of the rich narrative they'd begun to weave for me. I'm a white woman with two Black daughters who are dancers themselves. It is because of those founding Dance Theatre of Harlem ballerinas that today my girls and other young women of color can buy shoes and tights that match their skin tones. I think the Legacy Council's investment in my girls is part of the reason the women have allowed me so completely into their lives to tell their fuller story.

Over the past three years, as the five women invited me

into their homes and families and communities, they've shared stories about the enormity of their childhood dreams, the fight to make them real, the sustaining gifts of Mitchell's energy and vision as well as the cost of his ego and temper. They had decades-old wounds that needed airing and healing, and a present day that demanded processing. The world goes hard on us all, even mythical creatures like ballerinas. Their lives have been set to thunderous applause and the damp hush of obscurity. They once soared under the brightest of spotlights but have struggled since to find contentment and in some cases equilibrium and financial security. They drifted apart during their second acts, living in different countries, subsumed by the demands of motherhood and bills and illness and divorce and aging parents. But now they've embarked together on a third act of their own urgent making. Their power has always been in company with each other.

Some third acts begin in tragedy. Not long after that miserable year when Daniella went looking in vain for proof of her mother's past, Abarca hit her emotional and physical bottom. After surviving her darkest night, she received a four-page handwritten letter from her daughter, urging her to trust in the path ahead. "There's many chapters in life and this one you're experiencing now is called 'BREAKTHROUGH,'" Daniella wrote. She included in the letter a prayer she hoped her mother would get in the habit of reading aloud. Every night since, Abarca has recited the prayer, the power and vibration of her daughter's words allowing her whole body to relax.

Toward the end is a line that feels particularly resonant as five forgotten ballerinas risk entering the spotlight again.

"I bind love to me. I bind joy to me. I bind up negative thoughts and loose the peace of God in my life."

May this book be a literal binding of the 152nd Street Black Ballet Legacy Council's lives as artists and pioneers and wives and mothers and friends. May it acknowledge their intrinsic value as women as much as it celebrates their achievements as ballerinas. May it free them of plaguing thoughts so that they can release themselves of grievance and shame. May they find peace in the telling of their stories, and in the fact of our finally paying attention.

Act One

1

HARLEM KIDS LIVED IN A WORLD OF THEIR OWN MAKING. Not on the busy avenues like Broadway or Amsterdam, but on the quieter side streets, where there was more freedom. They played double Dutch and jacks and stickball. They hit the local playground, the Battlegrounds, for the monkey bars and swings, and for hoops if they could hold their own. They played street games, like the tag game Ringolevio or Hot Peas and Butter, in which the leader hid a belt behind a stoop or a trash can and then yelled out to the others, "Hot Peas and Butter, come and get your supper!"

They were kids with parents who expected them back inside when the streetlights came on and neighbors who looked down from open windows with chins in hands, ready to pull them out of trouble by their ears. Kids who knew when someone's older brother or cousin had started sniffing glue or trying heroin and would learn to avoid them when they got to acting like strangers. Kids who'd lived through six days of rioting in their neighborhoods in 1964, as people took to the streets to protest the murder of a fifteen-year-old Black boy who had been gunned down by a white police officer in front of his friends and a dozen witnesses. And kids who lived, too, through the awful spring of 1968, when Dr. Martin Luther King Jr. was murdered on the balcony of a second-floor Memphis motel room, just a few days before he was set to join a march on behalf of striking sanitation workers.

When news of King's death rained down upon Harlem, Lydia Abarca was seventeen. She remembers her mother, Josephine, crying at their kitchen table. "What are we going to do now?" her mother said. "They killed this one hope."

But two months after Dr. King's murder, one of Abarca's five sisters came home from her violin classes with ground-shifting news: "Lydia, they've got a Black man up there. He's going to be teaching ballet." Sandra, seven years Lydia's junior, had seen a flyer at Harlem School of the Arts, which was run out of the basement of the St. James Presbyterian Church on 141st Street and St. Nicholas. Somebody named Arthur Mitchell was starting a ballet program for kids in the neighborhood, and he wanted grown dancers too.

Lydia Abarca had let ballet go when she was fifteen, tired of giving her whole self over to something that never seemed to love her back. When she heard about Arthur Mitchell's new school, she'd just graduated high school and was headed on a partial scholarship to Fordham University in the fall. She was going to be the first Abarca to go to college—Josephine liked to think her baby could be a doctor—and in the meantime, she needed to make a little money working a summer job as a secretary in the lobby at a bank down the street from their projects. Monday through Friday, she'd rotate through her same three outfits—twelve years in a Catholic school uniform doesn't build an impressive wardrobe—for a paycheck doing work she hated and wasn't especially good at. When her sister told her about this Black man looking for dancers, she couldn't get the thought out of her head. "I'd never had a Black ballet teacher before," she says. "Maybe he would put a little soul in the steps to make them come alive."

Harlem School of the Arts was the creation of Dorothy Maynor, the international concert soprano and the first Black American to perform at a presidential inauguration (first for President Harry S. Truman in 1945, and then President Dwight D. Eisenhower in 1953). Maynor believed that all children, no matter their zip code, deserved world-class training in the arts. In 1963 she launched her arts education program out of St. James church, where her husband was the pastor, beginning with piano classes for a dozen students. As her ideals took root, so did her courting of Arthur Mitchell. She wanted him to lend his pedigree to the start of a dance program. It would take the assassination of Dr. Martin Luther King Jr. for him to answer her call.

Mitchell would bring ballet home to the neighborhood that had raised him, or, rather, that had witnessed his raising of himself. When he was twelve years old, Mitchell's alcoholic father went to jail after confessing to the murder of a numbers racketeer. "I called the family together and said, 'I will take care of everybody; don't you worry,'" Mitchell said in a 2016 recording with The HistoryMakers, a digital archive of filmed oral histories from prominent African Americans. He assumed responsibility for his mother, a coat-check girl at the "21" Club, and his four younger siblings. He took on his father's superintendent duties in their apartment building, got a paper route, and worked for a butcher. After he spent a year of studying tap and modern at the School of the Performing Arts, his teachers told him he would never be a dancer, not with his bad feet and tight muscles. Determined to prove them wrong, he threw himself so headlong into his training that he promptly ripped his stomach muscles apart. His work ethic was his superpower. For the rest of his life, he'd expect everyone else to match his zealousness of character.

And so Mitchell accepted Maynor's offer to lead the dance division of her arts center. He planned to build an internationally renowned school that would once and for all prove that a person's skin color was irrelevant to their right or relationship to classical dance. His guiding ethos was as simple as it was revolutionary: Ballet belongs to everyone. Ballet benefits everyone. The discipline it demands, and the beauty it gives back, can transform lives. As he put it more bluntly, "You're not going to stick a needle in your arm when your instrument is your body."

He called his friend and financial adviser Charles De Rose

for help. A street kid like Mitchell, De Rose was an Italian boy who grew up thirty blocks north in Washington Heights and climbed the ranks to become a partner in a Wall Street investing firm. At the height of Mitchell's City Ballet career, he had asked De Rose to put some of his money away so he wouldn't blow it. "Now he's calling me saying, 'I need my savings. I want to build a school. I need to buy the kids toe shoes and build a special floor,'" says De Rose. "I said, 'Arthur, you're coming to the end of your earned income life as a dancer. You can't lift the girls anymore, because your back is killing you.'"

But Mitchell felt divinely called to his mission and wasn't going to let any practical concerns cloud his vision. "We were offered to be a part of Lincoln Center," De Rose recalls, "to come under their umbrella, where they would do the fundraising for us. Arthur said, 'Why do people of color always have to go downtown? Why can't people start coming uptown?' He told me, 'Charles, what I want is for the Dance Theatre of Harlem to be like a little diamond on the beach. When people are walking by, they'll see something sparkling, and we'll make them come over and see what it is.' This was the burn-the-boats mentality he had. How do you not fight alongside somebody like that?"

That summer Mitchell juggled his early-morning swims at the Y, daily classes at City Ballet, and rehearsals for the Broadway musical revue *Noël Coward's Sweet Potato*, in which he acted, sang, and danced, all while getting his Harlem operation off the ground. In the first month of the school, a reporter captured him schooling sixteen little Black girls at the barre. "Now, I don't want to see spaghetti," he warned the children, who loved their boisterous new teacher but also complained to their mothers that he was mean. "I want to see straight knees. Keep that knee straight, Fatso!"

When Lydia Abarca first stepped into Mitchell's studio, that windowless basement of St. James, expecting to join a dance class, she saw a couple of lamps casting a dirty yellow glow onto the floor of the gym where the church's AAU team practiced. The only source of light in the room was Mitchell himself, a man with movie-star good looks, wearing flared trousers and a tight jersey shirt that appeared painted onto his lithe muscles. His style of speech was fast and clipped, every elongated vowel and sharp consonant potent with urgency.

"Kick off your shoes; let me see your feet!" Mitchell said to Abarca by way of greeting. She slid out of her street shoes and angled her stockinged feet for him, extending and arching them into the shape of perfect cashews. A dance critic would later praise "those feet, so curved and strong one can imagine her picking up the stage with them." Mitchell took in her willowy figure, her flute of a neck. His mind whirled with possibilities for this shy sundae of girl, standing before him in leg warmers she'd knit for herself on her living room couch. He told her to join the dancers he'd summoned to audition for the company the following day.

Abarca did as she was told. She returned to the studio the next day for the audition, looking upon the tiny group in awe.

There was Walter Raines, who had trained at the School of American Ballet. He had performed with the Stuttgart Ballet in Germany before the grind of trying to convince white companies of his talent led him to quit dancing. And Llanchie Stevenson (who would change her name to Aminah Ahmad after converting to Islam and retiring from dance in the early 1970s), who had graduated from the School of American Ballet only to be told that Balanchine wasn't ready for a Black ballerina to break the color line of his corps de ballet. "When I came up, I did not blend in," says Ahmad. "Raven Wilkinson could blend in when she was at the Ballet Russe de Monte Carlo. Janet Collins, too, at the Metropolitan Opera. I was darker." But Stevenson was able to find work as the first Black female dancer in Frederic Franklin's National Ballet of Washington. She'd been touring with the company throughout the United States for a year, resigned to the fact that in some Southern cities she'd be told during rehearsal that she'd have to sit out the evening's performance for safety reasons.

Mitchell spoke to them all with the passion of a preacher. He asked the dancers to consider the magnitude of his vision— a permanent Black company that would show all the institutions that had denied, tokenized, or marginalized their talents how much bigger and grander ballet could be. Mitchell had already enlisted Karel Shook, an early mentor whom he persuaded to leave his post as ballet master at the Dutch National Ballet for Harlem. His dancers would be groundbreakers, ambassadors, and most of all artists, whose destiny would be determined solely by their ability, their work ethic, and their commitment to excellence. "We're going to show people that Black people can do ballet," he told the dancers, still breathing hard from the exertion of his class. "We're going to shock the world!"

As Abarca packed her bag at the end of the rehearsal, her head spinning from the fervor of Mitchell's speech, he appeared at her side, tapping his wooden counting stick on the floor. When he told her to come back the following day at the same time, she explained that she was expected at the bank in the morning. Mitchell brushed off her concerns. He offered Abarca $150 a week to quit her job and let him transform her into a ballerina. "All I heard was $150, and I said, 'I'm here, I'm yours.'"

Her mother, Josephine, was apprehensive.

But when she told her husband that their daughter was quitting the bank to dance, he didn't interfere. Francisco, or Tito as he was known in the neighborhood, worked as a custodial engineer—Josephine hated anyone ever referring to him as a janitor—at Brooklyn College and at Macy's. With a seventh-grade education, Francisco wasn't a reader and talked even less. He relied on Josephine, a part-time telephone operator who worked two nights a week, to read him the want ads and fill out his job applications. He was a father who'd grown up without a father, so he left the emotional work of parenting to Josephine.

Born and raised in Puerto Rico, Francisco demanded that English be spoken in his house, which perhaps explained his lack of conversation skills. The only time he ever slipped into his native tongue was to bark orders at the kids. *Cállate la boca! Siéntate! No toques eso!* No reading at the table. No walking around in bare feet. When he got home from work, Francisco liked to disappear into his room to watch his science-fiction shows on TV. His days were long, and he wanted the house quiet at night. "Face the wall; go to sleep!" he'd shout if he heard any of his seven kids playing past their strict seven-thirty bedtime.

Lydia shared a room with her brother, Julio, the only boy of the family. (When Francisco finally got his son after five girls, he banged on every door in the apartment building to share his triumph.) While Julio slept, Lydia would stay up late reading library books—Nancy Drew, Greek mythology—under the covers with a flashlight, eager for a portal into worlds free from the sour smell of government cheese and powdered milk.

The family lived in a first-floor apartment in the Grant Houses, a public housing project on 125th Street and Broadway, with bars over three layers of windowpane that had always made Lydia worry as a girl about how Santa Claus would get to them on Christmas morning. In the summertime, they roasted from the heat with only a box fan for a breeze. Lydia was the ringleader of her six younger siblings, directing them in little dance routines and games of make-believe. They'd play on the concrete playground out front, hiding in the cement barrels or hanging on the monkey bars, but whenever it rained, four of the siblings inevitably started coughing and wheezing until their faces turned blue. Josephine would pile the asthmatics into a cab, and they'd rush over to Columbia-Presbyterian, where she had given birth to all seven babies. One night, triaged in a booth with an emergency-room doctor, Lydia was presented with the newly invented rescue inhaler that would save her again and again, no matter the weather.

The children were a tight-knit unit; Josephine discouraged them from looking outside the family for friendship. See how the other girls in the building took offense at Lydia's loose Puerto Rican curls, she pointed out. See how they'd look at her with curled lip. *You think you're cute 'cause you got that good hair?* they'd sneer at her. "They're jealous of you," Josephine warned. "You can't trust them."

Lydia spent hours sitting cross-legged in front of their black-and-white television watching frothy RKO musicals like *Top Hat* and *The Gay Divorcee.* Watching those movies on repeat made her fall in love with dancing. "I was a shy, quiet kid," she says. "You could say boo to me, and I'd jump. I was so skinny my knees looked at each other. But those movies lit up something in me. Dance was Hollywood and the gowns and the limousines and the big bands playing behind you. I didn't see any of that in my neighborhood, but I saw it in all those movies with their happy endings. And I wanted that for myself."

A family who lived on the other side of the elevator bank from their apartment had a record player. Josephine would let Lydia cross the lobby and dance along with them to the latest songs by Martha and the Vandellas and the Marvelettes. Celia, the second oldest, would sometimes look at her sister, marveling at the invisible string that seemed to keep Lydia hovering aloft from everyone else. "It was almost like Lydia was born to be a dancer," says Celia, who took a free dance class at PS 125 as a little girl. When the teacher pointed out that her leotard was on backward, she was so embarrassed that she never danced again. "My parents would always tell me as a child, 'Sit up straight!'" says Celia. "Nobody ever had to tell that to Lydia."

Every Sunday the Abarca family went to St. Joseph's Catholic Church, two blocks from their apartment on 125th Street and Morningside, where their daddy would nod off during the Latin mass, making his children giggle. Josephine found a way to send four of her seven kids to St. Joseph's Catholic School, where Lydia met her class for a half-hour mass every morning before school. It was a nun at St. Joseph's who first saw the ballerina inside Lydia, after choreographing a brief number from *The Nutcracker Suite*'s "Waltz of the Flowers" for her fourth graders to perform at a school recital. The sounds of Tchaikovsky on the fuzzy speaker, and the thrill of finding both freedom and order in a simple routine, released something vital in the girl. "I was in heaven. Whatever the nun gave us, she got 150 percent of Lydia doing it. And when we did the performance, and the steps matched the music, and there was a big crescendo in the music, it was all just so fabulous. At nine years old, I was fulfilled." Afterward the nun pulled Josephine aside and begged her to get her daughter into some formal training.

Resourceful to her core, Josephine discovered that Juilliard, at the time located just two blocks down from their projects on Broadway, was hosting auditions for dance classes. "You're going to go, and it's going to be a lot of white people sitting at a table," Josephine told her daughter beforehand. "I don't want you to be nervous, but you're going to have to perform for them." The little experience Lydia had of white people in Harlem—nuns, police, the dentist—had made her wary. But on the big day, she walked head held high into a room with a glittering chandelier, mirrors on the walls, and a grand piano in the corner. The row of white people holding pencils to paper vanished as the girl disappeared into melody. Lydia could sense when the pianist was wrapping up and decided to pull out her split for a grand finale, waggling her hands over her head as the judges peered down at her. She was awarded a full scholarship for Saturday ballet classes.

But, oh, how that first class let her down! A stern white man told Lydia to go stand facing the wall. She grabbed hold of a barre with the rest of the girls, their feet already planted in tight Vs. Bend your knees, straighten your knees, over and over. "Ma, I thought this was going to be a dance class," she fussed to Josephine once she was safely back in their apartment. "When do we dance?" Josephine waved her off, telling her, "Just do what they tell you to do."

Every Saturday for four years, Lydia stood at the barre, bending, straightening, wondering when they'd finally start dancing. She kept going because she understood the cachet of being a Juilliard student. One day, when she was swinging on the monkey bars at Riverside Park, a white couple walked by and noticed her pointed feet. "You have ballerina feet. You should try dancing!" the woman told her. Lydia loved calling back, "I go to Juilliard!" That meant something to the outside world, even if it didn't mean much to her. And the white girls in class were nice enough. She got friendly with one of them, who invited her to spend the weekend with her family. "But I almost felt like a little show-and-tell in their big old house," says Lydia. "So I just went the one time." She had her mother in her ear when it came to girlfriends. "Don't need 'em, don't trust 'em."

As the oldest, Lydia had always been tasked with the bulk of the babysitting and housework. By the time she'd turned ten, though, she'd just wanted to float away into her movies and her novels. So one afternoon, resentful of her load of responsibilities, she ran away to Grandma Goldie's apartment, twenty blocks uptown. Goldie took sympathy on the crying girl, and as a treat suggested they spend the afternoon with her cousin Iris. The girls were told they could go either to the Coliseum or to Radio City Music Hall. Lydia voted for the Coliseum because it sounded like the one in Rome she had seen in books, and what was so great about a radio station anyway? But Iris wanted Radio City Music Hall. Their grandma cast the deciding vote. The three headed downtown for an afternoon showing of the new Jerome Robbins movie, *West Side Story*.

Of course, this was no radio station. When the Rockettes performed, Lydia felt like she was watching the cast of one of her *Million Dollar Movie* films kick free from the television. And that was just the windup to the main event. When the lights darkened, the brilliant curtain opened onto a world of operatic tension and high romance, with Puerto Ricans and their working-class white rivals dancing and singing for their lives in a neighborhood that looked just like hers. Lydia was a goner. *I want to do that; I want to do that,* she remembers thinking. *The movie was dancing, and it told a story, and it's in Harlem, and it's about Spanish people!* Soon she had her siblings calling themselves the 550 Jets, in honor of their address, 550 West 125th Street. When her godfather gave the family a record player, she wore out the grooves on the movie's soundtrack.

In high school, Lydia Abarca was granted a scholarship to the Harkness Ballet's professional training program, which was run out of a four-story brick mansion on East 75th Street, just off Fifth Avenue. "I would get off the bus and be in another world completely," she says. "Doormen opening doors for you, taxicabs everywhere." After school and all day Saturdays, she diligently took her pointe classes, and adagio classes, and Russian character classes, enduring the stiffness of all that training without her teachers ever paying her proper mind, let alone giving her a reason for all her hard work. A dancer trains for the stage, yet not once during those years was Abarca given an opportunity to perform. Sometimes she'd linger outside company rehearsals, only to find herself shooed back to class. "Move on," they'd scold the curious Black girl. "Don't stand in the doorway."

Harkness soon shifted its scholarship program to the June Taylor studios on the Upper West Side. One afternoon while she was there, Abarca heard live drumming and music coming from across the hall. She sneaked out of her ballet class and discovered Jaime Rogers, the diminutive Puerto Rican actor who'd played Loco in her beloved *West Side Story,* leading a spirited jazz class. Now, here was some dancing. Abarca started sneaking into his workshop, desperate for some of that pulse and joy. But when school officials caught wind that Rogers had a stowaway, they marched Abarca back to her ballet class. Listening to their reprimand, she realized with cold certainty that she was finished pretending she was ever going to be a ballerina. Why train and train without the promise ever of a stage? "I'd become convinced that for a Black girl, ballet was an impossible climb straight to a dead end."

She was fifteen when she quit dancing. She focused on her grades. She took a year of Latin. She joined the drum corps in her school band. She got into college and picked her first-semester courses—economics, theology, Spanish, and philosophy. She fell in love with her first boyfriend and tried to keep him a secret from her father.

But now Arthur Mitchell was telling her that ballet was meant to be shared with audiences, that he was going to give her a stage. She hadn't realized the history of aspiring dancers being turned away from companies because of the color of their skin. Listening to Mitchell, she realized for the first time that ballet could represent something larger than a series of technical exercises to be silently endured. "Wait a minute; you're telling me I can make a living from this?" she remembers feeling. "You're telling me that we can shock the world and can show people that their blindness is their fault and has nothing to do with us?"

She begged her mother to understand that this wasn't just Arthur Mitchell's dream now but hers as well. "I got to do this, Ma. This is my one shot."

Ultimately, Abarca dropped out of Fordham after one semester. She'd failed two of her classes, after missing so many because of Mitchell's rehearsal schedule. Her brokenhearted mother ate the cost of the tuition not covered by scholarship. Abarca vowed to herself that when Dance Theatre of Harlem really made it big, she'd repay her parents with a house, by finally moving them out of the projects.

A month later, four of Mitchell's new dancers—Lydia Abarca, Llanchie Stevenson, Walter Raines, and Gerald Banks—made the three-hour bus ride to Rensselaerville, New York, to perform in front of a library audience. Mitchell was busy in rehearsals for his Broadway show, so Karel Shook accompanied the dancers to their first lecture-demonstration.

In their makeshift dressing room, Abarca applied some simple lipstick and mascara. When she looked over at Stevenson, who had laid a towel on top of a dresser and neatly unpacked her entire makeup kit, her stomach dropped. Rows of lipstick and eye shadow. Trays of false eyelashes, which Abarca had never even seen before. Stevenson had come up as the first Black ballerina to join the corps de ballet of Radio

City Music Hall, where she'd been expected to wear a full face of stage makeup that would last through the day's four shows. When she toured with the National Ballet of Washington, she'd traveled with her personal makeup case, knowing she was on her own in a white company.

In Rensselaerville, Abarca studied Stevenson's trays of false eyelashes on the dresser top and knew she was in trouble. (Mitchell eventually realized he'd have to spring for a company makeup class, in which a flamboyant older woman with ostrich plumes for eyelashes schooled the dancers. "There should be no line of demarcation," she'd shout about the art of applying base. "No line!") Raines, who was so skilled with makeup he could contour a cleft onto his chin, took pity on Abarca's naked face. "Walter told me, 'The audience has to be able to see your eyes and your mouth!' I'm telling you, he beat my face. I'm looking in the mirror as he works, going, 'Oh my God, I look beautiful. I've never seen myself look this good before!'"

When it was time for the performance to begin, Shook introduced the small audience of cultural elites who'd gathered in the library to Arthur Mitchell's four new dancers. The program started at the barre and then proceeded to center work, where the dancers progressed into more dynamic, full-body movements. Stevenson and Raines danced a pas de deux from Mitchell's *Holberg Suite*, still a work in progress then. And Abarca and Banks performed the pas de deux from what later would become the first movement of Mitchell's *Tones*. It was her first time ever dancing on pointe in front of an audience.

"By no stretch of the imagination could one have called this a good performance," Raines would tell Jacqueline Moore Latham for her 1973 PhD dissertation on Arthur Mitchell. "The four of us could hardly stand up, let alone dance. Llanchie and I had danced more than Lydia and Gerry, but that made little difference as we were literally falling all over the place." But Raines quickly realized he'd underestimated the emotional power of their raw artistry. "It was the reaction of the people after we had finished that struck me. It was the look on their faces—expressing that they had just witnessed one of the most beautiful things that they had ever seen in their lives."

Sitting among the audience that day was Abarca's grandmother Goldie, the only family member who could take the day to make the journey upstate. After the show, Goldie hugged her granddaughter tight. "You looked a little shaky up there," she told Abarca, her voice thick with pride. "But, honey, I can tell you're going to be really good."

2

THAT SAME SUMMER, SHEILA ROHAN TRAVELED BY BUS, ferry, and two different subway lines to get from Staten Island to Harlem. Her sister Nanette had sent her looking for a man named Arthur Mitchell, who was putting together what she understood to be a little theater group for Black people. When Sheila arrived, weary from the commute, having arranged with family beforehand to watch her three young children, she was taken aback by the scene at the church. *Oh my God, they're real ballerinas,* she remembers thinking.

There was Lydia Abarca, stretching her endless legs at the barre. And Virginia Johnson, who'd spent her childhood in Washington, DC, training at the Washington School of Ballet, only to be told by her teacher when she graduated that she would never have a career in ballet. Now she was a student at New York University, looking to avoid being shunted off on the modern-dance department. There was regal Patsy

Ricketts, who'd come up in Jamaica's National Dance Theatre Company and then trained at the Martha Graham School of Contemporary Dance. Meanwhile Sheila Rohan was a twenty-seven-year-old wife and mother who'd long since tucked away her pointe shoes and resigned ballet to a chapter of her youth. She had a part-time job selling insurance to help make her family's monthly rent of sixty-seven dollars. But when Mitchell saw her on the steps, he told her to go on already and find a place at the barre.

Sheila's mother, Marie Elizabeth, born on July 4, 1900, left the French side of St. Martin alone by boat as a young girl. Eliza, as she was known, landed on Ellis Island, then in quarantine, and finally with relatives in New Brighton, a West Indian enclave on Staten Island. Sheila's father, Frederick, who'd grown up with Eliza, would later immigrate to America and settle in New Brighton too. Reunited in a community so thick with relatives and immigrants it felt in its own way like their island village, Eliza and Frederick married. She would go on to give birth to eight daughters, one every two years for nearly two decades.

Frederick found work as a tailor, at a dry cleaner, and on the docks. Eliza—whose family and friends called her Za, or sometimes when praising her, "The Great Za!"—was a domestic worker. She cleaned the houses and helped raise the children of prominent Jewish and Italian doctors and businessmen in Staten Island's wealthy Todt Hill neighborhood. The family lived in a second-floor apartment, with floorboards so thin the sisters could spy through the holes at the congregation cater-wauling below in the storefront Pentecostal church. On Saturdays, the girls went to a neighbor and got their hair pressed. On Sundays, they went to the Bethel AME Church; Eliza was as devoted to the Sunday service as she was to the traditional full-course meal she prepared for her daughters afterward.

Shortly after Sheila turned one, Frederick died of a stroke. He was in his early forties. His body lay in an open casket in their tiny living room for the weekend, as family and neighbors gathered to comfort and weep. Eliza slept with the baby in bed with her, while the other seven sisters piled on top of each other like kittens in the second bedroom. They were never alone in their grief. Eliza's sister lived next door, and there were cousins and aunties all up and down the street who sustained them in their time of loss.

As a single mother, Eliza had to be strict, strong, and un-sentimental. "You'd better do it right when she said it" was how one of Sheila's sisters, Delores, described her parenting style. No rolling your eyes and putting your hands on your hips, or you'd get smacked with whatever she happened to be holding in her hand. Eliza had eight girls to raise and no time for foolishness. Even with all that responsibility on her shoulders, Eliza still made room for joy. In the summers, she would pack sack lunches and pile her daughters onto the train for day trips to Rye Beach or Bear Mountain. There were birthday parties at the apartment and New Year's Eve gatherings that could go on for days. Twice a year she'd have all the girls dress up, and they'd make the trek into the city for the big West Indian dances at the Harlem Renaissance Ballroom, where they'd reunite with cousins from other neighborhoods.

Everybody babied Sheila, and not just because she was the baby. She had asthma and was prone to bouts of pneumonia; every winter cold knocked her flat. She was the only one of Eliza's girls who fell victim to the polio epidemic that blew through Staten Island in the late 1940s. Seven years old, a bird of a child with legs suddenly caged in thick braces, Sheila had to miss an entire year of school. A nurse came by the house three times a week to exercise her limbs on the living room sofa. Delores remembers the time as awash in worry: a mother who couldn't skip work, and seven sisters trading off care. Someone was always telling the baby in the family goodbye, promising to play paper dolls later or read together that night. Somehow Sheila held on to faith that this, too, would pass. "I just kept thinking, *I'm going to get up and get over this,*" she says. "I always believed I would walk again." When she finally emerged back into the brightness of childhood, her legs were diminished but throbbed once more with feeling. The family doctor prescribed exercise. Movement was the only thing that would bring this child's body fully back to life.

Sheila's second-oldest sister, Nanette, had an idea for how to help. A lover of art and design, Nanette was a student at the Fashion Institute of Technology when she signed with the Harlem-based Ophelia DeVore modeling agency. She became one of the first African American models to book print commercial work, in advertisements for brands like Lysol and

Jaguar. At a fashion show, Nanette met Romare Bearden, the collagist and painter, whom a preeminent Manhattan gallery owner once referred to as "the pictorial historian of the Black world." In 1954, she married Bearden in her Staten Island church, then celebrated with a modest reception at Eliza's house.

Told of the doctor's orders for Sheila's recovery, Nanette found and paid for weekly tap and ballet classes at a storefront studio in Staten Island's Stapleton district. She bought Sheila her first leotard, tights, and ballet shoes. "I don't see how my mother could have afforded it otherwise," says Sheila. "Even if classes were only ten dollars. In those days, ten dollars was groceries."

Blessed by Nanette's generosity, Sheila developed a new Saturday routine. Each week she and Delores would set off on the three-mile walk over the hill from their home to the George Sturgis dance studio. Delores would linger in the cluttered space watching her sister, the only Black girl in the class, form her body in ways precise and new. At the spring recital, the whole family, which felt like half the neighborhood, really, came to watch Sheila's first performance. "I never wanted to dance," says Delores, who as a child chose the softball field over the dance studio. "But when Sheila was onstage, I could imagine myself up there. That's what she did when she danced. She let me be in my imagination for a bit."

It wasn't long before gentle Mr. Sturgis would pull Nanette aside, humble with the knowledge that he'd taken her talented sister as far as his skill set allowed. Nanette convinced their mother that Sheila, by now around thirteen, was old enough to ride the ferry into Manhattan. Nanette would meet her on the Manhattan side and escort her to private lessons she'd arranged in Midtown with the stern Italian instructor Vincenzo Celli, a former principal dancer and choreographer at La Scala opera house. She paid for the classes, the car services, more leotards and tights, and the first pair of pointe shoes, which felt like rocks on Sheila's feet. Nanette took Sheila to museums and concerts and plays and to Lincoln Center to see *The Nutcracker.*

The precision of ballet, the demands it placed on Sheila's muscles and line—it called to her, even if her ambitions were modest. She knew that Black girls weren't welcome in classical institutions like the School of American Ballet or Juilliard. That they couldn't even get an audition at American Ballet Theatre. She'd read stories about her hero Raven Wilkinson, who'd spent five years dancing with the Ballet Russe de Monte Carlo, facing ugly rejections from segregated hotels and narrow escapes from the Ku Klux Klan on tours through the South. One night in Montgomery, Alabama, Wilkinson was forbidden from performing onstage, warned by the company manager to stay in her hotel and not open the door for anyone. While the Ballet Russe de Monte Carlo enchanted the audience with their gift, Wilkinson watched a cross burn outside her hotel-room window. After being told it was too dangerous for her to continue traveling with the company through the South, she left the company and eventually found work with the Dutch National Ballet. She was never again hired by an American ballet company.

Sheila had no interest in leaving her life on Staten Island to join some white company abroad. "I was dancing for the love of this wonderful art, not to be onstage," she says. "I danced for my own self-expression and to help me come to a greater understanding of life." She was also the child of a deeply practical mother. Rohan was raised to graduate from high school with honors, then go on to college to study and become a teacher. That was the plan, and Eliza expected her daughters to stick to it.

But then Sheila met Ellsworth. She was sixteen, at a friend's house for a backyard barbecue. She stepped out the back door wearing a pink dress. The glow of her under the porch light nearly struck dumb a handsome and charming boy from the next neighborhood over. "My goodness," Ellsworth said to his friend. "That girl's the one for me."

When she got pregnant at eighteen, Sheila knew to expect Eliza's rage. "But then the worst thing was, she cried. And you can imagine how awful that was because Mama was not the type to cry." By then Ellsworth had graduated from high school and left for a stint in the army, working as a cook on kitchen patrol duty. But as one of thirteen children, family was the most important thing in Ellsworth's life, too, and he pledged to do right by mother and child.

The young couple married at Borough Hall.

Sheila brought her firstborn, a son named Gary, home from the hospital to Eliza's house. After Ellsworth got out of the service, they moved into a small apartment in nearby West Brighton. Charlene was born two years later, and Little Sheila arrived in 1965. Sometimes Sheila would practice ballet exercises in her kitchen while the children napped, but she assumed her days of classical dance were behind her. Nanette would call her up every now and then, telling her it was time to go on back to class. "Three kids!" says Rohan. "I'm in the kitchen washing dishes, and she'd be calling trying to pull me back. I think she wanted me to have the life because she wanted to be a dancer."

Then came the summer of 1968, when Nanette saw an advertisement in the *New York Times*:

"Arthur Mitchell, of the New York City Ballet, will hold auditions for Negro dancers next Monday at the Harlem School of the Arts, St. Nicholas Avenue and 141st Street, for a company being formed at the school. Both modern and classically trained dancers are invited, girls at noon and boys at 2 p.m."

She immediately called Sheila with the news. "There's a Black man in Harlem," said a breathless Nanette. "He's going to start a dance group. You got to go up there." She rushed out the bones of Mitchell's résumé—Balanchine, City Ballet, *Agon*. But none of that was what moved Sheila to leave the dishes in the sink and drop her children at her sister's house. It was the notion of dancing once more in pointe shoes, but this time with her people.

In the church basement, Mitchell promised to transform their lives. "His energy is what I remember," says Rohan. "'I'm going to build a company, and it's going to be a great company, and you're all going to be ballerinas and principal dancers!' That's when I realized this wasn't some little community organization." When Mitchell asked Rohan about herself after class, she lied and told him that she was twenty. She said nothing of her husband and children waiting for her back home. "When he said he was going to transform us into ballerinas, I had to make a conscious choice," she explains. "I wanted to stay there with everyone, and I knew that in those days, after a certain age it was considered impossible to dance let alone have a child, and I had three!"

That night she told Ellsworth she was going to quit her part-time job at the insurance company for one that would barely cover the cost of her new commute into the city. Mitchell had taken her on as an apprentice. She started commuting into the city several times a week, leaving meals in covered dishes for Ellsworth and the children in the refrigerator. Her feet screamed in pointe shoes, she was so unused to the torture of them. "Because she wasn't as experienced, the pain that Sheila went through was extraordinary," says Stevenson, who coached Rohan to wear her pointe shoes everywhere to acclimate her feet. "It was torture, but it went with the job," says Rohan. "We were working hours after hours, and Mr. Mitchell wanted us in pointe shoes all the time. It's not like he would let us mark the dance in our slippers and dance full out later. My legs and my technique needed to get stronger."

No amount of pain was going to stand in her way. She had until recently resigned herself to an ordinary life, clocking into a desk job for hourly wages. Now she took her place among dancers a decade younger on an unfinished platform stage, which had been designed by Balanchine—the completion of the stage would have to wait until Mitchell could raise more funds. The dancers would sweep away the rubble to make room for company class and rehearse for hours. Long after the sun had set, Rohan would take the trains, then the ferry home, where she'd soak her aching feet in a bucket of ice so she could do it all over again in the morning.

3

MITCHELL NEEDED HIS YOUNG DANCERS TO SEE THAT ballet was a performing art. The fact that Abarca, his most exciting discovery, had spent most of her childhood at the barre, and no one had ever thought to give the girl a stage, was unacceptable. Not long after they'd begun working together, he told her to meet him at the stage door of Lincoln Center, where he was performing with New York City Ballet. He'd have a ticket waiting for her there.

Before the performance, Lydia Abarca sat alone in the balcony, quietly soaking in the glamour of the evening. She was two stops on the express train and an entire universe from the Grant House projects. Let her siblings argue over who got to watch what on the television that night. She'd been invited here by one of the stars that this fancy audience had paid good money to see. A man who believed he could get her on a stage as grand as this one day.

The well-heeled crowd buzzed and hushed into their seats, a collective sigh of anticipation wafting over the room. Members of the live orchestra busied into position in the pit. Abarca was so engrossed in what lay ahead that she didn't notice the young woman peeking over at her from the end of their row.

Gayle McKinney-Griffith had rushed into the balcony, eager to find her seat before the lights in the theater dimmed. As a rising third-year Juilliard student, attending cultural events was part of her curriculum. Once she was settled into her seat, she was surprised to see a light-skinned Black girl with a long neck and limbs folded delicately into her chair down the row. Could it be that this girl was a bunhead like her? And if so, had she also started to wilt under the pressure of a doubting world?

McKinney-Griffith was too shy to introduce herself. Too tender to risk another rejection. "I dared not," she tells Abarca with a laugh as the two older women reminisce over the evening. "Suppose you'd said, 'Who are you? Mind your business!' I would've been devastated." It was enough to share space for the evening, to rise together to their feet and give Arthur Mitchell the standing ovation he deserved. He had performed his iconic role of Puck from *A Midsummer Night's Dream*, which Balanchine first choreographed for him in 1962, and which would later be captured in a 1967 film adaptation. Mitchell's Puck was like a lightning storm onstage. His lithe five-foot-nine frame, painted up in a sheen of glitter, shimmered as he raced about, causing mischief and havoc with Puck's plucked flower. "I've often threatened to attach a pedometer to my waist just to see how many miles I run per performance," he said. "It must be at least ten miles. But I love every minute of it." That night he left the audience in a swoon, no one more so than the two young dancers up in balcony seats.

"All those other people on the stage, and he was the shining star," says Abarca. "His dancing was down to earth, it was personable, it was clean, it was sharp. Oh my God! You can be real in ballet? It's okay to have Motown in your bones and do Balanchine at the same time? His character wasn't just this ethereal thing anymore. He was Puck, but then he'd drop the whole facade and go a little street. It all just clicked for me. This is what he wants me working toward."

That night Mitchell showed Abarca how much bigger and bolder ballet could be than she'd imagined. He freed the dance from the prison of the barre, a series of repetitive movements without pride or personality. He wasn't a Black man who dared to dance ballet. He was a dancer who dared ballet to see and celebrate his Blackness.

Mitchell's dancing left McKinney-Griffith similarly inspired. "The feeling of pride I felt was enormous," she says, her gentle voice still full of gratitude. "He was representing us. He was showing the audience that we could be ballet dancers too."

Some of McKinney-Griffith's fondest memories as a child were watching her parents get dressed up for nights out at the Savoy, the Lenox Avenue ballroom that the poet Langston

Hughes once called "the heartbeat of Harlem." Gayle's sister Maxine, fourteen years her senior, remembers her parents taking her there as a child to see the "president of jazz," saxophonist Lester Young, and the thrill of entering such a sophisticated world of cool. But however happy Maxine's childhood was, it grew tenfold more so when her parents brought her baby sister Gayle home from the hospital to their courtyard apartment on 111th Street and Lenox. From then on, wherever Maxine went, she took her sister with her in a stroller, though her parents drew the line when she tried to bring her to the Wednesday-night dances at Central Park's Park Palace.

When Gayle was five, her father, Harold, got a mechanical-design engineering job offer in Connecticut that he couldn't turn down. With his deep, resounding baritone, Harold interviewed for the position over the phone. He believed that the company thought it had hired a white man and didn't know how to turn him away when he reported for his first day of work. For most of his illustrious career, he was the only Black draftsman in his division.

In Connecticut, he bought a colonial-style house, to which Gayle would eventually return after her father's death to care for her mother, Millicent, until her death in 2019 at the age of 101. Maxine deferred her acceptance to Fordham University to watch over Gayle in Connecticut, while Millicent stayed behind in Harlem for a year, waiting for the telephone company where she worked to transfer her job. She finally was transferred, but she was also demoted to long-distance operator, which she attributed to the color of her skin. Without complaint, she worked the night shift, eventually marching her way back up the ladder to supervisor. "She surpassed all of the people that didn't want her to move forward," says McKinney-Griffith.

Harold and Millicent adjusted to life outside Harlem by pouring themselves into their new home.

It was Gayle who pined for Harlem. Her parents hoped dance might be a balm for their homesick daughter, who'd been taking dance classes at Carnegie Hall before they moved. They found a local studio run by an old Russian couple, Maximillian and Olga Froman, who had once performed with the Bolshoi. All the white girls in the new studio carried round, pink dance bags to match their pink tights and shoes. Harold bought his daughter a rectangular black-patent-leather dance bag and painted her name on it in his artful script. Every time she entered the studio, he wanted her to know that she was precious and deserving.

Connecticut wasn't Harlem, but the Fromans helped Gayle feel at home. Maximillian played the piano, and Olga taught classes. It was under their tender care that she fell forever in love with a room with a barre and mirrors. "There's some feeling of magic that comes over me when I walk into a dance studio," she says. "Maybe it's the smell of the wood, the cedar. But there's an atmosphere that surrounds you. My heart starts beating faster in my chest every time I get close to one." Olga took exquisite care of her new student's training, invested in every degree of her port de bras, and provided a safe space where her talent could bloom. Hearing of this woman's care with her friend, Sheila Rohan remarks, "Your teacher was a true dance artist. She wasn't seeing this little Black girl at the barre. She saw a dancer." By the time she was ten, Gayle began her transition onto pointe, funneled into an advanced group of demi-soloists. She was chosen to perform the "Four Swans" variation in *Swan Lake*.

There is a gracefulness to Gayle McKinney-Griffith's spirit that softens whatever space she enters. Throughout her childhood, people gravitated to her gentle and competent energy. She was elected secretary of her high school class, then president of the Waterford High Dance Club, and she received a scholarship to attend the annual American Dance Festival hosted by Connecticut College. There she took classes from the likes of the formidable Martha Graham, the mother of modern dance. She remembers Graham wielding her training stick like a weapon against mediocrity in the studio. "She would just hit you on the back, yelling, 'Contract! Contract!'"

Knowing her parents expected her to go to college, Gayle set her sights on Juilliard. The audition process was a three-day blur of anxiety. On the first day, she found herself assigned to the modern dancers, despite her extensive ballet résumé. After letting her talent speak for itself, she was allowed, grudgingly, she felt, to join the pool of prospective ballet dancers. She was the only dancer of color in the group, an exhausting fact for which she'd long since developed coping skills. "When you live in this skin, you grow up knowing you have a special position in the world that you must protect," she says. "I don't think that we're even aware of when we're doing it. But we're always protecting ourselves—in school, in different communities. You have to wear blinders and focus. When you walk into a room and you're the only Black person there, you right away develop this persona that is protective but also standing strong. You're used to thinking two things at once: *Yes, I'm the only Black person here* and *Yes, let's do this.*"

Gayle was accepted into Juilliard and moved into Maxine's family's three-bedroom apartment in Morningside Heights, sleeping on the pullout sofa in their den. Her dancing garnered immediate notice in her new school. The Uruguayan teacher and dancer Alfredo Corvino personally requested her in his ballet class, despite the administration grumbling about the extra course expense on top of her regular load. Anthony Tudor, choreographer emeritus for American Ballet Theatre at the time of his death in 1987, likewise asked for her to take his class, believing he could push her pointe work even further. Grateful for his encouragement, she tried her best to ignore the way her white male classmates flinched when they were told to partner her.

But no matter the potential these giants of ballet saw in her, Juilliard's administration wouldn't budge when it came time for McKinney-Griffith to declare a major. In a private conference, she was pressed to let go of her dreams of ballet. They told her she'd never get hired by a professional company. There likely wouldn't even be opportunities to audition. The fact of her talent, which seemed devastatingly beside the point, was never mentioned. It was time for her to be practical and move into the modern-dance department. It wasn't what she wanted, and it also didn't make sense. Her friends in the modern department were lifetimes ahead of her in terms of their training and passion for the form. She was a ballerina, not a modern dancer. She grasped for examples of women of color who had proved themselves exceptions. What about Maria Tallchief? Or Mary Hinkson? Or Kathleen Stanford Grant?

McKinney-Griffith left the office holding back her tears and sank to the floor of the hallway in defeat. "My God, this is not working," she remembers crying to herself. "Why am I even here?" One of her friends from the modern-dance department happened upon her that way, and after learning the cause of her distress, she pulled McKinney-Griffith to her feet with life-changing news. "Arthur Mitchell is auditioning today. For an all-Black ballet company. Stop your whining and go!"

As she emerged from the subway station onto familiar streets, she fell in lockstep with a graceful Black woman, who walked in the familiar slue-footed style of a ballerina, her toes turned out like a duck's. Virginia Johnson—another founding ballerina of Dance Theatre of Harlem—whom Mitchell would personally tap to revive the company as its artistic director in 2009, entered the church basement right alongside her. The ramshackle space was a far cry from Juilliard's gleaming studios. But the sight of all these brown and Black dancers, the kitchens on the backs of the women's necks pinned up like hers, allowed her to unclench. She could dance here without the weight of her armor.

"I don't know how to describe the feeling of looking around that room other than magical," says McKinney-Griffith. "The sheer numbers of us! I had never seen such handsome, sculpted men in my life. And then the women! All so statuesque and elegant. Everybody doing the same thing that I've loved all my life."

Karel Shook was leading the class with his trademark Kent cigarette hanging from his mouth, as he did for much of his tenure at Dance Theatre of Harlem, until he died of throat cancer in 1985. He was an intellectual man with melancholy eyes, whose wryness was a welcome counterpart to Mitchell's brio. He liked to lean in close to the dancers' ears and whisper a joke to test their focus. When he was feeling cheeky, he'd hold his lit cigarette underneath a dancer's leg as motivation for her to continue holding her arabesque longer than she'd ever thought herself able.

After class, Mitchell burst into the room, harried from another fundraising meeting. Shook introduced the promising new girl from Juilliard to him. "Hmm. Hmmm, put your pointe shoes on," said Mitchell. "Let me see you turn." Satisfied by the grace of her pirouettes, Mitchell handed her a piece of paper. "Go learn this dance. We're rehearsing the first movement of *Tones* tomorrow, so be here first thing in the morning." Then he marched off in his high-heeled boots to his next order of business. He didn't wait for her to tell him that she had class in the morning or to wonder if those few minutes before him counted as her official audition. The only thing she knew for

51

sure was that she had to find a way to stay in this room, where for the first time in her life as a dancer, she was one of many.

Gayle McKinney-Griffith showed up the next morning, just as she'd been told to, to learn one of Dance Theatre of Harlem's first ballets. *Tones* was the first ballet music composed by Mitchell's twenty-four-year-old accompanist, Tania León. A Cuban refugee new to the country, on a scholarship to NYU, she'd aligned with Mitchell by chance. She'd been filling in for a sick friend as a substitute piano teacher at Harlem School of the Arts on the day Mitchell was taking stock of possible studio space. She was noodling around on the baby grand piano during breaks between students, playing her own melodies, when Mitchell happened to pass by the open door, then passed by a second time to get a closer listen. She noticed the startlingly attractive man hovering outside. When he finally stepped forward to introduce himself, León could only hold up her hands and say, "No English." Mitchell made the motions of a telephone with his hands and got the phone number to the Bronx apartment where she was camping out with friends. Two weeks later he called her up and asked León in a garble of Spanish and Italian to come play for him again.

When León returned to Harlem School of the Arts, she joined Mitchell and four dancers who were waiting at a barre set up in the middle of the basketball court. Mitchell balked when León pulled out some of her friend's music books, asking her instead to pay attention to the movement and the sound of his voice. As Mitchell walked around the dancers tapping his stick and calling out "One, two, three, four!" she began improvising at the upright piano. "The four ballerinas were Lydia, Sheila, Virginia Johnson, and Patsy Ricketts," she says. "I still have a little Kodak picture of these four young women standing at the barre. He told me to follow his counts based on watching the movements, and I just started creating all these pieces."

After class, Mitchell talked to León about his mission and the opportunity he was trying to provide for Black classical dancers, and he offered her a job as his full-time accompanist. "When I found out that the whole project was to demonstrate that people of color could dance ballet, I got immediately hooked," says León. As a child in Cuba, her beloved grandmother had wanted her to learn ballet. But when she took her granddaughter to the dance school for classes, they turned León away because of the color of her skin.

As he did everyone else, Mitchell threw León onto his wild seesaw of approval. If León's playing was too slow for his liking, he would scream at her, "You're killing the dancers!" Other times he cried out with sunny approval: "Yes! Yes! Just like that, remember that. That's perfect!" But no matter his shifting mood, he recognized greatness in her. He called her Taniacita, and she became one of the founding partners of Dance Theatre of Harlem.

"After that Arthur made me do everything," says León. "I was the pianist. I was the music director. I was the head of the school. I was like an octopus person. Arthur said, 'Compose a piece for me!' Now I was a composer. 'You want to conduct the orchestra? You know all the ballets, you know everything, you can do it.' Now I was a conductor. It's like he could see into the future." León would go on to be awarded a Pulitzer Prize for her orchestral work *Stride,* and in 2022 she was a Kennedy Center honoree for her tremendous contribution to American culture, but to this day, when she steps in front of an audience, she hears Mitchell's voice in her ears: *"Always walk onstage like you are somebody!"*

For a few exhausting weeks, Gayle McKinney-Griffith tied herself in knots juggling a full course load at Juilliard with Mitchell's six-hour-plus daily rehearsals. Finally, fed up with her racing into the studio late and always leaving in a rush back to school, Shook and Mitchell cornered her at the end of a long afternoon session. Mitchell asked how much longer she was going to keep dragging her butt back and forth to Juilliard. She stammered over her idea of hanging on to both college and the company. "Well, I'm giving you an ultimatum," Mitchell said, cutting her off. "You're either going to dance here or you're going to dance at Juilliard. Now you have to make up your mind." Shook, sensing her torment, patted her softly on the back, but Mitchell barked, "Ding ding ding ding!" before turning on his heel.

That night she flopped onto her sister's sofa in misery. She couldn't bear disappointing their parents and wasting all that money that they'd spent on her tuition. And yet something vital had been restored in her under Mitchell's eye.

She called her parents with the news that she was dropping out of college. She told them about Mitchell, his exquisite vision, about Abarca and Rohan and Johnson and the rest of the artists who would dance that vision into existence. Her voice dripped with so much passion that all her parents could do was sigh quietly and tell her that they believed in her too.

Just two years after that phone call, Dance Theatre of Harlem would travel to Connecticut and perform at the college not far from the family's house on the hill. A widowed Madame Froman would sit in the audience with tears in her eyes. "Look at what you did!" McKinney-Griffith wanted to call out to her teacher during the company bows.

By the end of that first summer, student enrollment in Mitchell's dance program mushroomed to 250 kids. On warm days, he threw the bay doors open to sidewalk traffic for the breeze. He added live drummers to the mix of León's piano as a lure to anyone turned off by classical music. When neighborhood kids lingered outside the garage, mesmerized by the scene of beautiful young women in tights, Mitchell was able to entice them inside, assuring the boys they could wear their street clothes if that was their hang-up. "What's your sport?" he'd call out. "Basketball? What if I could teach you to jump two feet higher than anyone else on your team? All you need to learn is something called the plié." McKinney-Griffith remembers having to lead the occasionally unruly youth class. "They'd be chewing gum in their dungarees," she says. "'Whatcha mean, don't lean on the barre!'"

Meanwhile Mitchell was feverishly developing choreography for his rapidly improving company's repertoire. He finished the first movement of *Tones,* a neoclassical ballet of angles and form set to León's atonal score. His *Holberg Suite* was a romantic confection also choreographed in Balanchine's neoclassical style. He revived *Rhythmetron,* a ballet he'd first choreographed for the National Ballet Company of Brazil in Rio de Janeiro, set to Marlos Nobre's thirty-three-percussive-instrument score. The ballet fused classical technique with African ritual and would quickly emerge as the company's signature piece. Finally, he created *Biosfera,* a pas de deux also set to the Brazilian Nobre's music. He cast Lydia Abarca in the female lead, with Sheila Rohan as her understudy.

Mitchell told his dancers, and the world repeated the fact over and over, that there was nowhere else for them to go to realize their full potential. In a June 2021 interview for the *New York Times* about the Legacy Council, Virginia Johnson described the feverish time. "There was so much on the line! I think one of the beautiful things about those early years of Dance Theatre of Harlem was every single one of us had been told, 'No, you can't do this.' And then Arthur Mitchell gave us a place to do it and gave us a way to achieve a high level of excellence. So, yes, there was opportunity, but it was about grit. It was a fight. People had told us we couldn't do it,

56

and we had to show them we could. Remember, this was the middle of the Black Power movement. There were plenty of Black people who did not think that we should be trying to succeed in 'the white man's art form.' And there were plenty of white people who didn't think we should be either."

"We all understood this to be a higher calling," says McKinney-Griffith. "Suddenly that step on pointe made a difference. We were a group of brown people, of all different shades from different cities and countries. For those of us who'd felt for so long adrift and like a lonely standard bearer—to look around and feel the power of numbers was just extraordinary. We were en masse, so we were protected. Can you imagine the energy that freed up? The freedom to just focus on our craft. We never had to justify to each other our right to ballet."

4

"My Best Day—We went to the Dance Theater of Harlem.
I would like to be a ballet dancer. They used their feet
and legs. Sometimes the music went low and high."
—John, PS 161
499 West 133rd Street

"I did not like it for a while; then it was great. At first,
I thought it was going to be different, but it turned out
to be wonderful."
—Wendy, PS 161

"The performance you gave to us on Monday was
terrific. The dancers were all great. Someday, maybe,
I will be with your dance group."
—Eric, PS 161

D ANCE THEATRE OF HARLEM WAS FORMALLY INCORPO-
rated in 1969, with Arthur Mitchell assembling a power-
house board that included, among others, two of his dearest

friends, the celebrated actors Cicely Tyson and Brock Peters, as well as George Balanchine, Lincoln Kirstein, and Charles De Rose, who'd taken on what was basically a second job as the company's first treasurer.

Shortly thereafter Mitchell's relationship with Dorothy Maynor devolved into a clash of egos, and suddenly the dancers were out of a home. They relocated to another church basement, at the Church of the Master across the street from Morningside Park on 122nd Street, where as a child he'd once attended a free camp. Mitchell described their new neighborhood as "the worst dope area in Harlem." But he liked to brag that because of his alliance with a local gang leader who respected his hustle, vandals skipped over Dance Theatre of Harlem, and the dope dealers left the dancers and the kids alone.

The new space was beaten down to say the least. Leaking pipes overhead had left the floor badly buckled. The dancers had to pitch in their change to meet the costs of getting a new floor laid so they wouldn't injure themselves. The girls' dressing room consisted of costume and lighting crates for benches and a Chinese screen for privacy. But still, the basement blessed them with a large studio space with a raised deck that could accommodate up to sixty spectators. Soon after the move, Mitchell began opening their Wednesday rehearsals to an audience, as a shrewd method of community outreach.

Folks in the neighborhood came to recognize and look forward to seeing the dancers on their way to and from the studio. The women gave themselves away with their high buns slicked back in Murray's pomade, hurrying down the sidewalk on their orchid-stem legs, their feet turned out like ducks'. Each morning on her walk to work, Lydia Abarca passed the same drowsy clump of testosterone on a building stoop, sitting around listening to music and smoking cigarettes. "Hey, baby!" they'd catcall for her attention. "Hey, I'm talkin' to you! You too stuck up to talk to a brotha?" Tired of their baiting, she'd eventually reclaim control of the situation with one graceful swivel. "Hi, my name is Lydia, and I don't usually talk to strangers," she said, looking each of her antagonists in the eye. "I have to walk through here to get to work every day, and now that you know my name, I'll make sure to say hello." From then on, she found herself greeted with a respectful chorus of "Good morning, Lydia!"

Dance Theatre of Harlem quickly became an important symbol of possibility in the community. Says De Rose, "What Arthur did was raise people's pride. He said, 'This is what people said Blacks couldn't do. They never said we couldn't play basketball. They never said we couldn't box. They never said we couldn't tap-dance. But classical dance was a no-no.' And Arthur Mitchell said, 'Bull! Any child given the same opportunity is going to have the same results.'"

In his studio, every gesture, every tilt of the head, every step had to have a purpose, and it needed to be perfect. Rehearsals would be scheduled for an hour and last for five. If Mitchell wasn't tired, the dancers better not be either. "In the beginning, Dance Theatre wasn't mediocre; it was good," says De Rose. "But it wasn't up to world-class standards. Arthur was unrelenting. 'Your leg has to be higher; you have to be better; you have to be straighter; you have to walk better, your hands, your feet. You either hit the high C or you don't. Do it again! And this time, do it right! No, do it again! Again!' Arthur was no teddy bear, but he brought more out of you than you ever knew you had to give. And he did it by example. He was the first one into the studio, and the last one to leave at night."

After rehearsals, the dancers would freeze in a line, bracing for Mitchell's corrections. Nobody dared slouch or sigh or sneeze, lest they make themselves the target of his fusillade of judgment. "We got in trouble for everything," says Abarca. "If you didn't hold your passé, if you didn't hold your little toe by your knee, if you didn't hold your knee up, if your foot was sickled. Every little detail. You could never be good enough for him. But you also understood he was our third eye. If we could please him, we would please the audience." Mitchell would often echo the warning Kirstein had given him as teenager. "Everything you see them do," he'd say, referencing the top ballet companies, "you have to be ten times better."

The poison of his tongue would thicken depending on his stress level. "Sometimes he could just be goofing around with you," says Gayle McKinney-Griffith. "He had this big, wonderful, boisterous laugh, so if he was laughing, everyone was laughing." But inevitably, he'd turn on you. He'd arrive at the studio after what he thought was a lucrative fundraising meeting, only to discover that the promise of money at lunch had evaporated during his commute uptown—and his temper would hit like a fire hose. Remembers Sheila Rohan: "If your leg wasn't high that day, or your back was weak, Mr. Mitchell would pick on you. He would call you out by name. 'You, you with the butt! You with the thighs! You with the attitude!' I mean, he could absolutely destroy a person."

"I've been called an ogre, a taskmaster, and you better believe it's true," Mitchell once said. "Just ask the kids. Hey, I'm not running a party here. This is something very important to me, to Harlem, to Black people everywhere. No one's going to hand anything to us."

His philosophy was: better he be the one to grind a dancer's ego to dust than someone outside the family, of which he'd immediately cast himself in the role of formidable patriarch. He began boasting to reporters of teaching his dancers how to dress, where to buy their clothes, how he'd paid for some of them to get their teeth fixed. If a dancer ever showed up to class in raggedy leg warmers or tights, he'd make them go home and change. He wanted smooth ballet buns on every woman, forbidding them to wear their hair in cornrows or beads (though somehow Rohan, who had come into the company with a short Afro, was spared his disapproval). He'd insist upon meeting his dancers' boyfriends and girlfriends, telling them to dump suitors whom he found lacking. When reporters would ask Mitchell if he had any intention of marrying, his grin slid like an ocean liner across his face. "No, but I have thirty-one children," he'd respond, referring to his company of dancers and his lean support staff, who made up the scaffolding of his operation. Mitchell's most familiar refrain to his dancers was that they represented something larger than their individual selves. So they'd better get right with shouldering the pressures and responsibilities that came with being an ambassador.

Sheila Rohan always left the studio at the end of their marathon days in a sprint. "I got to get the boat!" she'd yell to those behind her, by way of goodbye. The younger dancers would be plotting their evenings, taking a quick nap before hitting a disco, or enjoying an hours-long soak in the tub with Epsom salts to baby their feet. Rohan had to race to the subway, which she took down to South Ferry, where she'd wait for the boat to take her back to Staten Island, where, as she puts it, she had to make sure there was peanut butter in the cupboard for the day ahead. If she ever missed the midnight ferry, when it switched to running on the hour instead of every half, she'd try to keep herself awake by reading on a bench, inevitably passing out from sheer exhaustion. Mitchell had begun throwing multiple ballets at them to learn in a rush. Balanchine had graciously given Dance Theatre of Harlem the rights to use some of his most popular ballets, beginning with *Concerto Barocco*, so they had been meeting with City Ballet dancers to learn the choreography. "You guys were dancing for your lives," Rohan's youngest daughter, Little Sheila, says now in a family conversation.

As their audience size increased, so, too, did Rohan's battle with stage fright. She questioned her talent compared with dancers like Abarca ("she had the beautiful face and body and extension"), Johnson ("so elegant and crisp"), and McKinney-Griffith ("her gorgeous technique"). Says Rohan, "I believed you really couldn't dance ballet unless you had complete control over it. I thought I wasn't ready or good enough to be onstage yet, and Mr. Mitchell was pushing us before we were ready. I was terrified I was going to make a mistake or knock someone over or go on the wrong side of the stage." (Once, during a performance in which she was dressed as a yellow canary, her worst fear came true. "I fell on my butt, and instead of just quietly getting up, I went *whoof!* on the stage," she says, laughing and covering her face. "It's bad enough to fall, but then the audience laughed! I played that one over and over in my head waiting for the ferry.")

Eager to develop tools to calm herself down, Rohan began reading about Buddhism and, along with several other company dancers, visited a downtown temple for meditation classes. She started chanting before shows—*"Namu Myōhō Renge Kyō"*—so that the vibrations might connect her to a higher level of consciousness. And she drew upon her fundamental sturdiness, which attracted the younger dancers to her. "She was our rock," says Abarca.

Rohan's children were mesmerized by what felt like sudden stardom for their mother. They delighted in the occasions when they could watch her on television, like when she appeared in a one-hour Christmas Eve special, *A Holiday Celebration with Ossie Davis and Ruby Dee,* dancing in an excerpt from *Holberg Suite.* Or on NBC on Thanksgiving morning, freezing alongside the other dancers in front of Macy's, performing *Forces of Rhythm*. The wind howled so fiercely, it wrapped a giant Snoopy's head around the cab of the helium truck, forcing organizers to remove balloons from the parade for only the second time in its forty-five-year history. They wanted a part in their mother's world.

So as she had done for their mother, Nanette paid for her nephew and nieces' arts training. She would meet them on the New York side of the ferry and travel with them up to Harlem, where Sheila's middle child, Charlene, was taking ballet classes. Their mother would have reminded them in the morning to address her as Aunt Sheila. If anyone asked, they were her nephew and nieces.

Charlene was eight years old when she first took a class with Arthur Mitchell. He'd spend half the time shouting at the children about the importance of alignment and posture and the other half lecturing about dance history and the personal dignity that flows from the practice of discipline. His classes were serious business, but as a teacher, he could be just as fun and funny as he could be mean. He was a tyrant, but you could tell that he was one of those rare adults who genuinely likes children.

After class, Charlene would linger to watch her mother and the rest of the company rehearse, drinking in the sight of her new favorite dancer, the young Lydia Abarca. "She was like our Barbie doll," says Charlene. "Everyone wanted to be her. She was the beauty, and she got to wear the best costumes and dance the best roles."

It took over a year for Sheila Rohan to confess that those kids who'd been hanging around the studio on Saturdays were in fact hers. Dance Theatre of Harlem had been accepted as one of the touring companies by the New York State Council on the Arts and then the National Endowment for the Arts, a huge honor considering that the bylaws of both organizations demanded that a company have a minimum of five years under its belt. Rohan needed Mitchell to know that while he had her full commitment, she was a woman with obligations. After her confession, Mitchell stared at Rohan in disbelief from behind his desk before letting out a sigh of exasperation. "If I'd known you had mouths at home to feed, I would've paid you more!" he snapped, sending her back to class. True to his word, there was a modest bump in her salary the next paycheck.

Throughout her time in Dance Theatre of Harlem, her mother, Eliza, who loved the Brooklyn Dodgers not ballet, remained skeptical of all the sacrifices her youngest daughter was making. "She had an immigrant mentality," says Rohan. "My mother saw me dance, but she wasn't sentimental. She didn't believe in art for art's sake. The fact that I had to leave my children to barely make a living didn't make much sense to her. And she worried about the fact that I was getting older. 'How long do you think you're going to be doing this? If you're not making money, why are you going on? You've got three kids. Go home to them.'"

She had no interest in meeting the great Arthur Mitchell, which was probably for the best. "If she ever heard him yelling at us the way he could, she'd have cursed him out," says Rohan.

"She was the type of woman who would've stood up in the audience and laid him flat. Of course, he probably would've loved her. Because she was gutsy, and she would've gave him word for word. I think he would've respected her."

But when money was tight, Rohan would worry that maybe her mother was right after all. She and Ellsworth would look at their bills spread out on the kitchen table, and she'd float the idea of quitting Dance Theatre of Harlem to find work as a secretary. Every time, Ellsworth would shake his head fondly and remind her of her purpose: "Sheila, you're one of the few people who get to do what they actually love. Do what you love to do."

Maybe she would've quit, if it weren't for her husband's support. Or if she hadn't trusted so completely in the purity of Mitchell's vision. Or if she hadn't been able to rely on the other dancers, who took turns crying on each other's shoulders and lifting one another's chins. "In rehearsals, Arthur would insinuate things about the other dancers," she says. "'Oh, look at her legs.' 'That's a fat one.' Just loud enough for them to hear. Or he'd be trying to start stuff between Lydia and Virginia. 'Oh, if you can't do that, maybe she can.' It hurt me to see my friends cry in the dressing room. But if this was what we had to put up with, so be it. The work was so hard that we had to come together as a force. We clung to each other. We were all in the same boat, and we had to survive this captain."

They lived in fear of the reflection of his square head underneath the EXIT silhouette at the back of a theater, where he would watch rehearsal. They feared, too, the shadow of his

Afro moving backstage before he stomped into view to deliver his corrections. "We knew that he loved us, but he was very, very stern with us," says Gayle McKinney-Griffith. "Everything was always upping the ante. 'Okay, you did this this way; you got to do it better tomorrow. You're fat today; lose that weight for tomorrow.' You were never good enough for him."

How easy it would have been to go back home, or to college, or to nine-to-five lives. They stayed for the promise of the next curtain rising, on stages bigger and grander with every passing month. "In the dressing rooms beforehand, we might've all gone quiet because of some big altercation," says McKinney-Griffith. "And then you'd just snap out of it and put your makeup on and go wait in the wings. All that noise, if you could just slip through it, you'd be fine. Mr. Mitchell couldn't touch you when you were onstage."

5

B Y 1970, WORD HAD SPREAD THROUGH NEW YORK CITY OF
Arthur Mitchell's mission to make ballet more inclusive.
Over one thousand children, some of them white, had enrolled in Dance Theatre of Harlem's school. When reporters
asked Mitchell about his intentions to integrate the company,
he balked at the idea. "I don't want an all-Black company, but
until other companies start to employ them, why should I take
a white dancer and put a Black one out of work?" Of the major
dance companies in New York at the time, American Ballet
Theatre had yet to welcome a Black dancer to its ranks, City
Ballet had one, and the Joffrey Ballet had two.

Wherever Dance Theatre of Harlem traveled, Mitchell
scouted for talent. When he recognized potential in a young
person, even in someone as raw as a kid who'd just volunteered to join him onstage during a lecture-demonstration,
he'd encourage them to move to New York so he could take

over their training. DTH would pay for their education at New York's Professional Children's School. Sometimes, if a dancer struggled to find housing, Mitchell would move them into a spare room in his mother's Harlem brownstone, which he'd purchased for her. As far as he was concerned, nothing was going to stand in the way of a child with talent and drive.

That year, when Dance Theatre of Harlem traveled to Cincinnati, ten-year-old Marcia Sells told her mother they needed to get tickets. She'd been the only Black student in her ballet classes since she was four years old. She'd never seen a Black ballerina perform before. This performance was about to change that.

Marcia's mother, Mamie, was her greatest defender. As a teenager, Marcia danced in the role of a snowflake in *The Nutcracker* with the Cincinnati Ballet. During intermission, Mamie, who had little patience for ignorance or unkindness, overheard a child whining to her parents about the "dirty snowflake" on the stage. "You've never seen candy dance, either," she told the family. All ballet is fantasy—a graceful unspooling of wonder and enchantment. If the child could accept a snowflake coming to life, surely her worldview could expand enough to allow for a Black girl in the role.

Mamie was a teacher and had always been adamant that her students be educated in Black history far beyond the perfunctory bullet points on slavery that made up the public school system's newly created Black History Week curriculum. At the time, some of Marcia's teachers weren't even ready to acknowledge that slavery had been an operation built on evil. Mamie expected her daughter to educate her peers in ways her teachers weren't. By the third grade, Marcia was teaching kids in her class about W. E. B. Du Bois and Booker T. Washington; the journalist Ida B. Wells and the first Black female lawyer, Charlotte E. Ray; and the singers Marian Anderson and Leontyne Price. There was greatness all around her to emulate, starting in the close-knit community of Black lawyers, doctors, teachers, and judges who composed their family's inner circle.

Mamie served on the board of the Women's Auxiliary for the Symphony and was a leader in the YWCA, a member of the Women's City Club, and in her later years, a columnist for the Black newspaper the *Call Post* and eventually for the *Cincinnati Herald*. Anybody who was anybody wanted to find themselves captured in "Mamie's Urban Scene."

Mother and daughter were each other's favorite dates to dance performances and cultural events throughout Marcia's childhood. They went to see *Swan Lake* when American Ballet Theatre came through Ohio. They saw Rudolf Nureyev dance in Columbus. They went to see the Cincinnati Ballet perform *Winter's Traces* to a Verdi score, taking proud note of Black dancer Dwight Hughes in the corps. They swooned at the ferocious talent of Judith Jamison performing with the Alvin Ailey American Dance Theater. They saw the Joffrey company perform at Cincinnati's annual May Festival, in a production that included Black dancers Gary Chryst and Christian Holder. With every performance, Marcia's fantasies of her future grew more extravagant. She imagined herself dancing iconic roles like Odette/Odile, the Sugar Plum Fairy, and the leads in Balanchine's *Serenade* and *Concerto Barocco*. She daydreamed about greeting her fans backstage, her arms heavy with roses. She was still young and well-loved enough to believe that even though she had never seen a Black professional ballerina, she could still be one.

When Dance Theatre of Harlem came to Cincinnati, Marcia Sells sat next to Mamie in a sold-out theater at the local university, both dressed to the nines. When the dancers first appeared onstage, the girl's jaw dropped and stayed that way until the very end of their chest thumper of a finale, *Rhythmetron*. "I just remember when the curtain came up and Patsy Ricketts was standing in the middle of the stage wearing the most immense cape in a golden-brown color," she says. "And then the rhythm of the music began. And the dancing that was all on pointe but also completely different from any other classical ballet I'd ever seen. It was electric, and the audience was going berserk. I remember saying to my mother, 'Look at this! Look at this!'" That night ballet revealed itself as something neither mother nor daughter had previously known it could be—dramatic, theatrical, spiritual, Black in both color and core.

"I've been the only Black girl in my ballet school for my entire childhood up until then," says Sells. "And now here comes Arthur Mitchell. A Black ballet company on the university main stage in my hometown. Lydia and Gayle and Sheila! Suddenly nobody will ever be able to tell me it's not possible for me too. Even if my ballet school doesn't imagine that for me, I can point to that stage and say, 'Right there—see! Those women, right there, already having an impact, even as they're just starting the company.'" It's a night she credits with changing the course of her life. "Because I don't think I would've gone forward if I hadn't seen Dance Theatre of Harlem in 1970."

After the performance, Mamie took Marcia backstage to congratulate and mingle with the company. The dancers were sweaty and exhilarated, the men as handsome as any she'd ever seen, everyone shining through the stage makeup they hadn't yet had time to remove. Arthur Mitchell preening in the center of it all. This was the backstage life Marcia had always fantasized about, but she'd never before imagined everyone in that fantasy could be Black. In front of her, collecting roses and words of adoration, was Lydia Abarca, who was even more radiant up close than she'd been onstage; Marcia didn't know whether to stare or look away. Mamie told her to go introduce herself, which struck Marcia as preposterous. She was so in awe of what felt like new dance royalty that she'd sooner approach the queen of England. "I remember I saw Lydia, and forget about it," she says. "I couldn't even talk properly. Even at ten years old, I knew a star when I saw one." She did manage to murmur some words of dazed appreciation to Gayle McKinney-Griffith, who smiled down at the child with her beatific warmth and spoke sweetly with Mamie about the excitement of being in the company.

Marcia hung close to her mother, who'd joined a circle of conversation with Mitchell, James Truitte, and Thelma Hill, the University of Cincinnati's new Black visiting dance professors, who'd been instrumental in bringing Dance Theatre of Harlem to town. They had been founding members of the Alvin Ailey American Dance Theater and a couple of Mitchell's early Harlem faculty hires.

Since they'd arrived in Cincinnati, they'd been keeping a watchful eye on Marcia Sells, the only Black girl in the college-preparatory ballet program. As a teenager in the 1950s, Hill had been one of five Black students at the Metropolitan School of Ballet, where she'd earned the lifelong nickname "Mother" for her nurturing temperament. She knew how lonely it could be for a Black girl in ballet, so she always encouraged Marcia to take sustenance in the careers of Raven Wilkinson and Janet Collins, to see the ballet technique in modern icons like Jamison and Carmen de Lavallade, who'd partnered with Truitte in the 1950s at the Lester Horton Dance Theater. Hill regaled the eager young ballet student with stories of her adventures in cofounding and performing with the New York Negro Ballet Company, whose one international tour in 1957 was cut unceremoniously short when the dancers ran out of money. Hill wanted this bright-eyed girl, who hadn't yet known struggle, to understand that the road ahead would be hard. But it had been traveled before.

When Mitchell joined their circle, Truitte made the introductions. Mitchell nodded down at Marcia, telling Mamie that he had taken notice of her in her dance class. "It looks like your daughter has some skill," he said, which, coming from Mitchell, was high praise. Mamie insisted he join them at their home for a family dinner the following evening after he'd finished giving a master class for the university's dance department.

Mamie invited Mitchell over for dinner for the same reason that Gayle McKinney-Griffith's family had hosted the company when it came through their town, with a potluck supper of dishes cooked by her mother's friends from the Methodist church. For them, in the Black communities they'd been raised in, it was just what you did. You gathered and offered warmth and fellowship and a safe space. "When someone like Arthur Mitchell comes to town, you're supposed to invite them," says Marcia Sells. "Because in the old days in the South, a Black person wouldn't have had anywhere else to go. My mother was born in Alabama, and my father was born in Oklahoma. This is what you did." At the time, though, she was horrified. "Ten-year-old me didn't understand this at the time like sixty-three-year-old me does. So ten-year-old me found the whole thing nerve-racking. It was like the principal of your school coming over—like, oh my God, what are they going to be doing in my house?"

The Sells family—Mamie; husband Halloway Charles Jr., who had a master's in social work and a PhD in sociology and organizational development; and Marcia's younger brother—lived in a three-story house on a picturesque cul-de-sac with two cars in the driveway, a library with built-in bookshelves, and a bay window that looked out upon an enormous apple tree. Throughout the meal of Cornish game hen, wild rice, and brussels sprouts, Marcia sat riveted by the fervor of Mitchell's storytelling and his bright-eyed attention.

Over dessert, Mitchell, who'd already examined Marcia's feet in the studio, declared that the next obvious step was for her to move to New York City to begin training full-time at Dance Theatre of Harlem. He already had a family in mind for her to live with, and she could complete her education at the Professional Children's School on West 60th Street. Mamie gave Marcia's father a sideways glance, a near-invisible shake of her head. No child of hers was leaving for New York City anytime soon.

After the meal, the children were sent upstairs so the grown folks could talk in peace. The adults moved to the living room, which held a piano and a couch long enough for Halloway, with his six-foot-five frame, to take Sunday-afternoon naps. After getting into her pajamas, Marcia crept down the stairs and peeked through the rails of the banister at Mitchell sitting in one of her mother's living room chairs, deep in conversation with her parents.

That night, with Mamie leading the charge, the group sketched out the initial plan for Dance Theatre of Harlem's next visit to Cincinnati. Halloway was the executive director of Seven Hills Neighborhood Houses, Cincinnati's largest social service agency, serving a socioeconomically disadvantaged community near the University of Cincinnati. Seven Hills would sponsor a five-day residency for DTH, during which Mitchell would direct master classes at the university, and the company would perform lecture-demonstrations for inner-city children at over a dozen public schools, then dance onstage at Cincinnati's big Music Hall for a heavily publicized one-night performance.

Marcia Sells listened for a while as all that business was sorted out in the living room, then retreated to her bedroom. She unfolded the three-panel black-and-white program on thick, shiny card stock from Dance Theatre of Harlem's performance the night before. The copy included a quote from a piece that *New York Times* dance critic Clive Barnes had published four months before Mitchell started DTH. "Few Negro children learn classic ballet," Barnes wrote about the exclusionary gates to the art form. "This is probably because there are few chances for Negroes to make their way in classic ballet, and unfortunately, those chances do not get any greater, because there are so few Negroes trained in classic ballet."

Alongside the text, the program featured individual photos of the company members, the women wearing black leotards and pink tights and pointe shoes, the men in fitted white T-shirts and black tights. She taped it to the wall between her twin beds, so that she could look at dancers like Lydia Abarca and Sheila Rohan and Gayle McKinney-Griffith as she fell asleep.

At ten years old, she had already transitioned to pointe work in her ballet classes. "It's like foot-binding," she says. "This tight little box squeezing your feet. It's all blisters and bruises and calluses and losing your toenails. You start at the barre with simple exercises—bourrées, relevés—then you graduate to doing a little center work. It's all incredibly painful, but you start building up strength in your ankles and calves and thighs. You get some momentum, and you're able to stand on pointe and do the pirouette. You feel the actual physics of it all. Suddenly you feel light. Like, *Oh my gosh, I'm now a ballerina.*"

Still, she wasn't ready to leave her family for New York, not that her mother would've let her. But the following summer, at age eleven, she attended Dance Theatre of Harlem's first-ever summer intensive program for talented ballet students. She was the youngest child in the Church of the Master studio, dancing on pointe alongside sixteen-year-olds. Mamie did volunteer administrative work for DTH while her daughter took classes. They stayed in Thelma Hill's apartment.

6

IN 1970, DANCE THEATRE OF HARLEM LEFT ON ITS FIRST major tour, a swing through the Caribbean that included stops in Bermuda, the Bahamas, and Antilles. For many of the members, it marked their first time ever on an airplane. Arthur Mitchell laid down strict expectations for company travel attire. From the moment they stepped out of their apartments until they found themselves on the subway back home, he wanted them dressed sharp, their hair and makeup perfect. "When you get to the airport, you'd better look like you're traveling in first class," he warned, "because they're going to be expecting you to come to the airport with fried chicken in your pocket."

When they arrived in Bermuda, and the dancers were checking in to their hotel, nobody volunteered to room with Lydia Abarca. A splinter seemed to have lodged between her and the other women. There were no petty squabbles or acts of sabotage, but Mitchell had placed her on a pedestal, creating a distance between her and the other dancers. "There was a clique and then there was Lydia," says Llanchie Stevenson. "Arthur was trying to do everything Balanchine did, so he had to have his principal ballerina. Lydia was the Suzanne Farrell of Dance Theatre of Harlem."

She was the chosen one. She got the best roles and the bulk of Mitchell's attention. There was a sense that she could conduct herself in ways that the other women never could, like missing the occasional company class for a modeling job. Abarca still remembers Sheila Rohan raising her hand during a company meeting to ask Mitchell why Abarca could miss class but the rest of them couldn't. Watching him brush Rohan off in response, Abarca wished for the studio floor to swallow her whole.

That first tour, though, Stevenson volunteered to room with Abarca out of pity for the younger girl. "I felt so sad for her," she says. "We're both ballerinas. We can room together. And that was the greatest thing I could've done because Lydia and I became sisters after that. And how can you dislike your sister?"

In Bermuda, the company premiered their first Balanchine ballet, *Concerto Barocco,* which had been coached on them by City Ballet's Melissa Hayden. There's a moment in the ballet in which the principal ballerina—here, Abarca—declares with an aggressive placement of her foot that she is superior to the second ballerina, Stevenson's role. In a conversation with the Legacy Council, Stevenson asks Abarca how she felt about her when they would perform the ballet. "Did you ever feel, when you put your foot down like that, did you think like, *Boom, I am the prima ballerina here. You might think you're so great, but I am better?*" The specificity of the questioning confuses Abarca. "Because when you watch the New York City Ballet," continues Stevenson, "Suzanne Farrell puts that foot down, and she's saying *I. Am. The. One.* Balanchine put that in her. But I never got that feeling from Lydia. Offstage, she was always like, *Okay, here I am, little Lydia.* It's like we actually enjoyed dancing together. When we smiled, we really were smiling at each other. But I still always wondered. Did you feel superior in that moment?"

Abarca grimaces, waving her hands as if to ward off the very idea. Sensing her discomfort, Rohan steps in. "You know what I really believe?" she says. "Lydia never knew she was on the throne."

A muse is a source, not a star. She's chosen to reflect someone else's greatness. It's a role assigned, and one that comes at a cost. Abarca was always shy about Mitchell's anointing of her, nervous that the other women resented her position. The question of whether colorism might have played a role in that status still makes Abarca uncomfortable. "I never took somebody's part," she says. "I never asked for a part. Whatever I had was given to me, without asking. And if it was trusted to me, I did my best to make it the best I could do to please Mr. Mitchell." But two things can exist at once: Abarca emerged as a magical force in the company, as did Virginia Johnson, another favorite of Mitchell's, and their light complexions played a role in his anointing of them. The indisputable fact of their artistry can live beside the dreary truth that Dance Theatre of Harlem wasn't immune to an early prioritization of Caucasian beauty standards.

Former principal danseur Mel Tomlinson described the bias he witnessed at the company in his 2018 memoir, *Beyond My Dreams*. "It was hard watching some brilliantly talented ballerinas be passed over repeatedly for roles because they were too dark in Mr. Mitchell's eyes," he writes. But in the very same chapter, he rhapsodizes over Lydia Abarca's singular appeal. "Everything about her, from how she moved her little finger to how she moved the souls of everyone who ever saw her, created an awe in me that I have never felt for any other ballerina."

In his interview with The HistoryMakers, Mitchell brushed off the accusations of colorism that dogged the company's early years. "'He only likes the light-skinned girls,'" Mitchell parroted when asked about the subject, his voice heavy with impatience. "I said, 'What are you talking about, the light-skinned girls?' I said, 'Sweetheart, you've got legs like a piano, no.'"

Indeed, Llanchie Stevenson felt Mitchell's lack of interest in her had less to do with her dark complexion than with her weight. "Lydia had the perfect body," she says. "Even though I had the technique and bah bah bah, I knew I would always be second fiddle."

At City Ballet, Mitchell had absorbed Balanchine's stern preference for ballerinas with pea heads on top of wraith frames. Clavicles popping out of necks like bicycle handles; tendons long enough to stretch beyond human limitation; all those thin, interchangeable buns holding back colorless sheets of hair. In earlier eras of dance, ballerinas were allowed curves and muscles, but Balanchine's taste for whitewashed slips of muscle and bone changed the art form's aesthetic ideal. Ballet still hasn't righted itself from his influence.

In Harlem, Mitchell may have preached about the importance of inclusivity on a classical stage, but he could be just as narrow-minded when it came to a woman's body. "On the one hand he's talking about Blackness and Black culture and beautiful Black bodies," says Sheila Rohan, "but in rehearsals he's talking about 'I want skinny, Balanchine-looking girls. Your butt is too big. You could get your leg up if you could lose the fat on your thighs. Wear a tighter bra to hold your breasts in.'"

"He was always slapping thighs," says Gayle McKinney-Griffith. "He hated butts. He wanted everyone what he called 'bone thin.' He could tell if you gained an ounce.'"

And so it was Lydia Abarca, not Stevenson, whom Mitchell chose to dance the pas de deux in *Agon*, the second ballet Balanchine gave Dance Theatre of Harlem. During rehearsals, Mitchell was exacting on every detail of her performance, down to the placement of her pinkies. "In *Agon*, there's a part where I had to take my partner's hand," Abarca says, holding her own wrist to demonstrate. In cascading fashion, she languidly curls her fingers down upon her wrist one at a time.

"He'd say, 'Finger, finger, finger. The audience has to see and think about what you're doing, what story you are trying to tell. You never just take your partner's hand! It's loaded. Do it with purpose and feeling.'" However shy and self-conscious she could be in everyday life, Abarca possessed a toughness in the studio. She could absorb Mitchell's criticism, his badgering, the furiousness of his attention, without it leaving a mark on her soul. "Hours and hours of private rehearsals with him," remembers Rohan. "I don't know how Lydia took it." It was because she hoped that since Mitchell had transformed himself into a star, he might do the same for her.

Early in the company's existence, Mitchell was talked into performing *Agon* for a one-time engagement in Atlanta, on a splashy bill that included Judith Jamison dancing her iconic sixteen-minute solo *Cry,* which Alvin Ailey had created for her as a tribute to his mother and the spirit of Black women. Mitchell chose Abarca as his partner and rehearsed her to death leading up to their performance. McKinney-Griffith recalls how heavily Mitchell's ego hung in the studio as he readied his muse. "This was his dream with Lydia. To be able to say, 'This is my partner. I've trained her. I've made her.'"

The *Agon* pas de deux is a test of extreme partnering. An austere tangle of body parts is set to Stravinsky's rhythmically complex music. The costuming is simple—a fitted white T-shirt and black tights on the man; a black leotard for the woman—so as not to distract from the intimacy of limbs braiding and stretching apart in dynamic lunges and sculptural shapes. There's a moment in Balanchine's choreography when the male leads his partner in a semicircle as if showing her off to the audience. When he first created the dance on Mitchell, Balanchine told him to picture himself like a trainer leading his prize racehorse back to its stall. That night in Atlanta, Mitchell's prize was Abarca.

Onstage, Abarca didn't feel nervous or intimidated. "When I danced *Agon*, I felt sexy, aristocratic, in charge," she says. She understood the honor of being Mitchell's first and only Black partner in a pas de deux that had been considered so scandalous when he'd performed it with white women. "But we weren't making a political statement together," she says. "It was just pure dance. The crowd loved it. Getting to do that with Mr. Mitchell was so special, even though as a partner he was a little pushy. Like, you don't have to hold my hand so tight. I got this!"

In 1970, Dance Theatre of Harlem participated in a week of showcase performances at Jacob's Pillow Dance Festival. The opening-night audience treated the dancers to nine curtain calls, with the remainder of their matinee and evening shows playing equally well to full houses. "And what was extraordinary was for some reason people came to see us, and they came very skeptical," says Virginia Johnson. "And you could feel their skepticism when the curtain went up. But you could also feel when their hearts turned, and they were with you.

And when that curtain came down at the end, they were standing on their feet cheering. And that happened over and over and over again."

Critics began writing about Mitchell's young company with a genuine sense of astonishment.

Said one critic: "This company of nearly twenty performers has obviously been beautifully trained, and we rather suspect, relentlessly. Good dancing isn't come by easily; and superb dancing such as this comes of long grueling hours of stress, strain, trial, and error until the fine finished product emerges."

Another reviewer marveled: "In a few years the Dance Theatre of Harlem will be able to mop up Leningrad, Moscow, London."

Dance critic Anna Kisselgoff declared, "No young company has made such progress in so short a time. . . . The troupe's members—some in their early teens—already have a performing presence rarely seen elsewhere and very much their own."

After reading reviews that referred to the miracle of his success, Mitchell was circumspect. "It is absolutely a miracle," he said. "But it's a miracle of purpose and dedication, not something that just happened and makes no sense. It is not a miracle for Black people to be fine classical artists. I have to laugh when people get excited about our dancers, as though a Black girl in toe shoes is a creature from outer space. Some of the reactions to us when we go out on the road are just incredible. People come expecting *Super Fly* and switchblades because, after all, it is Harlem. And then they see disciplined young dancers, and they can't believe it right away. But it's not incredible at all. There were always Black classical dancers in America. They just never got onstage."

In January 1971, Mitchell felt the time had come for Dance Theatre of Harlem to make its formal New York debut. Their three-night engagement at the Guggenheim Museum was sponsored by the heiress and philanthropist Alva Gimbel, of the Gimbels department store fortune. The elderly white woman had become an ardent supporter of Mitchell and his mission after attending an open Wednesday rehearsal at the Church of the Master. Afterward she summoned Mitchell and his treasurer, De Rose, to a private meeting in her suite at the Pierre Hotel. "What I want you to do," she told them, "is go out and find a building that you like and bring the information back to me."

Explaining why Dance Theatre of Harlem had become her favorite cause, Gimbel told the *New York Times,* "One of the reasons I wanted to help Arthur Mitchell is that I felt this was one solution to getting these young people in Harlem to have an inspiration in their lives. If they're going to be good dancers, they cannot run around, they cannot take dope, they cannot lie around, but must keep in perfect condition and work very hard." She invited the entire company to her two-hundred-acre garden estate in Greenwich, Connecticut. Clumsily eager to make her Black guests feel at home, she served a lunch of fried chicken and watermelon, which the women still laugh about today.

But Mitchell was going to take the money however it came. On a freezing January morning, a tip from a cab driver led Mitchell and De Rose to an abandoned garage and warehouse with two stories and a basement on 152nd Street between St. Nicholas and Amsterdam. As they walked through the hovel of a building, rats running over their feet, Mitchell said they'd finally found their permanent home. When he brought the news to Gimbel, she handed over a check for $110,000, saying, "I want you to cash it before my accountants know that I've written it." A $75,000 grant from the Rockefeller Brothers Fund went toward hiring architects; Mitchell booked the dancers for $70,000 of added performances. The renovations would take months to complete, but Mitchell could finally stop worrying about rising rents and hassles with landlords.

On opening night at the Guggenheim, Gimbel preened like a hen, her silver-top cane in hand as she held court with her fancy flock of friends. A half-moon stage had been built in the museum's rotunda. There were raised seats surrounding it for the audience, and spectators could position themselves around the apple-peel galleries overhead as well. The dancers had been rehearsing in the museum all day, as Mitchell restaged their performance to fit the round stage.

"This was make or break," says Sheila Rohan. "Our launching. Mr. Mitchell was intimidating us, telling us how many important people were there, money people. 'This is it! I got all these reporters here. You guys are dancing for your lives.' We understood we needed to make the audience take us seriously."

When it was time for them to take the stage, the dancers had to walk through the audience, padding nervously on their ballet shoes across the cold marble floor. Gayle McKinney-Griffith's nephew Todd, dapper in his new three-piece suit, cut through the tension when he hung over the parapet of the museum's spiraling ramp and waved at his aunt and her friends down below. "Look, there's Patsy! Hi, Patsy!" he called out to Patsy Ricketts, who was bunking with McKinney-Griffith on Maxine's pullout couch at the time.

The company performed three pieces, all of them Mitchell's—*Tones;* the premiere of *Fête Noire,* a party-setting confection choreographed in Balanchine's neoclassical style that was dedicated to Gimbel; and the crowd-pleaser *Rhythmetron,* which highlighted Mitchell's intention to produce dancers who were as fluent in classical idioms as they were in contemporary- and African-diaspora-influenced styles of movement.

After the performance, the roar of the audience's approval shot up the spiral of the building. Rohan remembers that the largely white crowd was so enchanted that they reached out to touch them after their bows, as if to see if the dancers were in fact real, their wonder almost fetishizing. "These white people were treating us like we were touched in gold," she says. "'You're so beautiful! Ooh, look at your legs!'"

Rohan has a picture taken of her and Walter Raines, the

elder statesman of the male dancers, beloved by all, in the dressing room beforehand. They're sitting next to each other backstage, both dressed in their simple pearl-gray costumes for *Tones.* His weary head rests on her shoulder, the front of his leotard soaked in sweat, while she sits drowsily upright, one of her arms resting on her knee. At the cocktail reception afterward, Raines broke down in tears, realizing for the first time that the company was going to make it after all.

Two months later Dance Theatre of Harlem debuted its first Broadway engagement, at the ANTA Theater, which included a premiere of another ballet from the City Ballet repertory, Jerome Robbins's *Afternoon of a Faun,* set to a Claude Debussy score. "From the time the curtain lifted until it fell for the last time, there were vibes in that theatre that I've never felt before while watching ballet," wrote Colette Dowling for *Playbill* magazine, of the experience of sitting in a theater whose audience she estimated was about twenty-five percent Black people. "In short, the place was *alive.* This was no passive reception of sights and sounds but a kind of living, breathing participation, so strong was the involvement between audience and dancers. Among the bravos that followed each ballet were shouts of, 'Don't stop!' and 'Right on, brothers and sisters!' "

Lydia Abarca danced a pas de deux from *Afternoon of a Faun,* about an intimate encounter between two dancers alone in a dance studio. Ripe with the bloom of beauty and youth, the man and woman gaze at themselves through an imagined mirror played by the audience. Robbins's ballet is as much about desire as it is about the curious fascination at finding oneself desirable.

To help Abarca unlock her character, Mitchell had asked his friend Cicely Tyson to help her feel the emotion beneath the choreography. Tyson urged the young woman to practice the movements at home in front of the bathroom mirror, taking notice of where and how her eyes moved throughout the piece. When she got in front of an audience, Tyson wanted the girl to be conscious only of her own imagined reflection.

Abarca was further helped along by having the ballerina who had originated the role with City Ballet in 1953 as her personal coach. Tanaquil Le Clercq's spectacular career had been cut brutally short after she'd contracted polio in 1956 while on tour with City Ballet in Copenhagen. She remained paralyzed from the waist down, still living in the Apthorp apartment she'd shared with Balanchine, her former husband, until he'd left her to chase after Suzanne Farrell. She hadn't been inside a dance studio in years until one day, she and Mitchell crossed paths at a restaurant in their shared neighborhood. Sensing that his former partner was floundering, he insisted she bring her knowledge and experience up to Harlem. After some initial resistance, she handed herself over gratefully, promising, "Whatever you want me to do."

Every day when Le Clercq arrived, the male dancers would lift her wheelchair and carry her up the narrow staircase, where she would teach surprisingly ferocious classes, zooming around the wooden floor, demonstrating the steps with her one mobile arm. Even in a wheelchair, she had the darting energy of a hummingbird. When she noticed a break in a dancer's line, she'd whip her chair to their side, take hold of the dancer's leg, and roll backward with it until they were in full extension.

In advance of the Broadway performance, Le Clercq was joined in leading rehearsal by Jerome Robbins himself, who loomed so large in Abarca's imagination from *West Side Story*. A photographer came to the studio to shoot them rehearsing as well. Antony Armstrong-Jones—Earl of Snowdon, then husband to Princess Margaret and a professional photographer—had adopted Dance Theatre of Harlem as one of his favorite subjects after attending an open-to-the-public Wednesday rehearsal. He captured an iconic shot of Robbins demonstrating how the man in the ballet is romantically obsessed with the woman. Abarca sits on the floor on her knees, dressed in pale tights and a black turtleneck over her leotard, her hair scraped into a high ponytail. Robbins crouches on his fingertips beside her, brushing her cheek so passionately with his lips, it's like he's trying to inhale her. Ignoring Robbins's kiss, she gazes upon her imagined reflection with erotic indifference.

Lord Snowdon was so smitten with Abarca that he later arranged for a photo shoot outside her projects, pulling up to the Grant Houses on 125th Street in a limousine. "All we knew was somebody by the name of Lord Snowdon was coming over," says Lydia's sister Celia. "Didn't know his first name. Suddenly he's just in our little kitchen surrounded by a bunch of us, looking around like he'd never been to a place like ours before. My dad didn't give him much thought. He didn't know about kings and queens and Europe. All he knew was that his daughter danced." Abarca has a Polaroid of herself sitting in between the queen's brother-in-law and her daddy on their family room sofa. She has a shy smile on her face, holding her hands relaxed at her side with her legs crossed. Francisco, his mustache so trimmed it appears penciled on, stares unsmiling at the camera. Snowdon, dressed head to toe in dark denim, looks warily at Francisco, as if sizing the other man up and finding his own self lacking. He would spend the morning shooting Lydia Abarca walking up and down 125th Street for a European fashion magazine, while his driver gave her younger siblings a ride to Corpus Christi School on 122nd Street in Snowdon's limousine.

Abarca felt like she was on the threshold of the life she'd long dreamed for herself. She began slipping out of her family's apartment at the crack of dawn in the morning after a big performance to race to the newsstand at the end of her block. "I'd tell the guy, 'Let me look for my name?'" Then she'd squeal and read the reviews aloud for him whenever she found it. On the day after the ANTA performance, she held her breath as she found her name again and again in the morning's pages.

"Especially entrancing as the girl who stirs a narcissistic ballet student (Clover Mathis) from his daydreams was Lydia Abarca, 19, a native New Yorker who has been dancing for less than two years," read the review in *Time*. "Lithe and feathery, she exuded a quality of virginal nubility—and she displayed the eye-commanding presence that is the mark of a potential star."

Abarca held the magazine to her chest, the wheeze of the downtown bus and squeal of the bodega's metal gate rolling up for the day like music to her ears. She couldn't wait to show her mother.

7

THE COMPANY WAS ON A SPRINT INTO PUBLIC CON-sciousness. After the Guggenheim and their Broadway en-gagement at the ANTA, they made a second swing through the Caribbean. Then came a two-week residency in Chicago. A day of free lecture-demonstrations on the campus of Columbia University for over three thousand inner-city schoolchildren, which was such a resounding success that the administration invited the company to return for an ongoing series. A trans-continental tour of the United States. All they did was dance, or travel from place to place, piled on top of each other on buses and planes, to dance some more. "I remember when we went to Buffalo, New York, in the winter," says Gayle McKinney-Griffith. "There was like six feet of snow, and we had to get off the bus in the night, unpack the bus with all the big bins of costumes and lights, then get back on the bus to check into our hotel, where Mr. Mitchell says, 'There's a ten o'clock class in the morning, good night!' That was our reality day in and day out."

In May, George Balanchine extended a historic invitation to his former protégé Arthur Mitchell. He wanted City Ballet to share the stage, during its annual spring gala benefit at Lincoln Center's renowned State Theater, with Dance Theatre of Harlem. For the first time in the history of his company, Balanchine would present his dancers in tandem with another company's, a group of Black artists who'd been performing for less than two years.

In preparation for the event, Balanchine and Mitchell teamed up as cochoreographers of a new ballet, *Concerto for Jazz Band and Orchestra*, a piece that fused classical ballet idioms with boogie-woogie jazz steps. *The Tonight Show*'s bandleader, Doc Severinsen, and his jazz musicians would play upstage while the New York City Ballet Orchestra played in the pit. Twenty-four dancers from each company would meet and merge onstage: City Ballet male dancers would partner with Harlem ballerinas and vice versa. "That night was the turning point that made others consider us big league," says Charles De Rose. "After that is when the Bolshoi started coming to our rehearsals to see what everyone was talking about. A new level of competition had arrived on the scene—dancers with athleticism and technique and exuberance and freshness and something to prove."

It wasn't being strapped to the rocket ship of Dance Theatre of Harlem that tore at the seams of Sheila Rohan's marriage, though the demands of company life did cause a strain in the household. "He would have to pick up the kids after school or from the babysitters," remembers Rohan. "Sometimes I would try to cook in the morning, but if I didn't, he would have to cook. And he was doing heavy-duty work as a janitor during the day; he wasn't sitting at a desk. There was tension, but we managed."

Ellsworth loved her dancing. He never once asked her to quit, not that she would have. "I was proud of myself," says Rohan, of making it as a professional dancer. "I was accomplishing something. I wasn't out in the street or working in McDonald's. The whole neighborhood was rooting for me."

But the childhood sweethearts had a history of separating and getting back together. Ellsworth had a wandering eye. When Charlene was four years old, she remembers her daddy coming to pick her up from her grandmother's house so he could walk her over to his new apartment. And when Ellsworth assisted Sheila's brother-in-law Romare on a work trip in California, he ended up staying for almost a year, missing the Guggenheim, the ANTA, and Lincoln Center. Sheila was tasked with holding down the fort on Staten Island with the three kids and a tour schedule that wanted to send her to Europe that summer for over two months—the company's first transatlantic tour. She had to find a way to make it all work.

The kids were divided up among family and neighbors. Gary went to one of Sheila's sister's houses up the street, Charlene to another sister. Little Sheila would sometimes stay with her grandma Eliza or Ms. Barbara, the neighborhood babysitter, who lived so close by that the families could practically share a clothesline. Sheila Rohan knew her kids were safe, but leaving them still scraped at her stretched heart.

As their trip to Europe approached, Rohan wasn't the only one in a flurry preparing to fly across the ocean for the first time. "We were all packing our bags, getting our outfits," says Gayle McKinney-Griffith. "This was the most exciting thing that had ever happened in my life." From the moment company members stepped out of the cab at the airport until they were safely out of Mitchell's sight back in their New York apartments, the dancers were expected to come correct, dressed in stylish clothes, with impeccable hair and makeup. "When we go on tour, people think the dancers are a group of models," Mitchell said later in an interview. "They're so beautiful. They have good taste. They dress, but they don't overdress. They have beautiful, marvelous bodies and can wear just about anything. Sure, I criticize them. I guess I'm against both the garret and garish looks. Poverty is where we come from. If you're beautiful, don't cover it up."

Cicely Tyson joined them for a portion of their tour, casting herself in the role of the younger dancers' academic tutor. Between Mitchell and Tyson, two celebrities whose entire careers were spent in service of breaking barriers in the arts so as to lift up their race, the dancers stayed on their best behavior for the entirety of the tour. "She was like the mother of the group, and Mr. Mitchell was like the father," says McKinney-

Griffith. "They were all eyes on us." Mitchell liked to brag that his young apprentices in the company had risen from D to B+ academic students once they'd come under his demanding gaze. Tyson was a rigorous tutor and, though she was encouraging of the dancers, an intimidating one. "You never stopped feeling starstruck around her," says McKinney-Griffith.

For the most part, the dancers took to the glamour of Europe immediately, but Lydia Abarca quickly crumpled upon their arrival in Italy, their first stop, pining for the safety of her family. Not even having her boyfriend on the tour with them, a male dancer she'd nicknamed "Frog Legs" because of his spectacular jumps, could soothe her. "Oh, God, once we left New York City, give me about two days, and you'd find me in a bathroom somewhere crying my eyes out," she says. "I would get so homesick. 'Where's Lydia?' 'In the bathroom crying.'" Mitchell called Abarca's mother in Harlem complaining that her daughter was depressed, and they needed to revive her. Without a word to Abarca, he told Josephine to get a passport for someone in the family. They needed to come to Italy.

Not long afterward Mitchell told his dancers that the company's wardrobe mistress, Zelda Wynn, needed to return to New York for surgery because her knee had given out—all true. Prior to her life at Dance Theatre of Harlem, Wynn had become famous for designing gowns for the likes of Josephine Baker, Dorothy Dandridge, Ella Fitzgerald, and Mae West, as well as collaborating with Hugh Hefner on what would become *Playboy*'s iconic bunny waitress ensemble. She joined DTH when she was well into her sixties, running the department out of 152nd Street's brightly lit basement, where she always kept a percolator of hot coffee running and was occasionally known to sleep on her large fabric-cutting table. Wynn—so deeply beloved by the dancers, despite her habit of sticking them with her pins and then saying it was their fault for moving—served as the company's main costume designer for thirty-one years, until she died in 2001 at the age of ninety-six.

Mitchell took it upon himself to shepherd Wynn safely back from Italy to the United States, promising his dancers he'd return in no time. Unbeknownst to them, he would return with family support for his sagging prima. Josephine had chosen her son, eleven-year-old Julio, who was out of school for the summer and didn't have a job, to make the trip to Italy. Mitchell met the two outside the gate at JFK before their flight to Rome. Josephine would later tell her son that when she watched the plane pull away from the gate with her only boy, she was so nervous that her knees gave out. Julio, for his part, was terrified for the entire flight, sitting next to Mitchell, trying not to bleed his anxiety onto his sister's boss. "I'm not even the kid who was into roller coasters at the park," he says. "So I'm thinking to myself, *What am I doing thirty thousand feet in the air for seven and a half hours with this stranger?*"

The company's tour was set to begin with ten performances at the fourteenth annual Festival of the Two Worlds, a major cultural event that draws thousands to the ancient Umbrian town of Spoleto. The town sat on a foothill of the Apennine Mountains—as far from the Grant Houses or Staten Island or Maxine's spare sofa as the women could imagine. Cobblestone streets, women with silk scarves in their hair, handsome men winking at them from convertibles, gelato stands on every corner. "It was like being on the set of an Italian movie, it was so glamorous," says Sheila Rohan.

Lydia Abarca was in rehearsal one day, upside down, stretching her legs on the floor of the theater, when she heard a high-pitched oohing and aahing in the hallway. Just as she righted herself to see what all the commotion was about, Julio burst through the door. She started sobbing at the surprise of having him in her arms, and her brother and Mitchell, who'd trailed in just behind him, sniffled right along with her. "I told Mr. Mitchell, 'You have no idea what this means to me,'" she says. "There was no way my family could have ever come see us in Europe, and now here was my baby brother standing before me." Says Julio, "Everybody in that room was crying. They were so happy for me and Lydia. Although I was probably crying with happiness because I was just so glad to be off that plane."

For the rest of the trip, Lydia survived on peanut butter sandwiches, reserving her tiny stipend for Julio so he could enjoy restaurant food. He bunked in a pensione with Lydia's boyfriend, who was two years younger than her, only seventeen. The boys would spend their summer jockeying for her attention. "Two's company, three's a crowd type of thing," says Julio.

The festival began soon after Julio's arrival. With Tania León conducting her first orchestra, the company performed *Tones* to a sold-out house. Recently Sheila Rohan's daughter Charlene found her mother a bootleg copy of their performance on the internet, and it remains Rohan's only recording of her dancing with the company. At the end of their performance, the crowd surged to their feet for a twenty-minute standing ovation, their voices united in a rhythmic chanting of *"Bis! Bis! Bis!"* Says Gayle McKinney-Griffith, "We thought they were calling us 'beasts,' but quickly learned it translated into 'More!'"

European audiences, so much less reserved than American balletomanes, waited in throngs to greet the dancers at the stage doors for their nine subsequent performances in Spoleto. They showered them with bouquets onstage or had them delivered to their dressing rooms. Some of the women took to wearing their flowers in their hair, thinking it made them look like Billie Holiday. "We were feeling like we were on top of the planet," says Lydia Abarca. "We felt so good, so special. Like real ambassadors, you know what I mean? It was like, wow, this is what happens when you demand a hundred percent of yourself."

After Spoleto, the company traveled by train for performances in Turin, Verona, and Florence, then up to Amsterdam and Belgium, before returning to Italy for vacation days in Rome. "I was on the adventure of a lifetime," says Julio. "We stayed in an apartment near the Spanish Steps. I threw coins into the Trevi Fountain. Went to the Colosseum, saw Michelangelo. We'd go on scooters down to the ocean, where my sister bought me a little blow-up canoe. All those pretty girls in the dance company. I was infatuated with one of them, I tell you.

"But the best part of it all, to tell you the truth—hold on a second," says Julio gruffly, as he breaks into tears. "Sorry, every time I think about my sister dancing it makes me cry. The best part of it was getting to see her dance. She was so freakin' beautiful. I would watch her from backstage. You wouldn't think an eleven-year-old boy would be into ballet, but that's how special she was. She was the gift. Everywhere we traveled was just the ambience." His big sister was like liquid magic onstage, so pure and effortless under the lights. In between ballets, he'd watch her jam her inhaler into her mouth, desperately trying to open her lungs, then go right back onstage for another ballet. He'd never seen anything so heroic in his life.

To this day, whenever Lydia and Julio are together, the conversation inevitably turns to the surprise of getting to experience Europe together. The trip marked Julio's first and last time on a plane. He grew into a man so afraid of flying that he won't go anywhere that he can't get to in the comfort of his own car.

When Ellsworth learned the kids were being cared for under separate roofs while Sheila was on tour, he finally returned home. "When my dad came back to Staten Island, he moved back into the house," says Charlene. "To my knowledge, my parents were back together. And that's when I remember the real shift in the home. Dad became the primary caregiver while Mom was traveling and dancing. I always say I learned to cook, clean, and sew from my father because he took care of us when my mom was touring. That was his sacrifice. He saw that my mother had a vision for her life, and he wanted her to do it. And he loved to watch her dance."

Some nights after local performances, Ellsworth would pick Sheila up at the theater in his old BMW. He never resented the beautiful men who spent so much time with his wife, embracing and lifting her up onstage. "Why would I feel jealous? I can't dance," he says. Through it all, he remained convinced of the value of her work. "A lot of that came from Sheila's family," he says with a laugh. "Eight women? I mean they'd have whupped my butt if I got in the way of her dreams. No, nunh-unh. It would have been ill-advised of me to try and stymie that kind of creativity. She had a true talent, and it had to be used."

On the weekends, Sheila's three kids continued their regular trips to the studio, at the company's new home on 152nd Street. The building had undergone extensive renovations, thanks to the grant from the Rockefeller brothers and donated performance fees from the dancers. "We needed everything," Mitchell would later recount to a group of students at Radcliffe College. "We couldn't afford to buy costumes, so I asked Singer to give us some sewing machines. Then I went to several textile mills and discovered that they threw away the ends of bolts of material—sometimes as much as a hundred yards a swatch. I got them to donate the leftover fabric. With the machines and the cloth, we started a sewing and tailoring program. We also trained our own electricians, our own sound people, our own lighting technicians."

"Tell me I can't, and I'll show you I can" was Mitchell's motto. He had built himself a three-story response to all the naysayers who said what he dreamed couldn't be done. The company rehearsed on the top floor of their new home, in Studio 3, which mercifully had a fire escape where the dancers could catch a breath of air or dry their tears of frustration.

During rehearsals, they danced to the pulsing beat and slap of basketball and handball games on the Battleground playground courts just outside the brick-walled studio's giant windows. Mitchell claimed a narrow space tucked into a former elevator shaft for his office, just across the hall from Studio 3. Younger students rehearsed in two smaller studios on the ground floor, and then in the basement, Zelda Wynn set up her workshop, where neighborhood housewives joined her students on the rows of donated Singers. The locker rooms were in the basement, too, as was Karel Shook's office, from which smoke poured like out of an oven. "Sometimes he'd work in there in the dark, so you didn't always know he was in there," says Marcia Sells. "But then if I was sneaking in late to class, I'd see the ember of his cigarette light up, and the vapors of smoke, like out of some film noir."

Sheila Rohan would go up early on weekend mornings for rehearsals, Nanette meeting her kids at the ferry later as they'd grown accustomed to, and escort them up to 152nd Street.

Sheila's son, Gary, took León's percussion classes. Little Sheila, meanwhile, just six years old, got herself kicked out of ballet for her habit of running her mouth and swinging on the barre, but she studied violin and guitar with León. Though she spent the bulk of her energies asking for pony rides on Mitchell's shoulders, hiding under the company's designer costumes, and sitting on the ballerinas' laps in the dressing rooms, messing up their makeup.

Sheila's older daughter, Charlene, had kept up with her ballet classes. She loved her mother's world so much that she took to spending entire days in the theater when the company was in season, listening to Mitchell yell—"Right! That's what I told you! You have to use your head!"—at his dancers. She saw how the other women would gravitate toward Gayle McKinney-Griffith in the hours leading up to a performance. "She never seemed to get agitated by Mr. Mitchell when he was barking," says Charlene. "She seemed to have this ability to calm the other dancers."

She and her cousins would watch rehearsals from the wings of the theater, nap in the shadows, and then wake up in time to watch the performance from backstage. Every season Aunt Nanette bought her a ticket to one performance so she could watch from the audience. Charlene's proudest moment was the first time she saw her mother dance in the role of the Bride in Geoffrey Holder's *Douglas*, which depicts the elaborate wedding ritual between partners of African and Indian descent. "Mom was the one being showcased as the prima in that particular ballet," says Charlene. "The guys carried her onto the stage. Two men had her by the arms while she was in an aerial split, and they twirled all the way around. It was heaven."

At home, Sheila had started reading Dr. Spock, the author and pediatrician who was making headlines for encouraging parents to talk more openly with their children and show them affection. But Ellsworth wasn't interested in evolving his parenting style. He'd bang on the walls to wake the kids up in the morning. Set their alarms for early Saturday morning to start their chores. "My children thought I was kind of hard," he says now. "We made it work, though. I think the one special thing about us is that no matter what we've gone through, we are family."

Sheila would go on to divorce Ellsworth, but the two found a way to stay forever partners. The health of the family unit took precedence over any heartbreak. "We started as friends, we fell in love, and we continued as friends," says Rohan. "Family is the most important thing in our life. He's one of thirteen. I'm one of eight. Children are the roots. So regardless of whatever was going on with us, we kept the family together. We're soulmates."

8

THREE YEARS IN, DANCE THEATRE OF HARLEM WAS SET-
tling into its permanent home on 152nd Street. Founding
company member Bill Scott, a young, brash, beautiful twenty-
one-year-old dancer and choreographer who fancied himself
a younger Arthur Mitchell, volunteered to step up as ballet
master, the person charged with helping to manage the daily
rhythms of company life. Impressed by Gayle McKinney-
Griffith's calm demeanor, he asked her to join forces as his assistant. For her part, she would have preferred to concentrate
only on her art. But the ask had been made, and the need for
extra hands was so apparent. She split herself in two for the
sake of the company.

Mitchell knew McKinney-Griffith was blessed with the
ability to learn and memorize steps quickly, as well as having a
little Juilliard training in styles of dance notations—a language
to document human movement in symbolic representation.

Even as she feared that he was overestimating the breadth of the skill set that she'd developed over a couple of college classes, he tasked her with capturing the choreography of all the new ballets he was throwing at the company. Suddenly, for large stretches of day, she found herself tucked into a narrow metal desk at the front of the studio with stacks of notebooks, feverishly recording choreography as it unspooled from the minds of Mitchell and the other great artists who worked with them.

As time went on, the constellation of her new role's demands continued to expand. She took over scheduling. She helped organize company rehearsals, ran them, and maintained the dancers' schedules. If Mitchell was displeased with a ballet's casting or a woman's weight or a dancer's bad attitude, he'd charge her with communicating that news to them. In her personal archives, for instance, McKinney-Griffith has a telegram from Hutaff Lennon in the costume department, sent while the company was on the road. "Dear Girls, Mr. Mitchell has instructed me to hold up on the issuing of pointe shoes. Please try to make do with what you have already been issued." Dancers on tour run through shoes like brushfire. When the shoe box wears thin, the dancer bears her full body weight on her unprotected toes. McKinney-Griffith pushed back on Mitchell to reconsider the seriousness of the ask, and he went ballistic. "He was just screaming at me," she says. " 'Do you know how much this all costs and you're complaining?' " He was too proud to let her know that when the company operated on a deficit, he was forced to dip into his own pocket to cover the dancers' salaries.

She was always being asked to do more, more, more. McKinney-Griffith remembers a time on tour when Mitchell burst into Bill Scott's hotel room, where the two were fine-tuning the day's rehearsal schedule. Mitchell exclaimed that he'd been invited to meet with some possible fundraisers at the last minute and was unprepared. "He said, 'I need to get some clothes! I need a haircut!'" McKinney-Griffith says. "Bill went, 'Oh, Gayle will cut your hair.' Um, thanks, Bill. I cut some of the boys' hair sometimes, so I had my scissors with me. I tucked a pillowcase around Mr. Mitchell's neck. And I told myself, *Gayle, if you make a mistake, this is the end of your life.*"

Mitchell loved being described in an early profile by the *New York Times* as "a controlled maniac," and he never stopped referring to himself as such. And McKinney-Griffith could handle him in ways that the more outwardly ambitious Scott couldn't. When the egos of the two men clashed, she served as the breeze between them. There's a gentleness to the soft-spoken McKinney-Griffith that's not to be confused with fragility. She knew what was worth fighting for—the greater health of the company rather than anyone's singular grievances, including her own—so she spared herself power struggles that she knew she couldn't win. When Mitchell was on a tear, she didn't engage. When she needed him to look at a problem from a different point of view, she came at him indirectly, so that he wouldn't feel she was questioning his authority. "Arthur would never say, 'Oh, you're right,'" she says. "But he might say, 'Well, come back and we'll go over it again.' As soon as he said, 'I'll think about it,' I felt like I had won."

And there were wins, extraordinary ones. The women in the company had long relied on relaxers or on Murray's and Vitapointe and Dax to grease their hair up into high buns, which they'd then cover with do-rags to make lie flat. But the natural movement was in full, glorious swing. Black women on the street and in cinema had started embracing their curls and Afros as sexy and free. "Cicely Tyson was wearing braids and Afros," says McKinney-Griffith. "The rest of us said, 'Hey, we want to wear Afros too.' We were tired of putting the grease in, and the spray and the pins. We talked to the guys in the company first and said, 'We want to see how our hair is naturally.' They were all for it, though behind our backs they were probably like, 'They're going to get killed.'"

McKinney-Griffith brought to Mitchell the idea of the women all picking their hair out. She pointed out that Rohan danced with her tiny Afro and hadn't faced any blowback from the audience or press. But the idea of an entire company of ballerinas wearing their hair natural was too much for him. "Mr. Mitchell was like, 'No, no, no, we're not going to do that!'" she says. "I don't think it crossed his mind that we could wear our Afros *and* be elegant. But we stood our ground. I told him, 'It's not permanent; we can change it. We just want to see how it looks.' Plus, we were having lecture-demonstrations, and I was saying it would just be really great to relate to the students because they know Afros." And so for a couple of years, the women of Dance Theatre of Harlem wore their hair free, though eventually they reverted to Mitchell's preferred chignons. He always won in the end.

When Scott moved on from the company, Gayle McKinney-Griffith was left to manage Mitchell alone, taking on the role of the company's first ballet mistress. Within his office's narrow brick-lined walls, she bore intimate witness to all his stresses and furies. Whatever triggered his upset—the perceived failings of one of the dancers, a board member daring to suggest how he should run a company that he'd built from the ground up, or the world in general for refusing to bend to his will—would rouse him from his desk, and he'd mount the hand-carved spiral steps that were bolted into the wall behind it, leading nowhere. Looming over her, he'd bellow about his various frustrations and condemnations, and she would silently endure his purge. Then she'd have to stand alongside him in the studio or theaters as he complimented the dancers or the visiting donors to their faces, and afterward she'd follow him out of the room and listen as he ripped them to shreds, often before they were out of earshot.

McKinney-Griffith had to find a way to hold on to the joy of dancing for Mitchell, even as he revealed to her the darkest sides of himself. But listening to him speak so caustically about dancers whom she'd come to think of as her brothers and sisters wore at her spirit. "I was privy to a lot of conversations about casting, and it was just horrible sometimes," she says. "I cried for people. I would never tell anyone the disparaging things he'd say. Sometimes it was too much for me, and I would just become stone, listening to him with a poker face. 'This one's too fat!' or 'If she can't lose this weight, I'm taking her out of this!' I would have to try to make him see reason. I'd have to say in my most diplomatic voice, not too aggressively, 'Well, we only have a certain amount of people. You can't take them out.'" She'd studiously record his demands in her notepad, already strategizing how to convey his messages to her fellow dancers in a way that would cause the least possible harm.

Whenever dealing with Mitchell became too overwhelming, McKinney-Griffith would run to Walter Raines, Mitchell's first hire in the company, to ground herself. Raines was as kind as he was elegant, a contemporary of Mitchell's rather than his creation. He was the rare dancer in the company who called the boss by his first name. Raines had traveled the world before landing at Dance Theatre of Harlem. He spoke German and French. He knew everybody, traveling in the same elite circles as Mitchell, and he had a way of adapting his personality to meet the needs of every individual lucky enough to call him a friend. He and Rohan thought of themselves as the seniors in the company, the mom—or "Mamacita," as Tania León called Rohan—and pop to the younger kids. Raines also took on the role of patient tutor to León, helping her with her English on her assignments for NYU, where she was still a student. And he provided a stiff shoulder for McKinney-Griffith to cry upon whenever she needed it, while offering wise counsel on how to deal with their mercurial leader.

"Walter would listen to me rant on and on and on. He'd say, 'You know, Gayle, just go on and do what you feel. If you think that he's wrong, then he's wrong. Don't let him try to insult you. Don't argue with him. Just say your piece and leave.'"

In the evenings, when the rest of the dancers packed up their bags to head home, McKinney-Griffith could finally pull herself away from her role as ballet mistress and remember that she was a dancer first. "It was so nerve-racking, because I couldn't always rehearse with the group that I was supposed to be performing with the next week," she says. "I would always have to beg the men to stay late with me. 'Please, let's just run through our pas de trois or our pas de deux.'"

When asked now if her tenure as ballet mistress cost her opportunities as a dancer, she goes silent for a beat. While she considers her response, the other women chime in, flanking their friend's younger self. "No, she was too good," says Lydia Abarca.

Smiling graciously at the support, McKinney-Griffith is sanguine on the matter. "I didn't feel denied, but I was so involved with the present of everything we were doing. Sometimes when we were casting, I would feel like I could have done one of the ballets that he never considered me for." When she'd suggest herself for a role, he'd usually cut her off with a quick "nah," without even looking up from his paperwork. She pleaded with Mitchell to consider her for *Le Corsaire*, in the pas de deux that's one of the most famous in the classical ballet repertoire. Each time he'd brush her off, insisting she wasn't yet ready. He had it in his head that the purple tutu that the dancer Laura Brown wore in the role wouldn't suit McKinney-Griffith. "He wanted me in harem pants instead for whatever reason," she says. "So that's how he kept me at bay. 'I've got to get this new costume.'" When Mitchell finally surprised her with the opportunity to don Brown's purple tutu for a matinee show in front of a small audience, she remembers fumbling her performance. "I'd been trying to rehearse at night, but my partner, Paul Russell, didn't want to stay late," she says. "He was such a great partner that I hoped it wouldn't really matter. But that day I messed up my solo. Brilliantly."

Ultimately, her greatest roles never came from Mitchell, but rather from outside artists who recognized her potential and had no qualms about potentially distracting her from her ballet mistress duties. James Truitte and Carmen de Lavallade, the original stars of Lester Horton's *The Beloved*, set the ballet on Dance Theatre of Harlem. They chose McKinney-Griffith as their star. De Lavallade, a dancer of such refined elegance and the wife of Geoffrey Holder, worked with her on the role of the abused wife wrongly accused of infidelity, while Truitte and Raines dissected the role of the rageful husband who ultimately chokes her to death. Her gentle friend Raines brought a Method approach to the part. "I remember coming up to Walter before showtime, and he was stalking the backstage. I touched his arm, and he yelled, 'Do not bother me! I do not want to see you until after the show!' I backed away from him slowly, thinking he was going to kill me." Onstage, he pulled and threw McKinney-Griffith violently around by her arms. It was a beautifully choreographed piece, the memory of which would haunt her in the future.

But of all McKinney-Griffith's roles, her friends hold up her pas de trois in *Forces of Rhythm* as a perfect union of artist and material. Louis Johnson, who'd studied at the School of American Ballet with Mitchell, was a genre-crossing choreographer for Hollywood, Broadway, and the classical stage. The former ballet dancer, who taught by flowing, bounding example, was coming into the studio to cast what would become one of the company's signature ballets for years. "Mr. Mitchell told me that we were going to have a new piece, and Louis Johnson was the choreographer, and I was to do all the notation," she says. So she assumed her familiar position at her desk, ready to record his choreography.

But to her shock, Johnson called her to the center when he was casting what would become the ballet's iconic pas de trois. "I wasn't warmed up. I was just sitting there writing away. But then Louis said again, 'Gayle, come on over here.' My heart was fluttering. A dancer always walks on eggshells because sometimes a choreographer will say, 'Step in here and do this,' and then change course. 'Okay, no, not you. You over there, come step in.' You don't want to ever get too attached."

She glanced over at Mitchell before setting down her pen and notebooks. Johnson paired her with two of the male dancers, Homer Bryant and Derek Williams. He looked at McKinney-Griffith through his squinting eyes and told her,

"Your character is searching, searching. I want you to run over to this side of the room, and pause, curious, then run over to the other and do the same." Something in her grace and yearning spoke to him. He had found his ballerina for the pas de trois, which he set to Donny Hathaway's version of "He Ain't Heavy, He's My Brother." The song is a bath of feeling, from the opening strains of piano to the stroking velvet of Hathaway's voice. *The road is long, with many a winding turn.* "Her style, Hathaway's voice, it was the perfect pairing," says Karlya Shelton. "Soft, delicate, and so strong at the same time."

In video clips, there's an exquisite sense of hesitation and longing to McKinney-Griffith's performance, as her character struggles to choose between two different paths in life, represented by her partners, Williams and Bryant. She flutters like a sparrow in a simple white leotard and ballet skirt, gently careening back and forth between the men as the music throbs to its crescendo. With one last longing look at Bryant, she turns away from him at a run and jumps. She appears to levitate backward as Bryant comes in underneath her and lifts her by her seat straight over his head. After that one gravity-defying motion, she perches delicately in the air, sitting upright atop the palms of Bryant's hands like a cloud. The famous sit lift tested her core strength—she had to somehow lean backward, with arms outstretched, without toppling over her partner's backside—as much as her courage. "We rehearsed that until we knew it in our sleep," says McKinney-Griffith. "Once the guy locks his arms in, you can lift up and open your arms. But before that you can't do anything. I've seen a dancer go over the head onto the floor before. But Homer never dropped me, not once."

McKinney-Griffith's nephew Todd went to all his aunt's New York performances. He remembers waiting breathlessly in the audience each night for the sit lift. "That was always the applause moment," he says. "The music would swell, and all of a sudden my aunt Gayle would be up in the air, and you wouldn't know how she got up there. She'd just be this ballet angel goddess sitting on top of a guy's hands. You would hear the whole audience gasp, and everybody cry 'Ohhhh!'"

To this day, McKinney-Griffith can't hear "He Ain't Heavy, He's My Brother," a song of gratitude for worthwhile burdens, without choking up. It transports her back to the wings of a theater, where she'd wait for her pas de trois. "I always felt my heart bursting out beforehand because it felt like the women onstage were calling me. Then I'd have a lump in my throat the whole time I was dancing from the weight of what was being sung. The verses. The lyrics. Louis knew how to combine classical music with contemporary so that it touched your soul. And he could dance every part. If he could've had a strong enough partner, he would've done the sit lift himself."

In 2020, Louis Johnson, acclaimed choreographer, dancer, and director, died at the age of ninety after testing positive for Covid-19. For all his professional triumphs, Johnson never got the opportunity he deserved to display his talent as a ballet dancer. Upon his acceptance into the School of American Ballet, the administration warned that they would never let him into City Ballet. "I don't talk about it much," Johnson once told a reporter. "But I knew it was because I was Black. I would love to have danced ballet more than I did because that was what I did so much of my life, and never got a chance to do it for the public. You say to yourself, *Gee, I wish people could have known I did that, and I really did do it well.*"

McKinney-Griffith, for her part, still remembers the nervous thrill of hearing Johnson call her name that day in Studio 3, rousing her from her scribbling. "I'll never stop being thankful for it. Because that was it for me—the epitome of dancing. I was okay after that no matter what. I'd made it. I was in heaven."

9

"The evening's honors went to Lydia Abarca, a lovely young dancer who could easily be a fashion model should she so desire. Well-partnered by Derek Williams, her Balanchinesque body, long-limbed and slender, easily assumed the proper line of the choreography."
—*Evening Bulletin*

"Abarca appears onstage like a Modigliani creation, combining a child-like vulnerability with finishing school gentility."
—*New York Woman*

"A siren to stop all traffic."
—*Chicago Sun-Times*

"When Miss Abarca, an alluring young ballerina, appeared onstage, her artistic charisma electrified the audience."
—*Daily Defender*

"Undoubtedly, Miss Lydia Abarca is the unbilled prima ballerina here, displaying incredible fluidity, pin-point perfection in her bone-cracking extensions, as well as a lovely sensuality, too. Pure visual joy."
—*Philadelphia Daily News*

LYDIA ABARCA HAD TO DO A DOUBLE TAKE WHEN SHE passed the newsstand on her way to the subway. It was January 1973, and she was on the cover of *Essence* magazine. She had signed with a modeling agency named Black Beauty and was booking regular print jobs. *Essence* had hired her as a hand model for an inside article in its special issue celebrating Black love. "But then I'm walking down the street, and I see me on the front of the magazine," she says. The cover showed her bare back and the profile of her face in a romantic embrace with a male model. "So I called the agency and I said, 'Excuse me, can you call *Essence* and ask if I get any extra money for that?'" They paid her an extra $300, which to her felt like gold.

Abarca didn't grow up like so many of the other middle-class girls in the company. They had doctors and dentists and professors and engineers for parents. "They grew up in homes with an upstairs and a downstairs," she says. "To me that meant you were rich. I remember the first time Gayle invited me to her parents' huge home in Connecticut for the weekend. When we walked inside the door, the first thing I blurted out was, 'You have an upstairs?!'" When she went on a road trip from New York to Florida with a few of the women in the company, they stopped along the way in Augusta, Georgia, to stay overnight with one of the dancers' families. "We went down this long driveway, and I'm looking at the building, and I say, 'Well, where's your apartment?' And she said, 'No, that's my house.' I was so embarrassed. I didn't know people had houses like that."

Abarca wanted that for herself and for her parents, who had given her everything they could for a shot at a bigger life than theirs. "We never wanted for anything growing up," she says. "But here's Lydia with these dreams in her head, always wanting more. I wanted to buy my parents a house. Get us out of the projects. I wanted a car, you know, regular stuff. I didn't want to have to live with roommates for the rest of my life."

But five years into her career at Dance Theatre of Harlem, with all the accolades that had piled up at her feet, she was making only twenty-five dollars a week more than what Mitchell first offered to pay her if she quit the bank. She didn't have a nickel for a savings account. Even when Revlon selected her as one of its original Charlie girls—alongside the first female jockey Mary Bacon and Alice Cooper's girlfriend Cindy Lang, whom *Interview* magazine dubbed "America's First Lady of Rock and Roll"—Revlon paid DTH instead of her.

"It was only when I was dancing that I felt like a star," she says. "Then to come off the stage to my little life was always shocking. I'm in the first successful Black ballet company. We're doing legitimate ballets, not some made-up dance recital stuff. But nothing changed. Maybe if I'd had a publicist or a manager who could have looked at me and said, 'Okay, we can do something with her. She's a commodity.' But the commodity was always Arthur Mitchell. This was his dream. And I understood that. My allegiance was always to him and to Dance Theatre of Harlem. But couldn't I have high hopes for myself too?"

Not according to Mitchell. His stated agenda was to lift the whole company rather than spotlight an individual. If there was going to be a star of Dance Theatre of Harlem, it would be him. To separate her ambitions in any way from him or the company could be seen only as a betrayal.

Meanwhile Llanchie Stevenson's dream was to have Mitchell look at her the way he gazed upon Abarca. She yearned for a shot at the *Agon* pas de deux—"that's the prima ballerina role," she says—but Mitchell never let her do it. She was over thirty years old by this point, tired of the travel and the hustling and the knowledge that the best roles would stay out of her reach. "The other dancers were all up to my level and past me now because I started getting lazy and tired of the whole ballet thing," she says.

And yet it was then, when she was feeling her most invisible to Mitchell, that Stevenson revolutionized the way Black ballerinas looked onstage forever. Traditionally ballerinas had always danced in tights and shoes that were the palest of "European pink," meant to enhance the illusion of women dancing on their toes without any shoes. At the time, ballet shoes came in just two shades—Capezio Pink and Freed Pink. Stevenson had taken to dying the straps of her tutu brown while she danced in the National Ballet, so the pale slashes of fabric wouldn't interfere with the line of her neck and shoulders.

At Dance Theatre of Harlem, she took it one step further, layering brown tights with the feet cut off on top of her ballet pinks in class until her muscles warmed up. The result, however unintentional, was stirring. "Wait, my arms now match my legs!" says Stevenson. "All of the sudden, I'm connected. I'm a whole body instead of half of one. Soon I couldn't rehearse without them. I couldn't do the three pirouettes on pointe if I wasn't in my brown tights!" The other women in the company were delighted with the visual effect. "Brown tights pulled our lines out," says Gayle McKinney-Griffith. "It made us look slender. Llanchie and I used to talk, saying, 'Look at my thighs! Look how great!'"

Mitchell so admired the uninterrupted lines of his dancers that he would eventually adopt brown tights and shoes as company-wide practice. They began a European tour in pink tights and completed it in flesh tones, declaring to the world that the lines of the Black body deserved the same care and respect as those of their white peers.

Once they were back home, the dancers began a ritualistic process of going through Zelda Wynn's meticulously calibrated colors of dye and tea leaves to find their own unique shade. Before every performance, they would use makeup powder on their shoes to ensure they still matched their tights exactly, just in case a snatch of pink was sneaking through the dye. After every show, they would spray shellac or Future floor wax inside their shoes and around the box and shank and let them dry and reharden overnight. Expanding the aesthetic of ballet wasn't an abandonment of tradition, they realized, but an act of vital expansion and inclusion.

But Stevenson, who was never credited publicly by Mitchell for her innovation, was stalling out in the company. "I thought if I had Gayle's feet, I would be so much stronger," she says. "Or Sheila's strength and how she could jump and leap. If I had Lydia's extension and body, maybe Arthur would look at me more." She convinced herself the problem was her weight. "So many dancers came into the company, and he'd tell them to lose ten pounds immediately. I thought if I was thinner, I would get more roles."

She turned to Nation of Islam leader Elijah Muhammad's book *How to Eat to Live*, thinking it would help her lose the weight and catch Mitchell's eye. But what it did instead was introduce her to a different higher power. She started attending Nation of Islam meetings, whose tradition prohibits women from dancing uncovered in public. She fell in love with a lawyer who accompanied Dance Theatre of Harlem on tour as a tutor, and after he converted to the Muslim tradition as she had, they married.

Today Stevenson, now Aminah Ahmad, speaks of quitting Dance Theatre of Harlem in 1973 with a sense of palpable relief. "With Arthur, it was never perfect," she says. "The pressure that was put upon us was so intense. No matter how well you danced, there was something else he thought you could've added. You never got to feel like *Oh, I made it!* He kept our egos down by wanting so much more and more and more all the time. I'd realized there was a superior entity that was above all that. When I did an arabesque, it was this entity that was holding up and helping me. I couldn't accept Arthur's criticism anymore. So that was the end for me."

That same year, on the Sunday before Valentine's Day, twenty-three-year-old Lydia Abarca married Frog Legs, Julio's nemesis from their summer in Europe. In interviews from around this time, she'd begun acknowledging the "pressure being one of the few Black ballerinas" and the need to always play the part of "poised prima." She hoped marriage could provide a stabilizing anchor to her life of constant striving. "I just wanted what my mom had," she says. "I wanted someone that loved me like my daddy loved my mother. She'd give him a can of SpaghettiOs, and he'd say, 'Oh, your mother is such a good cook.'"

The marriage lasted less than a year, though it would take her another two years to save up the money for a lawyer's fee to pay for a divorce. Abarca had been looking for a port in the storm, a sturdy and reliable force against the tidal wave of pressure that came along with being the prima. She'd wanted someone like her father. But Frog Legs, who had dropped out of the company to work full-time for his father's trucking business, was no Francisco Abarca.

And how Francisco loved his daughter, even as he didn't understand her new world. He came to see her dance just once. The company was performing at Brooklyn College, where Francisco worked as a custodial engineer. Abarca was dancing the principal role in William Dollar's *Le Combat*, playing a warrior during the Crusades who conceals her gender as she seeks to avenge her brother's death. In the climactic scene, Abarca and her partner, Paul Russell, who would soon leave the company over creative clashes with Mitchell, engage in a swordfight that mortally wounds her. "I'm on the floor, and I take my helmet off and throw it," she says of the drama onstage. "Paul's character has fallen in love with me, so when he realizes it's me, he's like, 'Oh my God, what have I done!' He picks up my body. I start quivering and finally die. Devastated, he starts swinging my limp body around. I'm telling you, every time the audience just went crazy."

As his daughter died onstage, Francisco gripped Josephine's arm, his cheeks damp with tears. Later, he would nod solemnly at Abarca. "Very good, Mama."

But of all Abarca's family members, it was her sister Celia who most loved to watch her dance. "I don't think I ever missed a performance," she says. Before Dance Theatre of Harlem, she knew nothing about ballet or classical music, beyond her parents' record of Georges Bizet's *Carmen*. Seeing her sister onstage opened a whole new world to her. Every time she'd go to the theater, she'd look for Mitchell's right-hand man Lorenzo James in the lobby, who'd be waiting for her with a loose ticket in his hand. She'd take her seat by herself in the audience, where she'd have eyes only for her big sister. "To see Lydia onstage? I can't express the pride I felt. After it was over, I'd hear people yelling behind me, 'Bravo! Bravo! Bravo!' She'd be the last one to come out and take her bow at the very end. 'Bravo! Bravo!' And I would see her looking for me in the audience, because she knew I was out there somewhere. And every now and then she would find me, and she would lock eyes with me and give me a wink or a little smile. I'd be saying to myself, *They're all loving her, all these people. And she is mine. She is my sister.* Then we'd get on the train together to go home from the City Center or wherever, because we didn't have money for cabs, and she'd still have all her makeup on and be carrying her bouquets of flowers. And it'd just make me so proud. Here I am with this beautiful person on a train full of bums."

By 1974, Dance Theatre of Harlem was working six days a week, forty-eight weeks out of the year. Mitchell decided his young company was finally equipped to face critics and audiences in England. "I didn't bring them to London before because I did not think they were ready," he told the *London Times* before their debut at Sadler's Wells. "It is a very young company, many of them only started to learn dancing five years ago. We have a girl only just fifteen, and a boy who has been dancing only one year." But clearly they were ready now. For DTH's three-week season, the theater was sold out to the rafters at 113 percent attendance. After breaking its box office record, Sadler's Wells invited the company to return to London for another week on the back end of its tour, following performances in Oslo, Helsinki, and Belgium.

And then that November the company returned to the

UK for a spectacle above all the others. They performed excerpts from two ballets—Mitchell's *Spiritual Suite* and Holder's *Dougla* in the Royal Variety Show—before the Queen Mother at the London Palladium. The dancers performed in between sets by the comedian Ted Rogers and the singer Perry Como. Much to their awe and excitement, Josephine Baker, one of the marquis performers on the bill, visited with the women in their dressing room during rehearsals, treating them to an impromptu concert of songs in different languages. "She told us how beautiful she thought we were," says Sheila Rohan. "She also wanted to borrow a hairbrush, which I immediately jumped up and gave her mine. She returned the brush with a few strands of her hair. I took them out and put them away. I kept them for a long time. Before the show, I remember she was standing in the wings waiting for her cue, leaning against the wall like an old lady. As soon as the music came on, she stood up, put on her famous headdress, and walked out on the stage like a goddess." Less than a year later, Baker would slip into a coma during her sleep and die at the age of sixty-eight.

Everywhere they went seemed an opportunity for new wonders, but the pace of their touring schedule was putting Abarca's asthma to the test. Ballets like *Le Combat* and Balanchine's *Concerto Barocco*, in which Lydia Abarca danced in all three acts, had her lunging for her inhaler backstage. "I call my asthma 'Miss Wheezy,' and if she showed up during a ballet, I would try my best to ignore her," she says. Sometimes Abarca would come off stage almost retching, unsure how she would muster the strength to return for her bows.

Her struggle continued once they were back in Harlem. She remembers one Sunday Open House at 152nd Street performing in front of a community audience that included her grandmother, feeling weak and hot, her legs noodling beneath her. She fell during a lift. She thought it was her asthma acting up again, but overnight her fever rose to 103, with a headache so bad it had her seeing stars.

At Columbia-Presbyterian Hospital, doctors diagnosed Abarca with bacterial pneumonia. In between bronchoscopies and breathing treatments, she had no choice but to let herself rest. Lorenzo James, acting as Mitchell's emissary, brought flowers to her hospital room. Cicely Tyson visited at her bedside, leaving a copy of the children's novel *Sounder*, the movie adaptation of which had earned her an Oscar nomination, on the side table.

The situation had Mitchell in a panic. The company's New York season was fast approaching, and he'd lost his star ballerina. Gayle McKinney-Griffith was able to settle him with the promise of reserves at the ready. "He was tearing his hair out. I kept telling him, 'We have it, we have it. We can do this. I'm here, Virginia's here, Sheila's here, Susan Lovelle is here. We can all go in, and we're ready, because I've rehearsed all the casts.'"

Abarca stayed in the hospital for a month, then eventually rejoined the company on tour in Mexico City. "I made it through *Concerto Barocco*, but it felt like my lungs were screaming," she says. "Mr. Mitchell came backstage and turned me upside down. He put my legs over his shoulders, and he starts bouncing me up and down like a baby, trying to help me breathe."

How intimate and vulnerable they must have appeared to the other dancers. A terrified father desperate to revive his favorite child. A ballerina gasping for air, helpless in his arms. An audience out of sight, waiting, expectant.

But no matter how he cared for her, Abarca knew that if she didn't improve enough to perform, it was only a matter of time before she lost her spot. Mitchell regularly threatened his dancers about the ephemeral nature of the job. "He used to say, 'Dancers are a dime a dozen,'" remembers Abarca. "Any time a new girl was coming, he would always say, 'Wait until you all see this new girl. She's got legs and feet! Just wait until you see her.'"

The show had to go on. She wasn't ready to be replaced.

10

IN 1975, *DANCE MAGAZINE* PUT A BLACK COMPANY BALLE-rina on the cover for the first time in its forty-seven-year history. Lydia Abarca was hailed as "the dreaming soul of dance," and the close-up image of her dressed in character for George Balanchine's *Bugaku* feels lifted from a fairy tale. Her long, elegant fingers flank her angelic face. A sprig of silk cherry blossoms lies tucked into the side of her smooth high bun. "*A* for Abarca places this dancer first on the roster," the writer raved inside the nine-page spread dedicated to Dance Theatre of Harlem. "And there she belongs! Her looks, her style, her manner have the harmony of sheer perfection."

Across the country, in her local Denver dance shop, seventeen-year-old Karlya Shelton stared in disbelief at the sight of this sylph with twin oceans for eyes on the cover of her favorite magazine. Shelton, the only Black dancer in the Colorado Concert Ballet, had never seen the face of a Black ballerina other than her own, staring back at herself in the mirror.

The feature rhapsodized over this thriving company of Black artists, describing Gayle McKinney-Griffith as "a doe-eyed dancer-actress of beguilingly various moods" and Sheila Rohan "a cool, exact, enigmatic beauty." Shelton read about the company's record-breaking visit the previous year to London's Sadler's Wells, its command performance in Oslo for the king of Norway, and its sixteen-day triumphant season in Mexico City. "Everywhere DTH is feted at Embassy receptions as ambassadors of American culture," the reporter wrote. And yet somehow, across the country, this was the first time Shelton had learned of its existence.

She raced home, eager to share the magazine with her mother, Jean. Together they pored over the photographs—Abarca, leggy and sumptuous; Rohan, gorgeous and regal as the Bride in Geoffrey Holder's *Dougla;* Arthur Mitchell, dashing and chiseled, holding court in the company's 152nd Street studio. Jean found herself exhaling as Karlya clutched the magazine to her chest. "My God, Karlya's been bringing home that magazine her whole life, and I've never seen a Black person on it," Jean remembers of the moment. "Perhaps there's a glimmer of hope for her after all."

Karlya describes her childhood as blessed. "We were not wealthy," she says, "but we didn't want for anything." Says Jean, "Karlya would come home before another production of *The Nutcracker,* saying, 'Mom, I need twelve new pairs of pointe shoes!' I'd tell her 'Kar, nobody orders twelve pairs of shoes.'

Well, we'd go to the ballet shop, and my husband would say, 'Whatever she needs, that's what she needs.'" Lloyd Shelton was a navy veteran, a towering man of substance, a hero to all who knew him. He rose before dawn for the early shift at the post office, came home for an afternoon nap, then headed out again in the evening to work a second job at the liquor store or as a janitor. Karlya and her little brother, Kyle, would ride their bikes with their friends for hours after school, never worried about getting lost. The mountains were always west, so if they could see them, they knew the direction home. When the streetlights came on, Lloyd had a powerful whistle that seemed to travel miles. On the weekends, before dance completely took over her schedule, Lloyd would take Karlya fishing down at the Cherry Creek Reservoir, where his own father had once worked to build the dam. When Lloyd wasn't fishing with his daughter, he could be found under the hood of the family car with Kyle. Their driveway became a kind of emergency room for neighborhood kids' bikes and skateboards and roller skates. Lloyd was a man who could fix anything. He was so good with his hands, so capable of focus, that he developed a hobby of carving intricate faces into the heads of toothpicks with an X-Acto knife. He'd sit in his chair or out on the patio making tiny little shavings until a recognizable visage appeared in the centimeter of wood.

Every summer the family went out into the bigness of the world together, packing up the station wagon with their suitcases and a cooler of drinks and fruit and sandwiches. Lloyd set a strict departure time of five in the morning, and they'd hit the road to visit relatives in his home state of Iowa, or to take in the Grand Canyon, or they'd head to California or Tennessee. When Karlya was fourteen, her parents realized that their growing children were aging out of the family tradition. As a last hurrah, they handed over control of the final journey to their kids. They could stay with family along the way or, if the kids were lucky, at a hotel with a pool. The siblings chose a route that had them driving up to Michigan, into Canada to Niagara Falls, then down through New York City, where Karlya announced to her family that she would one day make the city her home.

Early into her high school years, the Colorado Concert Ballet invited Karlya to join the company on a swing of Wyoming, New Mexico, and Colorado dates. The tour was down a couple of dancers because of sickness and injury, and Karlya's teachers trusted she knew the repertoire well enough to step in. She relished the opportunity to prove herself on a grander scale. Her legs had jump in them that would draw gasps from the audience. The other young women in the company were pleasant with her, even if their fascination with her hair and compulsion to touch it grated. Even though her whole ballet world was white, it never occurred to her that she didn't have a place in it too. She could do five turns in pointe shoes, so how could she not?

Shelton speaks of her time at the Colorado Concert Ballet with affection. The white artistic directors did their honest best to support her dancing, but they had their own limitations. Karlya would never dance the role of Clara in *The Nutcracker*, for instance, or the Sugar Plum Fairy, which she attributes to a failure of imagination. And she wouldn't cross the unspoken divide that lived between her and her white peers. There would be no talk of the civil rights movement in the dressing room or on the bus. Nobody ever mentioned Dr. King's assassination.

One Fourth of July, the Sheltons attended a cookout with other Black families in a nearby neighborhood. Kyle and the other kids were playing in the front yard when they saw a parade of Ku Klux Klan members streaming down the street. They ran to tell the adults barbecuing in the back about the specter of Klan members in hoods and cloaks. "My daddy and the other men came out with pans and skillets and whatever else they could grab in their hands," she says. "My brother was going, too, but my mother held him back. The men chased the Klan down the block and then some." It never occurred to her to share the story with her white dance friends. When asked why, she sighs. "I think it would have made them very uncomfortable," she says. "I don't think they would've wanted to get that far into my world."

Her dancing life in Colorado was kind, but lonely, and compartmentalized. When the majority in the room aren't curious, and then sturdy in that curiosity, "the only" learns to protect her vulnerable core.

When Karlya Shelton was seventeen years old, a teacher named Dolores Kehr, a former soloist with the Ballet Russe de Monte Carlo with strong ties to the School of American Ballet and the Joffrey Ballet School, took over training her and the other advanced ballet students. The worldly woman asked her new students about their plans upon graduation. It was Karlya who took the first step forward. "I'm going to be a professional dancer," she announced, with the same matter-of-fact authority she might have told the woman the spelling of her last name. Kehr looked at her through narrowed eyes. "How old are you, dear?" she asked. When Shelton responded that she was seventeen, the teacher gently winced. "Well, you're almost too old," she said. After that Kehr met with the dancers' parents and persuaded them to send their teenage children with her on a trip to New York City to make the rounds of the country's best ballet companies.

It was only days before that trip that Shelton discovered Dance Theatre of Harlem in *Dance Magazine.* Suddenly she was desperate for a chance to meet Arthur Mitchell and his company of dancers. She called Kehr to ask if there was any way her teacher might arrange for an audition. It turned out Kehr was friends with Violette Verdy, a principal ballerina at City Ballet who had danced with Mitchell. She told the girl she would try to take advantage of the connection but couldn't make any promises. That was enough for Shelton, who got busy in the bathroom mirror trying to style her bun exactly like Abarca's on the cover, biting her lip in frustration at the one puffy section on the top of her head that refused to lie flat.

In New York, the group from Colorado checked into the Empire Hotel across from Lincoln Center on a brisk spring afternoon. Kehr marched them through a three-day whirl-wind tour of the ballet world. Their first stop was Balanchine's School of American Ballet.

As Kehr escorted her giddy students through the venerated halls, the group passed the legendary Jerome Robbins. Kehr called a cheerful hello to the choreographer, asking if he might have time to greet some eager fledglings. As if batting at a cloud of gnats, he waved them off with an impatient grimace. His testy dismissal chilled Shelton. But she was here to dance. The kids shed their outer layers in the hall and joined three somber adults in a room. There was nobody at the piano, no music. They were told to line up at the barre and stand in first position. One of the women came around with a stick measuring the lengths of their necks, arms, legs, and torsos, and their hip-to-foot ratios. "What about talent?" asks Lydia Abarca, horrified by Shelton's retelling. "They can't measure that!"

After the dispiriting audition, Shelton looked for the dressing room to change out of her dance wear into her street clothes. She asked a couple of students in the hallway where the visiting Colorado dancers might change in preparation for their audition. When one of the SAB dancers pointed Shelton in the right direction, her friend shushed her, wrinkling her nose at Shelton. "Don't talk to her," the girl hissed, taking her friend by the shoulder and turning their backs. Shelton still gets steamed talking about it. "'Don't talk to her!' Might it have been because I was Black? Or was she just that easily threatened by the idea of new competition?" She knew then and there that this wasn't the place for her. "I would have been in fights all the time. The whole atmosphere was unfriendly. I was still naive at that age, but when you grow up Black, you know what racism looks like, what it feels like. It almost has a smell to it."

Happily, on their last day in town, Kehr announced that she'd managed to get Shelton an audition with Dance Theatre of Harlem. The company was busy preparing for their first season at Broadway's Uris Theater, so she was going to have to join the company class onstage. When they arrived at the theater, Kehr and Shelton's classmates found seats in the theater to observe. Shelton assumed a spot toward the back of the stage for the company class and found herself getting choked up standing in such a large group of Black classical dancers. For the first time she allowed herself to feel just how alone she'd been on so many stages throughout her childhood. "I remember wanting to cry out to my white friends in the audience," she says. *"See? See! I'm not alone! There's a whole company of Black ballerinas and danseurs."*

And then in came Arthur Mitchell. One always sensed him before he appeared. The threatening urgency to his approach announced itself like a crack of thunder. "You can always hear Arthur Mitchell coming into the studio or backstage because you hear the thunder of his heels going boom, boom, boom," says Shelton. "So everybody would stand up, and then when he enters, he's got this whole force field around him. He was just so powerful. And it made the whole thing real for me, like here is that guy from the magazine before me."

Mitchell surveyed the stage, taking in the unfamiliar girl,

then led the company in class. Shelton remembers there being a single white person onstage with them, a small man in glasses named George, who normally played the piano but this morning was shadowing Mitchell with a stick to keep time. After the class, Mitchell looked at Shelton holding her breath and told her to go put on her pointe shoes for center work.

While kneeling in the wings to lace up the pale ribbons of her shoes, Shelton noticed Gayle McKinney-Griffith and Sheila Rohan sitting on the steps applying brown makeup to theirs. As her eyes traveled up from their feet, she took in how the brown of their tights matched the hues of their skin. In all her years, she'd never considered that she might have a right to bend the art form to meet her, as these women were. "For so long I'd looked at myself in pictures knowing something's broken," she says. "The line is not right. 'Is that my leg? Because it's not the same color as my arm.' I didn't do anything, because nothing was ever offered as a solution."

Oh, this is where I belong, Shelton said to herself. She finished tying the ribbons of her pink pointe shoes, already knowing she'd outgrown them, and returned to the stage. Mitchell ran her through one of his center variations— échappé, échappé, passé, passé, changement to fourth, then two pirouettes—to see how quickly she could get up on her legs. Shelton repeated the variation four times for him, while the company stood back appraising her. Then he asked her to show him two pirouettes; she did three.

The next day she returned home to Colorado, where three scholarship invitations would soon arrive at her house. "I had offers to Joffrey and School of American Ballet. But after I saw Dance Theatre of Harlem, it was like knowing the difference between Godiva chocolate and Hershey's. I felt like those other companies were going to be just like where I had been. I would be limited, and I didn't trust that they would let me climb. There were going to be roles that I was kept from because of the color of my skin. They were going to keep me in the corps de ballet. Arthur Mitchell was offering me a chance to dance in a company where it would feel good to dance again."

When the Legacy Council talks now about the individual ambitions they had as young dancers, an obvious generational difference emerges. The first generation spent their childhoods training with a sense of possibility that the founders lacked. Sheila Rohan can't relate to Karlya Shelton's tour of ballet companies. "Didn't your mother tell you that no white company was going to take a Black ballerina?" she asks. Shelton responds, "Why would she? Because I already was dancing with a white company from the time I was twelve." Or when Marcia Sells tells the story of being called "a dirty snowflake" in *The Nutcracker*, Rohan says, "Didn't your mother warn you that would happen?"

Rohan grew up thinking of ballet as an art form that intrigued her but a tradition that purposefully excluded her. "Sure, I had read about companies in Europe—the Ballet Russe or the Paris Opera—and that there were Black ballerinas over there. But I wouldn't even bother to pursue dancing with a white company." Sells, nearly twenty years Rohan's junior, considers this for a moment. "I think my mother thought, *Maybe there's going to be a change.*"

By twelve years old, Marcia Sells was dancing in the corps with the Cincinnati Ballet. At fifteen, she was awarded a prestigious Ford Foundation national scholarship to attend the School of American Ballet's eight-week summer program in New York. Richard Rapp, a City Ballet soloist and SAB teacher, auditioned her himself. She was the only dancer from the region to be awarded the scholarship.

Marcia's mother, Mamie, took succor from the example of Debra Austin, the brilliant dancer who'd been handpicked by Balanchine, at just sixteen, to join City Ballet in 1971. But while Austin's accomplishment was indeed cause for celebration, the telling of the woman's triumph would bruise Marcia's spirit. Her white peers at SAB took a careless delight in repeating to her how after the light-skinned Austin danced for Balanchine in her audition, he was thought to have said approvingly, "Who is the girl with the tan?" His assistant was tasked with informing him, "Her tan is permanent." "As the lone Black girl in the school at that moment," Sells says now, "I immediately realize I'm in trouble. Because I'm a lot darker than Debbie Austin. You can tell I'm a Black woman from one hundred feet away."

Near the end of the summer term, SAB's associate director, Nathalie Gleboff, pulled Sells into her private office, ostensibly to discuss her progress and future with the organization. Sells had felt well respected in her classes, often chosen by her teachers to demonstrate technique for the other students.

Having a private meeting with Gleboff felt like an honor. But the air in the room felt chilly as soon as she closed the door behind her. The Russian émigré wasted no time getting to the point. "The teachers like you," she said. "You're quite competent. But you'll never be in the company." Sells sat absorbing these conflicting statements, her face flushing with confusion and embarrassment. The arbitrariness of the rejection landed like a smack. She was too tender and too proud to ask for an explanation. She needed to escape the flatness of this woman's gaze. In the doorway, Gleboff lobbed one more grenade. "Your rear end," she told the prepubescent girl who stood frozen with her back to her. "You'll probably have to have some surgery to have part of it removed. And your nose too."

The young teenager spent the rest of the day in a daze. She cried for hours to her mother on the phone. But then the next day she woke up and remembered that she was the daughter of Mamie Sells, and she'd spent the last several years sleeping beneath the guiding lights of Dance Theatre of Harlem's founding dancers. This old Russian woman wouldn't have the final say over her future. The following week Sells reported to 152nd Street for her final summer intensive, which she'd attended every summer since first seeing them perform in her hometown. The following year, when she was sixteen, Sells finally would join her childhood heroes in the company of her dreams.

That same summer that Marcia Sells studied at SAB—and was met with the harsh reality of how truly little the larger world of ballet had evolved—Karlya Shelton moved to New York City. Jean and Lloyd left Denver in their Pontiac Catalina, the trunk packed full of their daughter's belongings. They stopped at the Briansky Ballet Center in Saratoga Springs, New York, where Shelton had been chosen as the first African American to represent the United States at the international Prix de Lausanne competition. Then they drove their daughter into Manhattan, to The Webster, a women's boardinghouse in Hell's Kitchen, where they'd rented her a single room for thirty-five dollars a week.

The next morning Shelton emerged from the lobby smiling with a couple of other girls, whom she'd met at the Webster's daily breakfast and had been delighted to learn were also Dance Theatre of Harlem dancers. They all piled into the Catalina, the girls talking merrily over each other like old friends, as Lloyd drove them uptown.

The only impressions Shelton had previously had of Harlem were from media scare reports and popular blaxploitation movies that painted the community as a blighted wasteland, corrupt and hollowed out by crime and drugs. "I expected these dark, dirty streets lined with people up to no good," she says. Instead, she found herself enveloped into a bustling community that treated the dancers with genuine pride and affection. Mr. Austin, a gentlemanly neighbor in a car coat and a tweed fedora, served as a kind of cheerful sentinel to the 152nd Street studio morning and night. As the company's self-appointed doorman, he'd go on to greet Shelton every day, urging her to be her best, occasionally regaling her with stories of his own prowess back in the day dancing the Lindy Hop.

But that first day, Karlya Shelton hugged her parents tight outside the studio, clinging hardest to her father. "Daddy, can I call home every night?" she said as Lloyd patted his baby girl on the back, assuring her, "You can call as often as you want." Jean promised she would write and indeed would mail a letter to her daughter every single day for the first two years, all of which Shelton has saved in an old Capezio bag, and care packages of her favorite treats, drinks, even a birthday cake. And with that, they were off, trusting they were leaving their brave girl right where she belonged.

Or so she thought. Shelton was sure she'd been accepted into the company, but now the front desk was telling her she'd be training in the downstairs studio with dancers Mitchell envisioned becoming part of a second company rather than up in Studio 3. She didn't make a fuss. She joined the preprofessional group to which she'd been assigned. But she knew one thing for sure. "I didn't know how I was going to get there," she says, "but I was going upstairs where I belonged."

For three months, Shelton labored dutifully downstairs, training with teachers like Mary Barnett, who would go on to be the associate artistic director at Alvin Ailey American Dance Theater. Barnett taught her an important lesson about the pragmatic value of surrender. "One time this guy and I were doing a lift, and he let go of me and I fell," says Shelton. "Ms. Barnett looked at us both and said, 'You need to learn to fall!' I was like, 'Excuse me?' But she was right. Most people tense up and hurt themselves when they fall. She was telling me to just collapse into it, so I wouldn't hurt anything. Surrender! Which is a very hard thing to do."

At a Sunday Open House, Shelton finally had the opportunity to show Mitchell what she could bring to the company. Barnett had given her some allegro choreography that highlighted the power of her turns and jumps, and she executed it beautifully. The next morning an administrator called Shelton out from the downstairs studio and told her to report to Studio 3 for company class. Mitchell had decided to bring her in as an apprentice, another test she was determined to pass. "You know how tennis players yell 'Come on!' when they win a hard point?" she says. "That was me. So that's how I'm getting upstairs. Finally!"

The pace of company life hit Shelton like a fire hose. Lecture-demonstrations began as early as eight in the morning. Then came a two-hour class to keep the body stretched and primed for the day ahead. A theoretical lunch break followed, but ballerinas were trained to think of lunch more as a time marker than as an invitation to eat. Splibs, as apprentices were called, were expected to work in the studio through lunch, practicing their pointe and partnering skills, before a mandatory four o'clock class with Karel Shook. During the dinner break, the male dancers might enjoy a Jamaican meat patty or chicken dinner from the open grill on the corner counter storefront with a hand-painted sign that read FOOD or brisket from Sherman's Barbecue up the block. The women seemed to get by on Tab soda and Tropicana orange juice and cups of Yoplait yogurt in the lobby, where the ashtrays overflowed with Newport cigarette butts. Then back into Studio 3 for a two-hour evening rehearsal.

One of the first things Shelton learned upstairs was how to walk with the DTH tip. Ballerinas typically walk with a certain stiffness, an inaccessible chill. "Imagine trying to walk on half-point toe, without moving your hips," says Shelton. "That's not the way women naturally walk." Mitchell encouraged his dancers to bring the heat. He taught the women to walk high on demi-pointe in diagonals across the studio, as if the floor beneath them were lucky to bear their rolling steps. "It's a very feminine walk, elegant and regal," explains Shelton. "The hips are allowed to move naturally. It's also a cultural thing, maybe learned unconsciously from watching our parents. It's like when we're dressed and know we're looking good." Shelton remembers watching Lydia Abarca and Gayle McKinney-Griffith incorporate the DTH tip in ballets like *Agon* and *Forces of Rhythm,* thinking they were the epitome of Black Girl Magic. "I would point my feet on each step," Abarca says now, "stay up on half-point, and slightly sway my hips to make it sexy."

During the company's New York season, Shelton and some of the other apprentices were told to stay behind in Harlem to train with Alice Elliott, an imperious woman of Ghanaian descent who had trained at the Bolshoi. Elliott and the pianist Svetlana had a way of speaking and laughing with each other in Russian that let the dancers know they were being skewered. One afternoon Shelton had to pause in the corner while practicing bourrées and pas de bourrée couru, a series of fluttering tiny steps on pointe. "Carol," Elliott said to Karlya, purposefully misidentifying her, "why are you stopping?" When Shelton complained that her toes had started bleeding, the unimpressed woman demanded proof. "I took off my shoes and showed them to her, and she said, 'Too bad! Put them back on and try again.'"

Every night Shelton took the train back to Hell's Kitchen, having long since missed the dinner service that was included as part of her rent. She'd walk down Ninth Avenue with another dancer and buy fruit from a bodega to split for dinner. In her first year at the company, Shelton dropped fifteen pounds, prompting Mitchell to call her out in Studio 3 one afternoon in front of everyone. "Yeah, that's what I'm talking about," he remarked. "Before your behind was like two watermelons!" Shelton still flinches at the nastiness of his words. She'd had her fair share of personalities in teachers before, like an instructor in Colorado who taught while holding a hamburger and a cigarette in one hand and a drink in the other. But she'd never had someone try to humiliate her in the studio in front of her peers. It was the cruelty in his voice that could cut. "Some people could take his insults and let them just roll off like water. But for me it got into my core."

Gayle McKinney-Griffith had begun to take a special notice of Shelton, though—both her talent and the way she seemed to shrink from Mitchell's gaze. "Karlya had this spark and energy and strength that all the dancers who came up with her didn't have. But I worried she was shy." As ballet mistress, she worried that the new girl's deferential habit of standing at the back of the studio during class was doing her talent a disservice.

One morning McKinney-Griffith pulled Shelton aside before class started and told her to switch places with her. "Gayle told me, 'He needs to see you,' " she says. "She wanted to make sure that everyone that deserved to be seen was at least given an opportunity. She put me in her spot in the front row just off center. From that day forward I claimed it with pride and told myself to always work hard to do it justice, in gratitude for how much this gesture of kindness meant to me."

Privately, McKinney-Griffith urged Mitchell to give the new girl a shot. One of the women in *Forces of Rhythm* was injured, and the ballet mistress believed the young apprentice was ready to take her place. "I think Karlya's the best dancer to put in there because she's strong," she told her boss. "She remembers the choreography. She's perfect." She was careful to keep the tone of her voice even, lest Mitchell find her pushy and say no out of spite.

But Mitchell just nodded impatiently, his attention elsewhere. McKinney-Griffith moved Shelton into the ballet, and the apprentice did her proud. After the girl's first performance, McKinney-Griffith took her aside and praised her dancing and told her she looked like she'd been in the company for years. But then she gently explained that her Maybelline blue eye shadow wasn't her best option.

Apprentices were typically given a year to prove their stuff before Mitchell brought them on as full company members, which meant an increase in both status and salary. Throughout her first year, Shelton elevated the corps of every ballet in the repertoire—the precision of her dancing, the muscularity of her turns and jumps, the obvious joy she brought to the stage. But when that year passed, she received no word about her progress. She finally got up the nerve to approach Mitchell about whether she was a full company member. He looked at her, seemingly annoyed to be reminded of the missed timeline. "Oh, I thought you already were," he said.

From that point on, she told herself she wasn't dancing for his attention or approval. Earning it seemed like an impossible, wrongheaded goal. "I decided my job wasn't to make Arthur Mitchell like me, or to dance with the expectation of his praise," she says. "He wasn't out there when we were performing. So why would I dance for him? I danced for the joy of it, and for the pleasure and challenge of trying to make it perfect."

The women and men who built Dance Theatre of Harlem from the ground up were more than colleagues or peers or fellow artists. No professional identity could possibly encapsulate what they meant to one another during that first pivotal decade. In a perfect illustration, a few dancers spontaneously put together a family tree, assigning everybody roles under the patriarchal branches of Arthur Mitchell and Mr. G. Dancers were claimed as mothers and fathers, husbands and wives, brothers and sisters, and sons and daughters. "We were young and being thrust into the public eye and the critics were all writing about us," explains Gayle McKinney-Griffith, who took on Shelton as her little sister and considered Sheila Rohan her mother. "Mr. Mitchell was getting all the funding and putting his whole life and career on the line. But if the reviews weren't good, the weight was all on us. That's why we developed the family system—just to feel like we could run up under somebody's wing." To blunt the harshness of their temperamental father figure, they would remind one another of their innate greatness. The dancers devised group rituals, like the prayer they'd recite over and over onstage before *Dougla*:

I believe in God,
maker of heaven and earth,
and myself.
The whole world stinks.
But I am lovely.
I am gorgeous.
I am divine.

Whoever was playing the Groom in the ballet would call out each line of the prayer, and the other dancers onstage would repeat after him. "Then the curtain would rise," says Shelton, "and the audience would see us standing there like African royalty. So straight and tall and proud."

Mitchell had built a stage for these kids; he wanted them to stay on it, too, forever. That meant you could never doubt him. You could never argue with him. You could never leave him.

But one by one, of course, the women all would leave.

Because that's what children do. The leaving was often ugly, because Mitchell didn't know how to let people go. And that's when a new work began, the work of defining themselves as women apart from Mitchell, apart from Dance Theatre of Harlem. But who would they be if they weren't ballerinas?

Act Two

While setting the ballet *Ancient Voices of Children,* choreographer Manuel Alum practices a lift with Sheila Rohan. *(Photo by Martha Swope © The New York Public Library for the Performing Arts)*

Gayle McKinney-Griffith and Derek Williams take their final bow after dancing the pas de quatre in Arthur Mitchell's *Fête Noire*. (Photo by Martha Swope © The New York Public Library for the Performing Arts)

Gayle McKinney-Griffith, after the company's transition to brown tights and shoes, dances the pas de deux with Paul Russell in *Le Corsaire. (Photo by Martha Swope © The New York Public Library for the Performing Arts)*

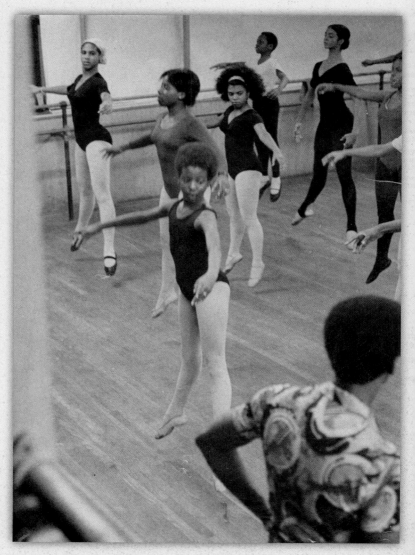

Marcia Sells, at age 10, practicing her sautés à la seconde in a studio full of older teenagers at Dance Theatre of Harlem's first summer intensive program. *(Photograph by Mamie Earl Sells, courtesy of Marcia Sells, private collection)*

In 1975, Lydia Abarca makes history as the first-ever Black ballerina in a traditional company to appear on the cover of *Dance Magazine. (May 1975 cover of* Dance Magazine, *featuring studio portrait of Lydia Abarca photographed by Kenn Duncan. Reprinted with permission from* Dance Magazine.)

When waiting for check-in at their Chicago hotel, the women opted for an afternoon in the park. Lydia Abarca set her camera on a timer, and they crowded in for a photo. *From left to right:* Virginia Johnson, Karen Brown, Gayle McKinney-Griffith, Karlya Shelton, Lydia Abarca. *(Courtesy of Lydia Abarca Mitchell, private collection)*

Sheila Rohan in the majestic principal role of the Bride, in Geoffrey Holder's *Dougla*, which became one of DTH's signature ballets. *(Photo by Martha Swope © The New York Public Library for the Performing Arts)*

In 1979, audiences were treated to the glorious sight of seventeen Black ballerinas standing in a state of luscious anticipation as the curtain rose on the first movement of Balanchine's *Serenade*. Here we see Karlya Shelton front and center. *(© Jack Vartoogian / Front Row Photos)*

Swan Lake dancers. From left to right at the point of the V are the four cygnets, Yvonne Hall, Terri Tompkins, Karlya Shelton, and Judy Tyrus. *(© Sharon W. Birthwright-Greco)*

Karlya Shelton in the principal role in Choo San Goh's *Introducing*.
From left to right: Shelton, Stephanie Dabney, Ronald Perry, Melva
(China) Murray-White, Hinton Battle, and Karen Brown.
(© Jack Vartoogian / Front Row Photos)

SHEILA

*I*N 1975 I GOT THE COMPANY SCHEDULE, AND IT WAS OUT-
rageous. *Touring all over the United States, Canada, Europe.
My children were getting older. Charlene was getting ready to
start high school. I knew I wouldn't be able to do it. Not with my
children becoming teenagers. Mr. Mitchell understood. Plus, I
was suffering from sciatica in my left hip. He said, "Come and
teach the young kids in the school." So Mr. Mitchell didn't really
lose me, or at least not right away.*

*I learned how to teach, which it turned out I loved. I was
reading technique. The other teachers were mentoring me. If
somebody in the company was out, I could fill in for* Forces of
Rhythm *or* Rhythmetron *as a swing.*

*Dance Theatre of Harlem was the highlight of my life—
without it everything would've been more minor key. I was sad-
dened to leave. I had a lot of respect for Mr. Mitchell, but he*

didn't hold power over my life. I never looked back. I wanted to stay dancing, so I kept learning.

I started full-time at the Nanette Bearden Contemporary Dance Theatre around 1977. At first, I was a principal dancer, then ballet mistress, and then school coordinator. I worked with a variety of choreographers; one of the more famous was Talley Beatty, who is considered one of the icons of the modern jazz dance genre. He set two works on the company. Talley was known throughout the Black dance world as a very difficult person to work with. He could be arrogant, mean, and disrespectful. He used to throw chairs. He had a bad temper and would throw a dancer out of rehearsal on a whim. They could get away with it back then. Not today. Arthur did see me dance again. I was doing Bill Scott's Every Now and Then *with Bruce Hawkins at my sister's company. There's a part where I go over for a penché, and I didn't make the six o'clock [in which a dancer's legs point straight up and down, like the hands of a clock]. I purposely didn't do it because this was a jazz piece, and I didn't think it was necessary. Afterward I saw Arthur, and he says, "Well, you know you should've made that six o'clock penché. There's no reason why you shouldn't have made that!" Well, okay, nothing about the ballet itself or the artistry or anything.*

We dancers had to make a living however we could because performing didn't pay very much in those days. It was common to know dancers who were with two or three companies and taught at several different schools. Nanette would sometimes pay my rent or my utilities. She always took care of me.

In 1986 I went on a tour of China and Korea with the Myung

Sook Chun Dance Company, a modern-dance troupe, for over a month. We got to live with the people. No hotels. We went to Beijing, Shanghai, up toward Manchuria. And we weren't always dancing on wonderful stages. Sometimes we were in barns in the backwoods. The people loved us.

I thought I was done with ballet. But then I got cast in Martin *[Gordon Parks's 1990 ballet film in which, at fifty years old, Rohan danced on pointe in the lead role of Rosa Parks]. The choreographer Rael Lamb contacted me about the production. He'd come to Dance Theatre of Harlem at times and knew Mr. Mitchell. Rael had also come to Nanette's and set a piece on us, so we knew each other. I wasn't nervous about my age. I never thought,* Oh, I'm too old. *I was in good shape and had never really stopped dancing, whether it was ballet, modern, jazz, or African. I was just surprised to be asked to perform a lead role.*

Mr. Parks was a quiet, distinguished gentleman. He produced, directed, and wrote the music. He wanted mature dancers. John Jones, who danced Martin Luther King Jr., was even older than me but still in good shape. I remember one day we were filming the first-act pas de deux. When we took a break, I noticed that the ribbon on one of my pointe shoes had come loose and was sticking out. This is a real no-no for a ballerina. I asked Mr. Parks if we could do the scene over. He just looked at me for a moment and said no. After the film came out, I was pleased to see that he must have edited over it or whatever they do. For years, PBS aired it every Black History Month. People would call the house and say, "I saw you on Channel 13!" I liked my performance too. This was the major dance role of my entire career.

Sheila Rohan's gravitas earned her the nickname "Pearls" in the Legacy Council. "Sheila doesn't always say a lot, but when she does speak, it's always in these pearls of wisdom," Karlya Shelton explains. "Maybe it's because of her age, or her experience, or her spirituality. Sheila's plane is very high. We all look up to her."

11

D ANCE THEATRE OF HARLEM HAD ARRANGED FOR MAR-
cia Sells to continue high school at the Professional Children's School, which had a flexible schedule that allowed for
full days of dancing. She enrolled as a junior, but because of
her high test scores and credits from her magnet program
back in Cincinnati, she was told that she could graduate by the
end of the year. The report cards of younger dancers always
went straight to Karel Shook, who was tasked with keeping
an eye on their academic lives. "So you got that B in history?"
he'd tease Sells while she was warming up at the barre. "Your
mother said you used to get As."

When Sells first moved to New York, she was placed downstairs with the ensemble, a ten-person preparatory group that
took company class but hadn't yet been called up to join its
ranks. Walter Raines, who ran the ensemble at the time, created a ballet to *Peter and the Wolf,* casting Sells as the Bluebird.

The ensemble toured the ballet throughout New York City's public schools, performing in front of thousands of students. "Mr. Mitchell saw when I danced the Bluebird at a Sunday Open House," says Sells. "Then he started to bring me out, because I was the baby, at the lecture-demonstrations. He'd use me, saying things like, 'Okay, she's going to keep her leg here, see, it's not going to move.' It felt like he was noticing me."

That October, two months after moving to New York, Sells was catching her breath in the locker room after a full day of classes when an administrator burst in the room looking for her. "Marcia, you have to go upstairs to Studio 3 right now. Mr. Mitchell wants to talk to you." As she got herself together, Sells worried over the urgent meeting, but upstairs, there was good news. "You are now an apprentice in the company," Mitchell announced. "You have to learn *Divertimento No. 15* tonight. Bring your pointe shoes and get ready. Rehearsal is at six o'clock."

Balanchine's *Divertimento No. 15* is choreographed for eight principal dancers, five women and three men, with a corps of eight women. Sells learned that one of the eight corps members had exited the company, just as Sara Leland, a former City Ballet principal entrusted with staging Balanchine's ballet on companies around the world, was wrapping up her final evening of instruction. Mitchell was in desperate need of an eighth for the corps, and he'd decided Sells was his best candidate.

"Fricking terror!" she says of being so abruptly thrown into Studio 3. "But I didn't have any time to get too insane with worry. Plus, I was already thinking, *Well, this is why I came here.*" In Studio 3, Leland directed Sells to her spot on the floor, where Gayle McKinney-Griffith and a couple of other dancers demonstrated a few steps for the section. Waiting for the pianist to dive into the Mozart score, Sells reminded herself that she had a history of meeting the moment, like when she'd been thrown at age twelve into the Cincinnati Ballet's *Concerto Barocco* after one of their dancers had injured her knee. By the end of rehearsal, Sells, a fast study with a photographic memory, was caught up with the rest of the company. "I remember someone going, 'Wow, the baby is smart. She picked this up really quick!'" The following month they performed a section of the new ballet at a Sunday Open House.

As ballet mistress, McKinney-Griffith pushed Sells to focus in rehearsals. "Marcia would be chatty and laughing, and I'd have to tell her, 'Marcia, sit down!' She was a baby, so Mr. Mitchell wasn't going to choose her for a lot. But I told her to learn all the parts that she could and be serious about it." Sells still thinks that a large reason Mamie let her leave home in the first place was because of the kind impression McKinney-Griffith had made on her mother backstage in 1970. "If she hadn't met Gayle and thought, *Oh, this is a really good woman, I can trust her with my child,* there's no way I'm in New York at sixteen." McKinney-Griffith was protective of all the younger girls who entered the company. Remembers Sells, "Gayle would forever be saying, 'Okay, we have to make sure the baby is taken care of. Don't anybody scare the baby.'" Says McKinney-Griffith, "I felt a responsibility to watch out for Marcia while she prepared to learn the repertoire and travel on tour. I didn't want to disappoint her mother!"

Sells got to take part in a *Dance in America* nationally televised special honoring Mitchell's triumphant company, performing in soft-shoe parts in *Forces of Rhythm* and *Dougla*. And then on Mother's Day, she performed in a specially choreographed concert at Avery Fisher Hall with George Benson, the thirty-three-year-old jazz musician whose album *Breezin'* had hit number one on the pop, R & B, and jazz charts. During rehearsals, Benson was playing his guitar in his dressing room when Shelton and fellow dancer Stephanie Dabney passed by. They followed the music inside the doorway, slid down the wall, and listened to him practice, basking in the intimacy of the moment. Mamie Sells was in the audience that special evening, having come to New York to watch her daughter on the big stage.

Life was grand, as far as Marcia was concerned. But then, right before what was supposed to have been her first New York season, came a rumble of trouble. Dance Theatre of Harlem's board of directors made the hard decision to cancel the company's scheduled spring 1977 season at the Uris Theater. The announcement in the *New York Times* explained that the company "cannot afford a deficit which might jeopardize existing funding," and it urged the public to donate "the price of the ticket you would have purchased, had there been a season."

Mitchell didn't explain to the dancers why the season was canceled or if they should worry about job security. "Think about a general on the field of combat that loses a battle," says De Rose. "He's thinking about the war. It was always 'We go forward.'"

Despite the cancellation of their New York season, the company marched on with its robust touring schedule. During a West Coast swing that summer, the dancers were invited to appear in the film *A Piece of the Action*, directed by and starring Sidney Poitier, alongside costar Bill Cosby. Filmed at the Royce Theater in Los Angeles, in the scene, the dancers performed in front of an audience, including Poitier's and Cosby's con men characters, who are out with their dates for an elegant evening at the ballet. As the cameras rolled, Marcia Sells was preparing to sauté under an arch of dancers' arms when, to her horror, she felt the snap of her pointe shoe ribbon. With her strap flapping hopelessly, Poitier was forced to call cut.

"I was dying up there onstage," says Sells. "I thought I'd sewed it well enough, but it was just one of those terrible moments. I ran and got new pointe shoes on really quick, thinking, *Mr. Mitchell is going to kill me.* Like, okay, this is it, I'm done. And Mr. Poitier, who was just a lovely, lovely man, came over to me and put his hand on my shoulder and said, 'It's okay. We'll just start filming again.'" The women shudder at the recounting of her narrow escape from Mitchell's certain wrath. "He beat Mr. Mitchell to you!" says Shelton.

Later that evening Sells called home to Mary Lane, as she did every night. "I met Mr. Poitier!" she exclaimed to her mother. "And he touched me!" When *A Piece of the Action* was released later that fall, Sells went to see it in the theater with her mother and younger brother. "When I do my grand jeté on screen," she says, "my brother stands up in the middle of the movie theater and yells, 'That's my sister!'"

After filming, the company moved onward to San Francisco, where Karlya Shelton performed in front of four generations of family—her mother, her grandmother, her great-grandmother, and her younger brother, Kyle. "I hadn't ever seen dancing as political, at least not in the sense that we speak of it now," says Kyle. "But when I saw all the other women dancing, I thought, *Well I'll be darned; they're all Black.* Because all those years I'd been going to see Karlya dance, I always knew when my sister was onstage. I couldn't help but see her because she was the only Black person up there! Now I got to see her with all these others up there and know she wasn't the only one. That filled me with a real sense of pride."

On a break before rehearsal, Marcia Sells and Shelton left the theater to grab breakfast. As they sat down with their plates of food at a window table in the crowded restaurant, Mitchell startled them by appearing on the other side of the glass. He pounded at the window, pointing down at their waffles and then gesturing at his behind, warning them to skip the meal. Shelton refused to look at him, the food in her mouth suddenly hard to choke down.

Sells knew she was on the curvy side for a traditional ballerina. "I had a butt" is how she explains it. But she was still so thin that, at sixteen, she hadn't even had her first period. "It's not like we were ordering French fries and cake and soda. But I was freaking out," she says. "Karlya was trying to school me and telling me to relax. 'Just look straight ahead. Don't let anybody know he's talking to you. No matter what, we have a right to eat.' Even when we walk back to the theater, she was still saying, 'Don't turn around, don't look at him. Just ignore him.'" Sells can laugh now telling this story, but Shelton doesn't crack a smile.

They had one day off while they were in San Francisco, and Marcia Sells spent it at a correspondence school, taking her final three exams so that she could graduate from high school. No senior prom for her. No cap and gown. She completed her exams and then overslept the following morning. She had a hotel room by herself because she hadn't been able to handle how anxious her assigned roommate had been about whether Mitchell liked her. So there'd been no one to throw a pillow at her head as she slept through her alarm. She woke to an empty room, realizing with terror that she'd missed the company bus to Berkeley, where they were scheduled to perform that evening. She took a taxi across the city, in a panic about how badly Mitchell was going to fine her, if not worse. When Gayle McKinney-Griffith saw her sneaking into the theater, she helped Sells gather money to pay the cab fare and distracted Mitchell while the girl got changed into her dance clothes.

Sells made it onstage in time for company class without him being any the wiser, wondering aloud to the other dancers, "Nobody noticed I wasn't on the bus?"

That night when Sells called home to Mary Lane, Mamie greeted her with unexpected news. A thick envelope had arrived addressed to her from Barnard College. "You applied to college?" Mamie asked Marcia. The head of the Professional Children's School, a Barnard graduate, always urged her students to take the SATs and apply to one or two schools, regardless of their professional ambitions. "I guess I forgot to tell you," Marcia told her mother. "I applied. Well, go ahead and open the letter."

As her mother read her the good news, Marcia replied, "Okay, that's nice. But I'm not going." She'd been in the company less than a year and had barely been given a chance to dance on pointe yet. She thought she was just getting started.

For Gayle McKinney-Griffith, though, that tour of the West Coast was her last. At twenty-seven years old, she'd been feeling for some time that she had reached the apex of opportunity in the company. "At that time, we thought twenty-seven was old and that we were at our end," she says. She'd always loved watercolors and drawing and now wanted to explore stage design. She invited Mitchell out to lunch in San Francisco to share the news that she would be leaving the company. "I was telling him it's come to a time that I think I should start looking around about what else I can do."

The previous day she'd gotten a call in her hotel room from Louis Johnson. He'd been hired for the movie adaptation of the hit Broadway show *The Wiz*. He was putting together a skeleton crew of dancers to set the choreography on during a summer of preproduction. "Louis said, 'I need you. I need you,'" says McKinney-Griffith. "I was the only one he was asking from Dance Theatre of Harlem, and I had always danced in his ballets. I always thought, *I'm his favorite*. I told him we were on tour, and I'd have to think about it, and he said, 'Well, we're going to start soon, so let me know.'"

Desperate for Mitchell not to feel like she'd been looking for work behind his back, she asked what he thought of her taking Johnson up on his offer. "And I remember he said, 'Oh Gayle, this is an opportunity for you! This would be good. You can branch out.'" After all, Mitchell had done Broadway and movies in the past. He knew not to squander good work when it came around.

They settled that she would leave the company immediately upon return to New York, but the door would remain open to her in the future. "We agreed on it, and he wished me luck," says McKinney-Griffith. "I didn't have any papers signed, because I didn't think I needed it."

Sheila Rohan sucks her teeth listening to her friend's recounting of such a cordial arrangement. "Oh my God," she says. "That's backstabbing." Because they all know now what would come next—Mitchell would twist the memory of their parting in his mind, casting McKinney-Griffith in the role of the abandoning child who betrayed her faithful father.

12

THE WIZ WAS ADAPTED FROM THE SEVEN-TIME TONY Award–winning 1975 Broadway musical of the same title, itself a Black reimagining of L. Frank Baum's *The Wonderful Wizard of Oz.* The Universal-Motown film, with Sidney Lumet directing his first musical and Quincy Jones serving as music supervisor and music producer, features Diana Ross as Dorothy, a naive Harlem schoolteacher dropped into the Land of Oz; Michael Jackson, making his theatrical film debut as the Scarecrow; Nipsey Russell as the Tin Man; and Ted Ross as the Cowardly Lion. Lena Horne and Mabel King play Glinda and Evillene, respectively, and Richard Pryor, wearing a twenty-five-foot-high silver head, was the Wiz himself. Though considered a box office failure at the time of its release, *The Wiz* endures as a treasured cultural touchstone for Black audiences. Here finally was not just a big, splashy song-and-dance movie but a declaration that the archetype of home could hang just as naturally on a rural Kansas town as it could contemporary Harlem and the comforting breast of Black family life.

Lumet had hired Louis Johnson to choreograph *The Wiz* because he was a fan of *Forces of Rhythm*. Speaking to a reporter leading up to the movie's release, Johnson recounted, "[Sidney] told me up front he's never done a musical before; he said he knew I had the scope, and the eye, for a picture on this scale. He left me alone to do my own thing, but he'd pop in the studio all the time and watch rehearsals and say, 'Louis, you're right on it.'"

In preproduction, he created choreography for elaborate production numbers like "Emerald City Sequence" and "A Brand New Day" on Gayle McKinney-Griffith and the rest of his skeleton crew, who would later be charged with helping set it on the cast. During a summer of early rehearsals in their oven of a studio space, Johnson, a former high school acrobat, led with the churning energy of soda trapped in a shaken bottle. "Louis would do all the steps, all the flips, the tricks, the pirouettes, everything," says McKinney-Griffith. "He'd tell us, 'Do it like this!' while we just stood there amazed. Then he would watch us through this big squint of his. When you'd make a mistake, his eyes would suddenly go really big, and he'd say, 'What was that? What was that you're doing?'" There was always the sense that if Johnson could have split himself in hundreds, he would've loved to dance the entire production himself.

Back at 152nd Street, Mitchell struggled with the loss of his ballet mistress. He'd send up manufactured flares of need, then fume when McKinney-Griffith didn't meet them. "He would tell me, 'Well, you have to come in and rehearse *Forces of Rhythm* with the dancers,'" she says. "They've already done the ballet four thousand times, and now he wants me to come in and rehearse it? I'd tell him, 'These dancers already know this. They've performed it.' He'd say, 'Nope. You have to come in and rehearse this!' I would try to explain that I had a new contract I had to honor and couldn't just take the day off. But I know it infuriated him that I wouldn't come home."

And his losses were just beginning. Over seven hundred Black dancers were pouring into auditions for *The Wiz*, from New York, Los Angeles, Chicago, and Europe. Even Sheila Rohan, who'd officially been gone from the company for two years by then, wanted a shot at it. But by the time she called Johnson to see if he could use her, he was already drowning in dancers. "He told me, 'No, darling, I have about two thousand dancers in here, and I can't take another one,'" Rohan says with a laugh. "He was a wreck!"

Lydia Abarca, meanwhile, was twenty-seven years old and still getting by on her $10,000 yearly salary when she heard about *The Wiz* and asked McKinney-Griffith for Johnson's personal phone number. "Me in a dance movie?" says Abarca. "This is what I've been working toward my whole life! We had been with the company twenty-four seven for nine years. This was another pioneering moment for a Black dancer in New York City. I was going to meet every dancer in New York, from all genres of dance. Arthur's done Broadway; he's done movies. He knows! Come on, that's fair!" There was no review gushing enough, no part Mitchell could give her challenging enough, to persuade her to stay. Her bank account was begging for her to make a break from ballet.

Her timing worked out well, sadly. At the end of the summer, Dance Theatre of Harlem had scheduled a group of performances at Columbia University's Ferris Booth Hall, as part of a special community dance series. "This weekend may well be the last chance for New Yorkers to see the vibrant Dance Theater of Harlem in Manhattan for at least a year," wrote the *New York Times*. "The company has no plans to perform in the city outside its own school building until after September 1978. And it does not have any other bookings scheduled except August 19–20 at the American Dance Festival season in Newport, Rhode Island. Money, or the lack of it, is at the root of this sad state of affairs. The company has been experiencing financial crisis since last winter, when it canceled a season at the Uris Theater and went into a period of retrenchment."

And so whether they were simply avoiding the unemployment line or chasing Hollywood dreams as Abarca was, that summer ten more dancers, many of them men, eased on down the yellow-brick road to join Gayle McKinney-Griffith at the Kaufman Astoria Studios in Queens. Mitchell had lost nearly half his company. Says De Rose, "Did it destroy him? No. But it did demoralize him, yes. He felt like we were a family. An army. 'We had gone on this mission together, and you desert me now?'" No matter how mad he got at them, though, how crudely he would demand them to return to him, those eleven dancers had signed contracts with the film. They weren't coming back until it was over, if ever.

While Gayle McKinney-Griffith and Lydia Abarca worked on the film, Karlya Shelton stayed behind in Harlem. She saw the thinning of company ranks as an opportunity for those left behind to make themselves more valuable in Mitchell's eyes. She grew familiar with the regular faces at the local unemployment office on West 90th Street, which the dancers referred to as Club 90.

Johnson knew Marcia Sells from when they'd worked together on a ballet for the Cincinnati Ballet and had assumed she would want to be a part of the movie, but she remained in the company as well. "I'll admit, I was too afraid of Mr. Mitchell to leave," she says.

The following year, during a lecture-demonstration at Columbia University, they were both onstage with Mitchell when he spotted one of the dancers who'd left him for the movie in the back of the theater. In front of the oblivious audience, Mitchell interrupted the proceedings to acknowledge the dancer trying to slip into his seat quietly. "Oh, here comes one of the Dumb Eleven," he spat, disdain thick in his voice.

"That was one of the times I really saw how ugly he could be," Shelton tells the women. "I think he was just afraid of losing control, so he made himself the victim."

That same fall McKinney-Griffith dropped by Dance Theatre of Harlem to say hello and gather some of her things she'd left behind. As she was coming up the stairs, she spotted Mitchell coming out of his office above. "Mr. Mitchell!" she called out happily. He recoiled at the sight of her, raising his hands up into a defensive posture. "No, no, no, no, no!" he snapped. "Get back! Get outta here! Go home!"

McKinney-Griffith kept following him up the stairs; it was inconceivable that he could be talking to her in that way. With mounting confusion, she reached out toward the man she'd worked tirelessly alongside for a decade. "I thought he was joking at first. I was still smiling because sometimes he could really clown around. And then he said, 'No! I don't want to speak to you. I don't even want to see you.' He put his hands up to block me from coming toward him."

Woozily, McKinney-Griffith made her way to the blue doors leading into Studio 3. "I was in a dream state because I didn't understand his rejection. I could not connect that this was Mr. Mitchell talking to me." Inside the studio, a room full of unfamiliar dancers stared uneasily back at her. She followed Mitchell's retreating back into the studio, mortified as he slipped out a second exit into the music room.

Humiliated, McKinney-Griffith fled the studio, leaving behind a decade of notebooks and files and old pointe shoes that would never be returned to her. Outside on the street, she let the tears she'd been holding back rain down onto the sidewalk.

McKinney-Griffith called her parents that night, asking to speak to her father because she knew the story would upset her mother so much that Millicent would want to drive into Harlem to curse Mitchell out. "Whether Arthur is acting a fool," Harold counseled his daughter, "that's his thing, not yours."

McKinney-Griffith would later hear that Mitchell had condemned any dancer from *The Wiz* who hadn't returned to him tail tucked, begging for forgiveness and reentry into the company. He'd forgotten, or chosen to forget, the collegial lunch they'd had in San Francisco, his excitement over her fantasies of stage design, his delighting in her opportunity to work with Johnson.

Years later, when she shared the story of her departure from DTH with the Legacy Council, it was the first some heard of the messy details of her exit. "I had no idea it was so bad," says Lydia Abarca. "I mean, you must have been devastated. That was family. How could Arthur have done that to family?"

Sheila Rohan rolls her eyes at the question. "He was thinking, *How could they do this to me?* Because we were his children. So, *how dare they disobey me?* He took it as a personal insult, a betrayal. I can't say I was surprised, but Gayle had given this man her life. She really was the epitome of a ballet mistress. Bah! He lost a gem."

A couple of years after *The Wiz*, Mitchell would speak magnanimously about the eleven company members who'd left to do the movie, in an interview with *Ballet News* magazine. "I just couldn't compete with the salaries that Hollywood was offering my dancers. Anyway, for a lot of those kids, DTH was the only world they had ever known. They needed to branch out and experience new things. It's hard to lose dancers whom you've spent so much time training, but a good teacher doesn't try to hold his students to his breast and keep them at home. He encourages them to venture out and try new things. Sometimes it's the only way for them to grow."

GAYLE

*W*ALTER RAINES CALLED ME EVERY DAY. HE'D SAY, "AR-
*thur's crazy. He's on his own planet." He would go on and
on, trying to soothe my feelings. And my "Sheily." Sheila would
talk to me for hours, just to give me strength and get me out of
that funk I was in. Finally, I became defiant. I told myself,* Arthur's not going to destroy me.

*In 1979 I had the papers to enroll in stage-design courses
when a friend called me out of the blue. Germany's Theater des
Westens was inviting a group of dancers from the United States
to be in different musical productions. They wanted three Black
men and three Black women. My friend told me one of the
dancers had dropped out. "You got to go see this man coming
from Germany. You get paid!" It was going to be carte blanche.
Beautiful hotels. Health insurance. Quadruple the salary of
Dance Theatre of Harlem. They were talking thousands when
I'd been getting hundreds.*

In Berlin, we became a part of the German ensemble. A lot of the ticket sales were ambassadors and the military. They gave us the German text, and we learned everything phonetically. Our first musical was Show Boat—*that was horrible. I hated that show. I said, "Oh my God, we're back in slave times! Good thing this paycheck is hefty."*

I thought I would stay in Berlin for six months, a year maybe. I married a man who went over with me for the Theater des Westens. My beautiful children Don and Khadija were born in Germany and attended the John F. Kennedy Schule, where I taught an after-school dance program for the students from kindergarten through high school in ballet, jazz, and modern movement. Khadija is a dancer, too, so eventually she would teach classes there with me.

My husband and I wanted to create opportunities for dancers and artists of diverse backgrounds. Unfortunately, my marriage was not always kind. If he was being horrendous, I told myself, that's just on him. I placed my energies and attention into my children and the projects that I was doing. If I didn't have a project, I would create one. I taught in several German cities as well as Italy, Switzerland, Liechtenstein, and Austria. I started the ballet department of what has become Tanzforum Wien. We started a youth dance program called Space and Time, working with social workers. Our goal was to keep at-risk kids off the streets and guide their energies into the theater and more creative outlets.

"I don't think growing up I understood all my mother had accomplished in her life," says her daughter, Khadija "Tariyan"

Griffith. Khadija liked to run around the apartment in her mother's pointe shoes as a child, but she wouldn't show any interest in lessons until she was ten. Even then Gayle chose not to enroll her into a rigorous program. "She said, 'I wanted to protect your spirit,'" says Khadija. "I was a sensitive child, and she didn't want me in a strict space that would try to mold me. It was always, 'Look what I can do, Mom!' And she'd say, 'Beautiful!'" When she was twelve, Khadija happened upon a showing of *The Wiz* on TV, stunned to see her mother in a gold designer gown and planet-size hat dancing atop a grand piano with Quincy Jones on the keys. "I chased Mom around the house, like, 'What do you mean you were in this!?'"

In 2015, Khadija was cast in NBC's television production of *The Wiz Live!* She called her mother and her brother, Don, in a three-way call in which they joyfully celebrated the full-circle moment. "It was so powerful and surreal," says Don, a Connecticut attorney and former semiprofessional basketball player. "Whatever unfinished business Mom had, it felt like Dija was taking home." At the first table read, Khadija stood up and introduced herself as the daughter of one of the dancers in the original movie.

In 2016, Gayle survived a final physical confrontation in her marriage. *It was spousal abuse. I had to leave Germany, my beautiful apartment, all my friends, the life I'd built there for over thirty-five years. I was devastated, but I just wanted to get out and be with my family and my children. I haven't spoken to him since.*

I've been surprised by how people can change. How they can turn on you. But I did feel like I got my apology from Arthur. I was at book party for Alexis Wilson, the daughter of choreographer Billy Wilson. Arthur was ill at the time. He was walking with a cane and really struggling. I was there with my daughter, so I said, "Khadija, I want you to meet Mr. Mitchell." And he goes to her, "Oh my goodness, you are so beautiful." And then he said, "I would like to tell you that I'm very sorry that I hurt your mother." And she's just standing there because she didn't know our history. I never talked to my children about that because what would it get me, telling all my woes? I was shocked. He never really looked at me but just kept telling Khadija that he was sorry.

Then he said, "Come on, Gayle, come on and sit with me." I didn't want to, but he said, "No, no, no, come sit with me." We were right in the front. Alexis was telling us all about the history of her book, and he's talking to me and laughing, disturbing me from listening. At the end, I got up and moved around, but then he was just there. He couldn't walk around. He just sat there for a while. So I said, "Arthur, do you need help?" He said, "I don't need any help!" I stood him up and said, "Well, do you want me to go down with you in the elevator? Is your car there?" "No, I can do it! I can do it!" So I just said goodbye, and the doors closed.

Back in Connecticut, I went in for my annual mammogram, and they told me I had cancer. I couldn't believe it. I had just gone through that big blowup in Germany. I was taking care of my mother. What was happening to me? My nerves were like *razor blades. The doctors told me it was spreading into my lymph nodes, and it was going to be in my bloodstream. They wanted to operate right away. But because of what happened in Germany, my knee was injured, and I first had to have that surgery. Then I hobbled into the cancer center and had three operations in there. They put me on a cocktail of chemotherapy that just flattened me. I lost my hair, my eyelashes. I lost all my strength. I couldn't take care of my mother. It felt like all my walls had come crashing in and there was no floor. I just felt emotionally broken. I don't have any history of cancer in my family, but I'd been under so much stress and then my broken heart. Through all my upheavals, I would talk to Sheila. My friends. My mother. My children. When I wasn't strong enough to walk around, my son would carry me into my appointments.*

"Talk about redefining strength," says Don. "I grew up with a different idea of what strength was. Now I realize that it's my mom who truly embodies strength. She has this quiet ability to weather any storm and come out the better for it. It's not loud and in your face. It's stay the course, stay disciplined, come out better. And that's what she's done. She doesn't break."

I got through it. Yoga and meditation helped. I don't have the energy and strength that I used to have, but I started teaching ballet again at the Dance Extension in Waterford [Connecticut]. I'm a substitute ballet teacher at Connecticut College. I feel my peace returning. My son, Don, proposed to his girlfriend, Katy, who's going for her PhD in education, on a beautiful beach here in Connecticut on the fiftieth anniversary of the Loving v. Virginia *Supreme Court decision. They mar-*

ried a year later. At the reception, I heard Don say, "Mom, have I got a song for you!" It was "A Brand New Day."

Tragically, in the years after the Legacy Council brought light again to that part of McKinney-Griffith's story, her cancer returned, metastasizing in her spine. She spent weeks in a state of numbed paralysis, unable to speak the words aloud. *I was trying not to put the news in the air. If it goes in the air, she told herself, it'll get a power of its own. If I kept it contained, maybe I could squeeze it dead.*

When she finally found the words to share with the others, steady and wise Sheila Rohan surprised her by having the biggest emotional response, crying visibly on-screen during a Legacy Council Tuesday meeting. McKinney-Griffith's eyes welled, remembering Rohan's tears. *She's my heart.*

I've had to come to terms with, yes, I have this again. It does overwhelm you. Sometimes it's the physical pain where I'm just wiped out. But mostly it's emotional because I say, "Jeez, I've got to do this again?" I'm trying to hold on to the part of me that is still me and knows I can fight through this. But when a cancer metastasizes, where does it go? It can go anywhere. I don't know how to fight it. So I'm relying on my meditation, breathing, yoga, movement, all these plant-based diets. My kids are focused on getting me through this. They're going to research and talk to the doctors and give me orders. I'm blessed. Coming from my marriage, I just know how to appreciate people. That taught me a big lesson. Never use anyone. Respect people. Understand that you're not the biggest fish in the sea. My work now is to hold on to some optimism. The treatments that I'm going through are supposed to keep me alive for a period of time. It might not kill the cancer forever, but I'm going to do everything I can to augment that thought process and keep it positive. Your body knows. Your soul knows.

She shakes her head, squeezing gently onto the tops of her arms. *If I had not danced, what kind of condition would I be in right now? All this pain. These pains let me know that my body is still trying, that it's still living. You live long enough to appreciate what you have and be thankful that you can still go for a walk outside. Every time I'm at the clinic, they ask me, "Do you need a cane or a wheelchair?" And I'm thanking myself constantly for being able to say "No, I'm okay." As a dancer I honed this body for so many years. When you're younger, a decade younger even, you think to yourself,* I don't like my hips. I don't like my legs. *I can't do an arabesque anymore. I can't lift my leg up. I get a cramp when I point my foot. But I'm okay. I'm okay. I'm okay. I wish there was something that we could say to people to remind them, "Your body is your house. Just be thankful for it and to it."*

But after months of treatment, McKinney-Griffith ultimately has to choose her words carefully to share news with the Legacy Council that she knows will be hard for them all to hear. *I'm at stage four. There are no more stages to go. They're trying to do as much as their knowledge allows. I'm still looking at other doctors and treatments, but my body is pretty fed up with all of this.*

Sheila Rohan leans closer into her camera, the power of her gaze tunneling through the screen. "Well, this is when your spirit takes over," she says. "And you're a very spirited person, Gayle. This is why you were always special to me. That's part of my attraction to you. You were the person that we all were drawn to. There you are. You have it in you."

I'm not going to give up, McKinney-Griffith tells her friends again, her voice taking on a reassuring heft of stubbornness. *I think about our group, and I think about our work. That's what keeps me going. At least they'll know I was here.*

Gayle holds up a photo of her nineteen-month-old grandson, Emmitt, Don and Katy's child. He's wearing a black onesie with the words READ TO ME across his plump little chest. The brightness of his wide-open smile could power the sun. From the Tuesday when she first announced that she was going to be a grandma, to her announcement of Emmitt's first words, to his first steps, to his first faceful of cake, the Legacy Council has celebrated each milestone right along with her. There is comfort in the knowledge that this child will grow up knowing everything his grandmother did as a girl, and then as a woman. Gayle McKinney-Griffith has put her story down on record. *It brings tears to my eyes when I think that I've done some work that he can be proud of one day.*

13

B Y THE TIME DANCE THEATRE OF HARLEM WENT ON HIA-
tus in 1977, Marcia Sells had already deferred her college
acceptance to Barnard. With the future of the company uncertain, she thought about trying out for Alvin Ailey in the
meantime. But she knew she wasn't a modern dancer. She
considered auditioning for Broadway or moving to Europe.
"But at seventeen, I just didn't have that level of risk in me," she
says. "I'd built this life for myself in New York around family,
friends, and safety. All this thinking around auditioning made
me realize I'd gotten spoiled. I'd always been good enough to
just get asked to do the work. So when DTH stopped performing, I had to really think, *How do I find a home?*"

After hearing that Marcia was considering pulling up
stakes for Europe, Mamie reminded her daughter of a more
practical next step. "Well, you already got into college," she
said. "Why don't you call Barnard?"

And so in January 1978, Marcia Sells entered college as a midyear freshman. Eager to throw herself into the full college experience, she moved into a dorm for the semester, before transitioning to a two-bedroom first-floor apartment on West 110th Street that was a block away from Karlya Shelton's apartment building. When fall rolled around, a year since Dance Theatre of Harlem had been on tour, Sells signed up for another semester with a full course load. She arranged her schedule with the precision of a surgeon so that she wouldn't miss Karel Shook's daily company class or Arthur Mitchell's evening rehearsals.

Mitchell had spent the last several months building back up the company ranks with fresh young apprentices he called up from the school, some as young as fourteen. A couple of dancers returned from *The Wiz*, though he'd humbled them with a grueling reaudition process. Of all the dancers who joined the movie production, it was Lydia Abarca whom Mitchell chased after to return. Before she left for *The Wiz*, her company salary had risen to $350 a week. Mitchell offered to make it $450 if she'd only come home. But her experience on that movie set had reminded her of sneaking into that jazz class back when she was just a teenager looking for magic. She wasn't ready to give it up.

Abarca had spent ten years dancing for Mitchell. She'd had a decade of rave reviews and modeling jobs and the occasional magazine cover. Yet she was still broke. She had to share an apartment with her sister Celia and brother, Julio, to make rent. "What's recognition unless it brings a lot of money with it?" she once asked a reporter. "One day I'm going to make so much money, and then I'm going to buy my parents land and a house and everything they want."

Going home to Mitchell felt like taking a step backward. She had to try something new. "I was this little mouse who knew what she wanted but had no idea how to get it," she says. Besides, she'd already helped build the company the first time around. She wasn't up for the rebuild, not when she finally had other opportunities to choose from.

On the movie set, Abarca had met a performer named Smokey, who'd starred in the original Broadway production of *Bubbling Brown Sugar*, the great Billy Wilson musical revue about the Harlem Renaissance nightlife scene, back when folks drank bathtub gin and scotch out of teacups. Smokey told her the show's producers were looking to launch a two-week engagement of *Bubbling* at Paper Mill Playhouse in New Jersey, with the legendary bandleader Cab Calloway headlining. "Here was this jazz, this jazz in my life that I've always been missing," says Abarca. She took two days to cram in new tap-dancing skills and landed the role of Sophisticated Lady, the woman from the title of Duke Ellington's song whose elegant fur stole and opera-length gloves belie a broken heart.

After *Bubbling*, Abarca got word that Bob Fosse, the man who had literally brought jazz hands to the Broadway stage, was looking for dancers. The legendary choreographer and director of *Cabaret, Liza with a Z,* and *Pippin* was getting ready to make *All That Jazz,* his semi-autobiographical movie starring Roy Scheider and Jessica Lange. "There were about five hundred dancers in the theater," Abarca says of the audition. "The first routine that Bob Fosse always did is a ballet routine. I was in the front, and after my group finished, he said, 'Wait a minute, wait a minute. You. What's your name?'"

But Smokey, who'd been sweet on Abarca since *The Wiz* and finally won her heart on *Bubbling,* had been cut after the first round of the *All That Jazz* auditions. He had it in his head that his new girlfriend should follow him right out the door. He signed on to an international company of *Bubbling* that was heading to Europe for the summer, and he persuaded Abarca to bail on the movie and join him abroad. "Smokey kept telling me, 'You're just going to be in the chorus,'" she says now. "'You got a chance to be the Sophisticated Lady in Europe. You know how they love Black dancers over there!'" When Fosse got word that she was turning down the movie, he called her personally to urge her to reconsider. Abarca can't help but cry when she recounts the brevity with which she told him no. She left for Europe, already worried that she was making the biggest mistake of her life, and all for the love of a man who liked her but loved cocaine more. "I turned down the movie for all the wrong reasons. I just didn't know how to be a star."

Mitchell, aghast that she'd chosen Europe over Harlem, would've agreed with her. Whether he liked it or not, he'd have to rebuild without his muse.

That fall Marcia Sells began dreading the studio, knowing she'd have to deal with Mitchell's judgment. "I had gained the

Freshman Ten. Which at my height is still the weight of a thin person, but not ballet thin. I'd gone through puberty and filled out a bit. Honestly, it just made me look normal. I knew I was going to have to make some changes physically. I'd hit that point in my life where weight was suddenly going to be an issue." She never made herself throw up, like some of the other dancers, but she started skipping breakfast and lunch, relying on Tab soda for shots of energy, and experimenting with protein diets. But no matter what she tried, the fact was that she no longer had the body of a young girl.

"I think the piece that I still haven't fully come to grips with," she shares with the Legacy Council, "is that although we were a Black ballet company, we were still always confronted by the imagery of what white women dancers look like. I truly believe that Mr. Mitchell was still comparing some of us to that. It's why he'd choose girls I came up with who looked like a washboard over me, even though I would compare my pirouettes to any of theirs."

Sells was confused by Mitchell's seeming lack of faith in her. Occasionally in lecture-demonstrations, he let her get up on pointe. She got to perform the pas de neuf from *Holberg Suite* for an audience of children. She understudied for one of the eight corps de ballet roles in *Concerto Barocco*. But for the most part, Mitchell consigned her to soft-shoe ballets like *Caravanserai* and *Dougla*. She couldn't help but wonder if it was because of her body type and also the darkness of her complexion.

"Yes, there was colorism at Dance Theatre of Harlem," says

Sells. "It was hard, and it was sad. I remember doing Skirt Girls in Louis Johnson's *Forces of Rhythm*." (In the ballet, the women cast in the role of Skirt Girls wear full-circle ankle-length skirts and kerchiefs and dance more modern choreography; Ballet Girls wear short ballet skirts and pointe shoes, dancing allegro variations with fast footwork, jumps, and pirouettes. Sheila Rohan, who started as a Skirt Girl but eventually was recast as a Ballet Girl, says the latter was the more coveted role.)

"I remember thinking, *I'm really talented; why am I doing Skirt Girls and not Ballet Girls?*" says Sells. "But it was all the light-skinned girls in Ballet Girls and all the darker-skinned girls in Skirt Girls." She points out that her mother had been denied admission to Spelman College years earlier for failing to pass the paper-bag test—the discriminatory practice within the Black community in which a person's skin tone was held up to a brown paper bag. "Colorism was not just a problem for Arthur Mitchell," says Sells. "This permeated Black life, period."

Years later she would write to her mother describing how her passion for ballet dwindled under Mitchell's care. "Somehow my growth as a dancer regressed once I joined the company," she wrote in the letter. "I think my emotional and mental growth started exceeding my growth as a dancer and affected my dancing. As my emotional attitude toward dancing changed, my satisfaction with DTH decreased. My weight then proceeded to increase. This combination of events had a profound effect on how I saw DTH, and they saw me."

That fall Mitchell called Sells into his office, informing her once again that she needed to drop weight if she was going to stay in the company. She remembers feeling bruised and angry but not ashamed. "I'm deep into feminist literature at Barnard by this point, and I had this amazing professor, Cate Stimpson, who is one of the leading feminist scholars, teaching me in a class. So I'm rethinking everything and asking myself, *Do I have it in me to still listen to him talk about my weight?*" She laughs, remembering the time she responded to one of his lectures by saying, "You know, you're not really being helpful to my emotional health right now." He was so unused to being talked back to like that that all he could do in response was sputter for her to get out of his office. Years later Mitchell would tell people of Sells, "Oh yeah, she used to be my smarty-pants."

Mitchell remained obstinate that Sells couldn't balance college life with the task of getting back into performing shape. Dance Theatre of Harlem was getting ready to embark on a West Coast tour. One morning Sells rushed up the stairs, knowing that she'd overslept after staying up late the night before studying and had missed the start of rehearsal. She stood against the wall leading into Studio 3, waiting for a chance to slip in among the dancers. When Mitchell noticed her standing there on the landing, he shook his head in exasperation. "What is that girl going to do?" he demanded of the studio. "Would that girl just make up her mind?" Sells felt her face go hot but forced herself not to cry or flee in embarrassment. "I would've walked out of class, but I didn't want to give him the satisfaction."

After rehearsal, Mitchell called her into his office. The two sat looking at each other, each painfully disappointed in the other. "I was just so sad and angry that he was making me make this decision to quit dance that I didn't think was actually necessary," she says. "I could've just taken a deferral from school and stayed. But at that point I was just so mad at him. I remember saying to him, 'You have psychological problems,'" she says, amused by her younger self's chutzpah. "I was eighteen years old. Disappointed, disillusioned, and feeling my oats of what I was learning in school. So yeah, *'Mr. Mitchell, you have psychological problems, and this is just ridiculous.'*"

Then she walked away from the life she'd dreamed about since she was a child, without the comfort of knowing she'd reached the limits of her potential. Besides the death of her mother, it would be the great loss of her life.

MARCIA

WHO WAS I GOING TO BE IN THIS WORLD NOW? I'VE invested all this time into ballet, and who was I without that? *After college I went to Columbia Law School, where I started my switch into what my other life was going to be. At the time I'm thinking,* Oh, I'll be an entertainment lawyer. That's how I stay in dance and the art world. *But then I intern at the NAACP Legal Defense Fund, the Cincinnati Institute of Justice, the NOW Legal Defense Fund. I turn in some ways to the social justice issues that my parents have always focused on and find my identity there instead.*

I become an assistant district attorney trying rape and child abuse cases for the Kings County District Attorney's Office. I have to say my mom was really quite proud of me. I used to talk to her on the phone and run through my summations with her, and she would give me pointers. The biggest case I won was helping to convict the Flatbush rapist who had committed four rapes. I was twenty-seven years old, with three years of experience under my belt. A win like that gives you a mixture of feelings. It's sad to see people go to jail. For me, it's still sad. But it is also important that people believed the women, one of whom was maybe just eighteen or nineteen years old, who got up to testify.

When I went to the DA's office, I knew that I'd found my purpose. Not just because of those cases. I knew I could develop the tools and the language of law. But the reality of being a trial lawyer is also having the ability to communicate with people who are not trial lawyers. The performance part made me comfortable. I knew how to connect with an audience, a jury, on things I felt righteous about. It goes back to Mr. Mitchell's training. His core thing was you had to move. If you're a tall person, you couldn't shrivel. You couldn't look like you were static. Commit to the movement. You had to expand your arms. Take up space. That idea of taking up space has stuck with me my entire life. I try to walk into a space feeling like I know I'm going to own the room. Not from the standpoint of I want everyone to know me, but I'm here to learn something about people. Around this time, there was a story in Smithsonian magazine about Dance Theatre of Harlem. I remember reading it at my mother's house. In it, Arthur Mitchell mentions, "Yes, one of our former dancers is a prosecutor in the Brooklyn DA's office." Like, wow, I thought this man who had once been a father figure to me had no idea what I was doing, nor cared. When I read that he actually claims me as one of his own, it warmed my heart.

After my parents divorced, my mother started her own

human resources consulting business to push matters of diversity, equity, inclusion, although the work wasn't called that then. She worked with companies like Procter & Gamble and the University of Cincinnati to recruit and keep minority hires. But when her health started really failing, her health insurance plan was expensive. I left the DA's office for a corporate job that paid triple my salary because the bills were just too high.

I was blessed with this huge apartment, so as my mother's health failed, she used to come and live with me for four months out of the year. I was in my twenties, and I had to get an oxygen tank, and we had the emergency numbers for all the doctors. Even toward the end, when she was on oxygen twenty-four seven, literally rolling an oxygen tank, she was determined to live. She made me move her back to my grandmother's house in Ohio because she wouldn't let me live with her as her health was really declining.

At the end of my first year as dean of students at Columbia Law School, I remember coming back to Ohio for a visit. Friends of my mom greeted me at the airport. They told me she was in the hospital, and they needed to take me directly there. And that was it. She was in the ICU for three weeks, and she died in July 1992. I now realize just how young my sixty-two was compared to hers. She was robbed.

For most of my career. I didn't put my performing background on my résumé. I thought it might make me sound unserious, to be frank. I thought people might think it was silly. But then when people did find out, they'd be like, Oh my God, you were an actual ballerina! *I realize now that the discipline* of ballet—every single day you go to the barre, and you start all over again, and you keep repeating the movements—gives you a real grounding in terms of how you tackle life. Music will come on, and parts of the steps will come up for me, even whole sections of the ballet. You have an emotional and physical body memory of that time, even though you can't do it anymore. American Ballet Theatre is doing Swan Lake at the Metropolitan Opera, where I was appointed to the role of chief diversity officer in 2021. The music is piped into my office speakers. "Oh, there's the dance of the four swans, the échappés." You remember it, always.

14

IN 1978, JUST FOUR MONTHS AFTER LEAVING NEW YORK for the European tour of *Bubbling Brown Sugar,* Lydia Abarca was on a plane back home, crying over her tray table. It had been sweet for a while. Escargots and champagne during rehearsal weeks in London. A show opening in Amsterdam, before moving on to the Théâtre de Paris. Then she says her boyfriend, Smokey, had persuaded her that they should call in sick from a performance and take a day trip to England to hang out with the London cast. When they returned to Paris, they discovered that the show's producers had ordered all their belongings packed up. Their ruse of illness had earned them an immediate dismissal from the show. Abarca, who'd never been fired in her life, was humiliated, furious at herself for listening to her boyfriend again. They'd stay together for a while longer, but the honeymoon was over.

Arthur Mitchell gave her a hard time, but for better or for

worse, Abarca could always count on him to take her back. "Lydia wanted so much more for herself," her husband of forty years, Al Mitchell, explains, "and Arthur held on tight to her and acted like a tyrant. But no matter how crazy he acted, he would always have open arms for her when she would come back. She'd leave and come back, leave and come back, and he would always take her, which he didn't do for everyone." But when she asked if the offer to pay her $450 a week still stood, he laughed in her face. She'd come back at $350, as punishment for choosing Europe over him.

"I think the one thing everyone at the company knew is that nothing bad was ever going to happen to Lydia," agrees Karlya Shelton. "Arthur was not going to ever be truly mean or ugly to her, because she was his prized person. That's who he always wanted at the top of the Christmas tree for the company."

Since Abarca had left, Dance Theatre of Harlem had added another Balanchine ballet, *Serenade*, to its repertoire. Mitchell immediately recast her in the principal role of the Dark Angel. He divided his ballerinas into a tall cast and a short cast, with the latter always relegated to second cast and understudy roles. Abarca, Virginia Johnson, and Lorraine Graves—five six, five eight, and five ten, respectively—danced the principal roles of the Dark Angel, the Waltz Girl, and the Russian Girl. At five three, Shelton was assigned to the second cast, understudying Graves.

Serenade opens on the transcendent scene of seventeen

women onstage, swathed in the palest and pearliest of blues, the tulle of their long skirts dusting the tops of their ankles. The soft blue lighting hits the women like moonlight. They stand with their right arms raised, their palms extended as if to gently hold back the weight of the stars. The Tchaikovsky score is luscious, feminine, a hymn to all things lovely and romantic. "As soon as the curtain went up, and the audience saw us all standing there, there would always be an immediate applause," says Shelton. "Your skirt would softly blow because the curtain produces a little bit of wind. You're standing in that opening position, and then there's that first move with your hand, that break of your wrist as you bring it to your temple. It's all so lovely and indulgent. Every night you felt beautiful."

Shelton says there was something magical about their corps de ballet. It wasn't just the depth of talent onstage, the mastery of technique and precision. "We just loved dancing with each other so much," she says. "'Oh, what is your arm doing? I'm going to put my arm just like that. Let's make sure we match. Let's make sure we're all together.' In *Serenade*, we had a little competition. 'I'm going to do a triple pirouette here. We should all do triples here!'"

Privately, though, Shelton yearned for a chance to step out from the corps into principal roles. If only Mitchell would see in her what she knew she had to give! On tour in Dublin that fall, she finally got a chance to shine.

A few hours before showtime, Mitchell got word that Lorraine Graves, whose career as a principal ballerina and ballet mistress at Dance Theatre of Harlem would span eighteen years, was down with a bad case of food poisoning. Shelton was out on her dinner break when Mitchell made the cast change. When she returned to the theater, the stage manager met her at the door with her marching orders. She had two hours to get ready to go onstage in the technically challenging role that's full of multiple pirouettes and quick footwork. She rushed out of her street clothes and rehearsed some of the passage's spacing with Abarca and Johnson and practiced the lifts with her partner. To add to the challenge, the Dublin theater had a raked stage typical of European venues. In America, the house of a theater is on an incline and the stage is flat. Across Europe, it's the opposite, which left company members fearing "the rake monster." Explains Shelton, "The closer you danced toward the mouth by the pit, the more it felt like the monster would swallow you." Turns suddenly felt more treacherous. A dancer would have to adjust their spotting, raising their head and upper body slightly so as not to go tumbling down.

But that night onstage, Shelton remembers feeling so focused, so alive and in flow. "I wasn't going to let the rake freak me out," she says. Afterward all the dancers clapped for her backstage. "You did it! You did it!" If Mitchell approved of her performance, he didn't tell her. But she didn't care. Shelton had danced in a role that she'd coveted since she was a child, and she knew she'd done it justice.

Just as Shelton's ambition was peaking, so was Lydia Abarca's sense of restlessness. In a profile that winter, *People* magazine bemoaned the fact that "time is about to catch up with Abarca, 28. For almost a decade she has been a prima but little-celebrated performer." In a *Washington Post* feature titled "On the Brink of Stardom," Abarca gave voice to her growing impatience: "Time is short. Ballet is like athletics; there aren't that many years to get what you want." When the reporter asked what exactly she wanted from the world, Abarca was charmingly blunt: "I'm just ambitious. I want to be a star."

The day after the *Post* story ran, Mitchell, likely still smarting over the Dumb Eleven and Abarca leaving him for Europe, called her in for a meeting. He brandished the newspaper like a weapon. "You don't want to be a star!" he yelled, stabbing at her words on the page with his finger. "You want to be an artist!" Abarca couldn't believe his outrage. "An artist? A starving artist, I guess. All I did was share my childhood dream. I wanted to be a star, and I didn't know how or when it was going to happen doing *Concerto Barocco* for him."

Dance Theatre of Harlem had always billed itself as an ensemble company, without the traditional stated hierarchy of principals, soloist, demi-soloists, and corps. Mitchell wanted the only star to be the institution itself and thus, by extension, its creator. "He saw himself as God-appointed," says Charles De Rose. "Arthur was narcissistic in a way. He didn't like others getting any undue recognition. He thought everything should be about Dance Theatre of Harlem. As a dancer, you were part and parcel of the package. This wasn't a star system like at American Ballet Theatre. You weren't supposed to stand out as a star like Misty Copeland. The more people who came to see Lydia, the more butts we put in the seats. But he never allowed anyone to get a big head."

In that same *Washington Post* interview, Abarca crosses her fingers for the role that would change her whole trajectory. "Hopefully one of these days I'll be getting that one ballet that will knock everyone down. And then everyone will have to say wow!"

Mitchell, too, was looking for an iconic piece. With the company's ten-year anniversary behind them, he felt that DTH was at a crossroads. "I want to make this a great company," he told the *New York Times* before the start of their new season at City Center. "Although we have lots of fans, I know we're still not a truly great company. To say that we are is like comparing a sapling to a mighty oak. Yet I think we can be a great company one day." Becoming one meant swinging for the fences with the same spirit of gusto and fearlessness with which he had started the company. "The time was right for us to do the classics," said Mitchell later, reflecting back on that moment. "We had to do them."

And so in January of 1980, Dance Theatre of Harlem gave its first two performances of nineteenth-century Russian classics: a divertissement from *Paquita,* staged by former Ballet Russe de Monte Carlo stars Alexandra Danilova and Frederic Franklin, and the drama-packed second act of *Swan Lake.* The decision was a bit of an about-face for Mitchell, who had long said he had no interest in the company ever attempting one of the Romantic-era ballets in which the female corps were costumed in white tutus, their limbs powdered white to heighten the dreamlike atmosphere. Now he'd decided audiences were ready to have their preconceptions of the *ballet blanc* aesthetic expanded. To help ease them out of tradition, DTH's *Swan Lake* would not be tied to the specific time or setting of the original German fairy tale. The program would be changed to identify the villain as "the Sorcerer," rather than Von Rothbart, and the leads as "Swan Queen" and "Prince," rather than Odette and Prince Siegfried. Finally, it was decided that white tutus on the dark skin of the sixteen swan maidens would appear glaring under the stage lights. So Mitchell and his costume designer settled on tutus in gradations of blue. The darker the woman's skin tone, the deeper her blue.

"I got tapped for the Swan Queen," recalls Abarca with a groan. "And that's when I realized, this is not what I want." Mitchell paired Abarca with Ronald Perry for the grand pas de deux, making them the first Black couple to dance in the ballet's leading roles. Says Abarca, "I remember Geoffrey Holder coming up to me saying, 'You look like an exotic bird.' I wasn't trying to be a bird. I was trying to be a swan!" Abarca felt like an imposter in a role she neither desired nor trusted that the world would let a Black woman claim as her own. "The Russians start learning this role in their bassinets," she tells the Legacy Council. "I didn't want to be held up against those dancers. Why were we doing this? It felt like, *Oh, we'll do* Swan Lake, *and then we'll be considered a real company.* Like, come on! How many years have we been trying to prove ourselves? We're Dance Theatre of Harlem. We do our own thing. This is stupid. Don't compare us to American Ballet Theatre."

On opening night, just before curtain, Abarca found herself surrounded by some of the most powerful men in ballet crowding her head with a flurry of last-minute instructions. George Balanchine, who was there for moral support, wanted her to make the dance brighter somehow and pick up the tempo. Mitchell was after her to find a place to add the Zah! moment. Franklin told her to go out onstage and melt like butter. "When the curtain went up, I didn't know what to do," she says. "I was lost. I heard the overture, and somebody had the nerve to come over and say, 'Good luck, Lydia!' I'm not Lydia! I'm trying to be the Swan."

But after their grand pas de deux in the first performance, the applause lasted for so long that it interrupted the ballet. Mitchell had so drilled into his dancers' heads never to make a move without his consent, they remained paralyzed in the wings, unsure if they should return to the stage to acknowledge the crowd. "If we hadn't practiced a bow, we didn't do one," she says. "We didn't know what to do, because they would not stop clapping."

However much the audience loved it, critics were decidedly muted in their appreciation. "Although Lydia Abarca has a beautiful body, she doesn't so much dance as enact a ritual learned second-hand," said the *Christian Science Monitor*. "Abarca looked like a beautiful Swan Queen, and caught in isolated movements, that is what she was. But neither she, nor her prince, Ronald Perry, tried to link those moments," wrote the *New York Times*.

Sheila Rohan winces as she talks about being in the audience on the night of the premiere. "From the moment I heard that Dance Theatre was doing *Swan Lake,* I thought it was ridiculous," she says. "And then I saw it, and I was embarrassed. I'm sorry, Lyd, this is nothing personal against you. The production was weak. The older ballerinas and us that came were like, *Oh well, he had to try.* But I left there feeling a little embarrassed that Arthur had felt the need in the first place." She pauses to check in with Abarca, to make sure she hasn't hurt her friend's feelings.

"I love your honesty," promises Abarca. "I have absolutely no ego around this. You do certain ballets, and you feel great about them. That one, my heart wasn't in it." Abarca danced in just two performances of *Swan Lake* before being taken down by a flu that was sweeping through the company. Her illness gave her a few quiet days away from the bustle of the theater to confront an irrefutable truth—she was finished with ballet.

On the morning she was due to return to class, Abarca remembers crying into her breakfast sandwich, pacing between the bodega across the street from her apartment on Riverside Drive and the stoplight on 157th Street. Avon Long, a famous vaudeville performer who lived in her building, stopped her on the sidewalk on his way to the subway to make sure she was okay. "I think I'm going to quit Dance Theatre today," she cried to him, the words gathering force as she let them tumble out of her mouth. Long gave her shoulders an encouraging squeeze. "Good for you!" he said. "We need to see more of you."

That afternoon she knocked on Mitchell's office door and

started crying before she'd even taken a seat. She told him that after all this time in the company, she could still barely make her rent, forget about her dreams of buying her mom a house. She was getting ready to turn thirty. She had to do something else while she was still young enough to try. "And he just started screaming at me," she says. "'You're just lazy! You've got to work harder is all, and you don't want to!' But everything he was saying was exactly why I was leaving. I'd had a chance to work with people who didn't abuse me like that for $350 a week. Every time it seemed like the door was going to crack open a little bit wider, it never happened. So why was I working, working, working to do this bird ballet that I couldn't find the jazz in anywhere?"

She left him fuming in his office. Out on the street, the air had a sudden freshness to it, the promise of possibility. "I had given Dance Theatre of Harlem everything I had," she says, "and now it felt like the rest of my life was about to begin."

Abarca had heard that Bob Fosse was looking to replace dancers in his Broadway musical revue *Dancin',* which had cleaned up at the Tony Awards when it premiered in 1978. After blowing her first chance to work with him, she wasn't going to let such an opportunity pass her by again. He'd come to represent the pinnacle of everything that that little girl who grew up on *Million Dollar Movie,* who sobbed over *West Side Story,* who'd wanted to be a star since she was in the fourth grade, and who still believed in happy endings, wanted from the world.

Abarca joined the show in an ensemble position, but not long afterward Fosse needed to find a permanent replacement for the Trumpet Solo, which he'd originally choreographed on Ann Reinking. The great smoky-voiced singer with Trans Ams for legs had made famous the two-minute dance number, a riotous, hair-whipping, high-kicking explosion set to Benny Goodman's "Sing, Sing, Sing." Abarca auditioned and won the coveted part. Fosse called her into the rehearsal studio to see how he might tailor the choreography to best suit her style. He encouraged her to tone down the sharpness of some moves, leaning instead into her slinky sex appeal. "When I was done rehearsing," says Abarca, "I overheard him say to the drummer, 'Wow, she's beautiful.'"

Abarca was dancing in the part of her dreams—and suddenly pulling in a $500 weekly paycheck. "They had a chair in the wing when I came off because I had to catch my breath. There was a part where I had to run and slide on the floor next to the trumpet player. I kept banging my knee, and the dance captain said, 'Well, we can modify it,' and I said, 'No, no, I'll be okay.'" When City Ballet's Jacques d'Amboise greeted Abarca backstage at the Ambassador Theatre after her first show, he exclaimed, "I didn't know you could do jazz!" "I told him, 'I could always do jazz. Arthur just never let me.'" After being kicked out of jazz class all those years ago for taking advantage of her ballet scholarship, she was finally in the center of the action.

* * *

Six months into her Broadway run, Abarca found herself increasingly unable to put weight on her right leg. When she could no longer dance through the pain, she went to see a doctor. Tests revealed torn cartilage around her right knee. The repetitive slamming down on the boards at the end of the Trumpet Solo had steadily chipped away at her bone. On the operating table before the anesthesia fully kicked in, she heard one of New York City's top arthroscopic surgeons mutter to his nurse, "Well, what does she want me to do with this? She's too old anyway." When a tearful Abarca returned to the Ambassador on crutches to pack up her things, the wardrobe mistress hugged her tight. "Oh, Lydia," the woman sighed. "I'm so sorry."

Her knee was busted. "She knew she was never really going to be able to dance again," says her sister Celia. "That was heartbreaking. All she knew was pointing that foot, that toe. Dancing was her whole world. We knew she was smart, but she wasn't prepared for anything else."

Abarca spent eight weeks on crutches in the first leg of her recovery. Every afternoon she'd take a cab to her cousin Iris's brownstone, where she'd watch hours of soap operas with her grandmother in the basement. During a commercial break one day, Goldie, who'd been in the audience for her granddaughter's first lecture-demonstration, at an upstate New York library, looked at her with worry in her eyes. "Oh, Lydia, how are you going to get along without the applause?"

LYDIA

I DIDN'T DANCE FOR A WHILE. MY KNEE WAS JUST STARTING *to get better after two years when Arthur called and asked me to come back for* Scheherazade. *The part was in heels, so I wouldn't be on pointe. I was stable enough to do it, and I loved the ballet. But taking a warm-up class and trying to do the développés and everything . . . I couldn't. I didn't want to. The* New York Times *did a story: "Lydia Abarca is back!" No, I wanted to tell them. I'm not.*

I got a job on the movie The Cotton Club *[directed by Francis Ford Coppola], but it took forever to make because they couldn't get the books straight. We still hadn't shot anything yet, and I was pregnant with Daniella. I'll never forget when I finally had to say to Mr. Coppola, "I'm sorry, I just cannot dance the fast numbers anymore." I remember Gregory Hines was like, "Good for you. You have that baby and take care of it." The cast threw Al and me a surprise baby shower and gave me a crib, all* the linen, even savings bonds. I got a credit for the movie, but you can't really see me because I'm hiding in the back.

My parents finally got out of the projects. They ended up getting a house in Paterson, New Jersey. But I had nothing to do with it. They had to put their pennies together. That was a huge disappointment for me.

Al and I got a little starter house five blocks from them. I opened a dance school at Daniella's Catholic school. It started out with me just doing talent shows with the kids. I'd spoken to the principal and said, "If you let me use the cafeteria, I'll only charge the kids five dollars a class and give the school a dollar for each one." At the end-of-the-year recital, there were so many people who wanted to see it we had to do it two nights in a row.

When I was forty, Geoffrey Holder called and put me in his production of House of Flowers. By that time, I had two kids, and it was nice to do something. My kids came with me to rehearsals. Walter Raines, my former partner, called me one night to say, "I wanted you to know that Arthur and I came to see the show. He didn't want me to say anything to you, but he said, 'She's still got it.'" Of course, Arthur didn't say anything to me, so it meant the world that Walter shared that.

I wasn't really dancing anymore, but I had my brain. I'd taken Latin for one year in high school. I taught myself medical transcription. Al tapped me around this time and said, "We're moving to Atlanta," because his job for IBM got transferred. My New York life was over. I got a job as a medical transcription-ist at a doctor's office down here. It was fine. I can always find something to enjoy where I am. People ask me, "What'd you do before this?" And I'd kind of mumble, "I was a ballerina." "Yeah, well, can you type?" I thought office work was the easiest thing in the world after dancing. Everyone would complain, "Oh, I can't wait for five o'clock!" Please, you don't know what hard work is.

I started coaching for Ballethnic Dance Company here in Atlanta in 1993, which was started by two former Dance Theatre of Harlem dancers, Nena Gilreath and Waverly Lucas. Since then I've helped run the rehearsals for their productions of Urban Nutcracker and The Leopard Tale. Coaching for them has made me feel like I've kept a toe in ballet. It taught me a whole new skill of how to try to get results like Arthur did, but without being mean. He was always that third eye for us. Now I'm trying to see the dancers from the eye of the audience that paid money for tickets. This past year I caught myself in rehearsal sounding like Louis Johnson on The Wiz: "Bring your brains, people. Bring your brains!"

When I first started reading about Misty Copeland, I was like, "Wait a minute. . . ." I did the ballets. I did Broadway. I did movies. I did everything except stand on my head. And it all just went away? I guess it was my mistake and vanity to think history would remember the first prima ballerina and all the other beautiful ballerinas and fabulous male dancers of Dance Theatre of Harlem. It doesn't feel as good when you have to toot your own horn. Humility was just so drilled into us. Even our bows were very much like, Oh, me? Thank you. I just think it's

sort of sad that because we were so quiet and so humble that
nobody knows about us or can appreciate what we did and how
hard it all was.

"We all felt that Lydia could've been Misty Copeland," says her
sister Celia. "And, you know, Misty was doing *On the Town*
on Broadway back in 2015. My cousin bought me a ticket. I
really didn't want to go, because of that jealousy that I had.
That could've been Lydia up there. But then again, it's a whole
different time. Fifty years have gone by!"

Abarca struggled with an emptiness she'd felt since she'd
had to stop dancing. The joys of her family helped fill it. So did
working with the dancers at Ballethnic. Even though her office
job was tedious, she took pride in a job well done. But as her
kids got older, and she crept up in years, she found herself self-
medicating more and more with alcohol. She'd put in her eight
hours typing away at the office, then come home and watch
TV alone upstairs with glasses of rum and Coke for company.
Al, who'd lost his father to the bottle, didn't know how to reach
her.

Everything came to a head when Abarca discovered that a
younger woman she'd been tasked with training at the office
had been hired to replace her. It felt as if the world was getting
ready to dispose of her again, to replace her with someone
younger who could do the work because she showed her how
first. Forget she had ever been there, while she floundered

without a plan B. All that anger and helplessness she'd been stuffing down for so long came roaring to the surface. She screamed at her manager and left the office in a blind rage.

Earlier in the day, in a terrible confluence of events, Al had been admitted to the hospital with heart palpitations. She took their son, Eric, to visit him in the emergency room, where they were told he needed to spend the night for observation. She went home bereft. She took a full bottle of Bacardí out of the closet and locked herself in the guest room. *I was drinking and feeling so bad for myself, you know? This girl stole my job. What am I going to do? Al's in the hospital. I just started talking crazy.* She drank and she drank. She smashed a lamp across the wall, shattering the base. A terrified Eric, knowing that his mother had pills in the room with her as well as alcohol, pounded on the door, begging her to come out and talk to him. She just kept screaming and sobbing that she wanted to die. Eric called his aunt Celia, who told him to call 911 immediately.

At the hospital, Daniella spent the night going back and forth between floors to visit both of her parents. It took Abarca several hours to sober up. When Eric first came to visit her, she'd looked at him meanly from her bed. "What are you doing here?" she teased. She says now that she meant it as a joke, though to him it came out like an accusation. Unwilling to be cast as the bad guy after the ordeal she'd put him through, Eric turned around and left the room without a word. Later that night she called him and sobbed that she was sorry, that she loved him, and then she thanked him for saving her life.

Around four in the morning, she was transferred in her night-gown and flip-flops from suicide watch to a nearby rehab facil-ity, where she stayed for eight days. She started going to AA meetings. She hasn't had a drink since, hasn't even wanted one.

In 2017, after Daniella blasted me for keeping all my his-tory packed away, we took a road trip as a family up to New York. We went to Dance Theatre of Harlem. There's no more pictures of me anywhere, but I got to see my four-year-old granddaughter running around Studio 3. Afterward we went to the library at Lincoln Center, and I showed my kids an old black-and-white recording of my pas de deux in Combat. *They lasted about two minutes because you could barely see me. It's just little figures on a stage.*

Then Al said, "Call Arthur." Arthur answered the phone, and I said, "Mr. Mitchell, hi, it's Lydia. Can we come by?"

I'd only seen Arthur here and there. We never talked on the phone. Never went for a meal or anything. But now we're in his apartment. He'd just gotten out of the hospital. I think he was on dialysis. Both hips had been replaced. One of the first things he said was "Who's that?" about my granddaughter. And he said to her, "Come here, let me see your foot! Stand up straight!" I heard how terse he was: "No, the foot! Turn this way!" Then he told my family all these nice things about me, and that I had been his star student. "All the ballerinas still ask, 'Where is Lydia?'"

I don't know why I'm crying. It's funny, because I think of myself as the kind of person who when I leave a situation, I just wipe the dust off my hands and move on. But I guess all those feelings were still trapped inside me. I was just so glad we got to meet with him. That was closure. For my family to meet him, and to hear him talk like that, was so special. I guess there really was a love for each other there.

I've been blessed in my life, I know that. Broke, but blessed. You have to understand, I had such big dreams for myself. So much emotion came up for me when Misty Copeland started getting all the stuff I wish I had gotten. I wish her the best. It's her time. But damn, I wish I'd had a publicist back then. Somebody who could argue with Arthur and tell him, "She's going to Hollywood to do this quick movie. She'll be right back."

I work as an extra on movies sometimes, which is so tedious. Long hours, and you're not ever sure if you're going to get any face time in the finished product. But I've never given up. I've never given up. That's why I've stayed a size eight all these years. Recently I got an agent and started taking some acting classes. Who knows? Maybe one day somebody will say, "Oh! Lydia. Let's have her come in."

15

C OME 1981, THE FORD FOUNDATION PULLED ITS SUPPORT
for Dance Theatre of Harlem. Arthur Mitchell was growing more ornery and more arbitrary with age. He frequented
psychics and told Charles De Rose they'd warned him that
people would try to take the company away from him. "He had
such an insecurity about losing control," says De Rose. "So when
people tried to help him take it to next level, he couldn't let go.
When there were ways to make Dance Theatre's administration
more sophisticated, with computers and technology, Arthur
wouldn't let anybody do anything he couldn't understand."

He fought and he fought and he fought to stay alive. Even
as the debt accumulated, Dance Theatre of Harlem was per-
forming at the Kennedy Center in front of President Ronald
Reagan and First Lady Nancy Reagan, and Vice President
George H. W. Bush and Mrs. Bush, in the presidential box.
And a few weeks later, in February 1981, Karlya Shelton was

one of a handful of dancers chosen to perform at the White House during the Reagans' first state dinner welcoming British prime minister Margaret Thatcher.

That summer Dance Theatre of Harlem returned to London, where it became the first Black dance company to perform at the Royal Opera House. The thirty-eight dancers performed fifteen ballets over their two-week engagement.

But just a few months later, the *New York Times* ran a story under the headline "Dance Theatre of Harlem Cuts Back." Classes for as many as one thousand students a year had been dropped, along with the sewing and tailoring classes, the percussion ensemble, and the choral ensemble. A company statement declared that over the year, "The Dance Theatre of Harlem experienced a thirty percent drop in private support and a twenty percent increase in expenses." It needed to raise $200,000 by the end of the year "to maintain its current level of operations."

Everywhere they traveled—Australia, Japan, Italy—they broke box office records. But the stress of money always kept Mitchell dangerously on edge. Shelton, never one to back down from a fight back then, had a limit to how much she was willing to ignore. "All the dancers would tell me, 'Don't take it personally,'" she says. "But to me it was personal. I would always try not to cry in front of him, because sometimes it felt like tears gave him power. 'See, I can break her down.'"

Mitchell believed deeply in astrology and was known to

ask dancers to reveal their sign upon first meeting. He was an Aries, like Shelton, who would get a tattoo of the zodiac constellation on her right arm when she turned sixty. "We were similar personalities in a way," she says. "When something happens that makes an Aries mad, you snap and slash. If I was like a bonfire on the beach, he was that blazing fire that ate up all the trees."

Shelton remembers taking a day off in Israel, where the company had performed at the Tel Aviv Opera House. "I wasn't dancing that day, so one of the ladies cornrowed my hair into a low bun in the back," she says. "Arthur Mitchell came up to me and said, 'Why do you have your hair like that?' And I said, 'Well, it's my day off and it's hot.' And he said, 'Well, you'll find out when you get your pink slip.'" Shelton refused to budge. "I said, 'Give me a pink slip, because I'm wearing my hair the way I want to on my day off.'

"After he made that scene, I went back to the dressing room, and I was so mad that I actually hit a dressing room mirror and broke it," she says. The other women on the Legacy Council gasp at her revelation. "It's a good thing you didn't get fined for that," says Marcia Sells. Shelton shakes her head as if to clear Mitchell's voice reverberating inside. "I was so angry that my face was paralyzed."

A great dancer rises to the level of expectation set for her and the quality of the roles she's given. On a transcontinental tour that would include a stop in Denver, Shelton pleaded with Mitchell to let her dance a principal role in Balanchine's *The Four Temperaments* in front of her hometown crowd. He let her go on as Choleric, a role that suited her fiery temperament. "The movements are sharp during the solo, and there are lots of turns. Her movements are slightly sensual." She and her partner, Eddie Shellman, had come up as apprentices together and had practiced a series of lifts on their own when the ballet was first being set. "We had worked it out so that he would throw me and let go of me, and I'd freeze in the air," she says. "Then I'd descend, and on the way down, he'd catch me, and we'd go on to the next and do it again. We never tried it again until that Denver performance. At the top of the lift, Eddie took his hands away so that it looked like I was suspended in air, and I could hear the audience gasping. It was a perfect performance. Afterward Arthur Mitchell said, 'Very good. I didn't know you could do that.' And I remember saying, 'Just let me out there. I can do a lot more than that!' "

But Shelton felt forever resigned, in Mitchell's eyes, to the second cast, the short cast. "I wanted to do *Allegro Brillante*. I would've loved to do the second pas de trois in *Agon*. But I don't think he ever saw me as a 'leotard and tights' dancer. I never felt he was comfortable with my body shape. I'm five foot three. Even though it wasn't big, I had a shapely butt." She was envious of dancers who could eat anything they wanted without gaining weight. "I told myself I would get really thin and maybe he'd let me do *Firebird*." But he remained a withholding force, never giving her the opportunities she craved.

After *Swan Lake,* Mitchell reversed course once more and ushered in a new era of American story ballets at DTH. Its revival of Valerie Bettis's *A Streetcar Named Desire* premiered during its season at City Center in 1982. The repertory shift scraped at Lydia Abarca's heart when she heard the news, as Mitchell publicly explained that story ballets "would serve as major vehicles for our dancers. . . . It is time to establish our dancers as individual artists, and we've provided them with roles of star caliber." He declared that Dance Theatre of Harlem had long since proved that Black dancers can do classical ballet, so it was time to shift the narrative from social to artistic resonance.

The following year the company premiered *Fall River Legend*, Agnes de Mille's devastating take on Lizzie Borden and the 1892 Massachusetts murder. "Ms. de Mille was a hoot!" says Shelton. "One time in rehearsal she got coffee on her glasses. When she realized, she said, 'Oh my God! No wonder you all look darker.'"

By then the company had a new teacher and coach, William Griffith, or "Mr. Bill" as he was known, a trained concert pianist turned ballet dancer who'd taught company classes at American Ballet Theatre and the Joffrey Ballet. He came to Dance Theatre of Harlem in the early 1980s as Karel Shook's health deteriorated. Mr. Bill had the body of a football player, all broad shoulders and narrow hips, and a commanding, deep voice. "He could say two words to you, and you knew what he meant," says Shelton. "He would say 'something here' and point to a part of your body. And you would just know. Or there'd be something in the music, and he'd tell you, 'Change

the accent.' He could unlock the mystery. I felt like he saw me."
It was ultimately he, not Mitchell, who would help push her dancing to the next level.

Raw from breaking up with her boyfriend, who was also her frequent dance partner, Shelton had a private rehearsal for her variation in Balanchine's *Pas de Dix* with Mr. Bill. At the end, he shared some advice she's never forgotten. "You need to develop a sense of loneliness," he said in his dry tone of voice. "You have to learn to be alone and pull from that to develop your artistry." At first, she was insulted. Mr. Bill was well versed in the company drama and knew about Shelton's heartbreak. She let his words marinade before coming back to him a few days later, eager for his approval. She pretended that she'd understood what he'd been trying to tell her. "No, you don't," said Mr. Bill with a patient smile. "If you knew what I meant, you wouldn't have to come and tell me."

But with time, Mr. Bill's message took on a new meaning. She realized how much she'd loved dancing with her ex-boyfriend, working on their variations together. He was one of her favorite partners. He had made her feel special, chosen. She realized she'd given over her power to him as a partner, onstage and off. "It felt like Mr. Bill was telling me, *You have to find you. And you have to develop you. Without this one or that one. It's just you,*" she says. "I became more gathered after that and started to find my footing again. All the noise that was out there, I didn't have to hear it. Mr. Bill handed me this big nugget of gold that became a part of who I grew into as an artist. I took that mental shift with me everywhere—in class, in rehearsal, outside rehearsal. I could've just stayed floundering, but he reminded me I needed to find me. That's when I truly became a ballerina, I think. She was always in there. I just found her and let her go. My dancing did change after that. And then one afternoon in class, Mr. Bill just looked at me and nodded. He recognized it too."

She started getting more principal roles in the new ballets. "Though every larger role I ever got was because of someone who saw me in class other than Arthur Mitchell," she says. She calls out choreographers Choo San Goh (*Introducing . . .*), Terry Orr (*Graduation Ball*), John Butler (*Othello*), and Domy Reiter-Soffer (*Equus*), all of whom successfully lobbied Mitchell to cast her in their ballets' principal roles.

Shelton danced brilliantly in the New York premiere of *Equus,* in what she calls one of those flawless performances a ballerina doesn't take for granted. Afterward she was celebrating with her partner outside the theater, the two of them basking in the knowledge of a job well done. Later she was told that after their final bows, Mitchell had searched for her in the dressing room. "He was looking for you," a dancer told her. "He had tears in his eyes he was so moved."

In the May 1983 issue of *Dance Magazine,* she got one of the best reviews of her career. "Karlya Shelton is the most sweetly, lightly authoritative junior Mistress of Ceremonies one could imagine," praising her work in the *Graduation Ball* ballet. "Her variation, with its jumps, pirouettes, and extended hopping on pointe is so beautifully, unaffectedly phrased that it registers not as the usual display number but as part of this girl's special, mischievous nature." And later, singling out her "piquant" performance in a *Pas de Dix* solo, *Dance* described her as an "extraordinary performer." The dancer who lived within was now getting the chance to exalt onstage.

That fall there was another fallow patch on the company calendar. The dancers were again placed on hiatus, which meant a return to Club 90. During the monthlong break, Karlya Shelton fell in love with a handsome man who worked in finance and wined and dined her at the finest restaurants in town. By the time Mitchell called the company back into the studio, she'd put on ten pounds of courting weight. Mitchell was disgusted. He banned her from traveling with the company for dates in Arizona and benched her until he deemed her body acceptable to go in front of an audience.

By the time the company returned to New York, Frederic Franklin had begun casting a production of the full-length version of the classic Romantic-era ballet *Giselle.* The story of love and betrayal was originally set in Germany, but Mitchell ingeniously reimagined it in the bayous of Louisiana, set among a community of free Black people. Virginia Johnson, as gifted a dramatic actress as she was a ballerina, was cast as the titular peasant girl who's driven mad by betrayal and then haunts the man who broke her heart from beyond the grave.

Shelton returned to the studio on the day Franklin was casting dancers as the friends of the peasant girl. Her mother, Jean, happened to be visiting New York at the time and was sitting quietly in Studio 3's observation gallery. As Franklin eyed the line of dancers, he called Shelton's name, beckoning her from where she stood at the barre to the center. "And that's when Arthur Mitchell went off," she says. "He started yelling in front of the whole room, in front of my mother, 'Oh no, I don't even know where you've been! You haven't come up here once for class. You're not doing this ballet!'" She stood there stunned, as all the air went out of the room. Franklin looked down at the floor, aghast at the scene playing out before him. The other dancers grimaced and bowed their heads. Jean rose from her chair, unwilling to sit and watch her daughter being berated.

Mitchell stormed out of the studio, and Karlya snapped out of her paralysis. She followed him, but he shut his office door in her face. "I remember sitting outside in the hall hearing his voice get louder and louder," says Jean. "I'm just throbbing mad, but she told me to let her handle it."

After years of sucking back her words, Karlya entered his office and let it all pour out. "There weren't many opportunities at Dance Theatre of Harlem to say what you wanted to say. I was finally going to take my opportunity." She stood over his desk, forcing him to pay her mind. "How dare you do that to me!" she cried. "You put me on hiatus! You never told me I had to report here for class!" The more she spoke up for herself, the angrier it made him.

"I want you bone thin!" he finally yelled. "Don't come back until you're bone thin!"

Karlya looked coolly at Mitchell's midsection, which by

that time was no longer the washboard of his youth, thanks to his ice cream habit. "It's not that easy to be bone thin," she reminded him. "You should know that, right?" Desperately trying not to cry in front of him, she turned to leave the room. "I will not be back," she said, her hand on the doorknob, "because I won't be treated this way ever again."

"Kar comes out of the office," says Jean, "and she's crying. I said, 'I can go talk to him. When I get through with him—'"

But Karlya shook her head no. "This is my fight," she said. "I'm done."

Jean followed her daughter downstairs to the locker room, where Karlya packed up all her things, gifts from the dancers, the company photographs taped to the front of her locker. She stopped at Zelda Wynn's costuming room, telling the older woman, who had kept her looking so beautiful, that she was leaving and never coming back. Ms. Wynn enveloped her in a hug, promising the weeping girl that she would be okay.

Outside on the corner, Jean held her daughter's hand and suggested the two go for a drink. "She knew this was my whole world," says Karlya. "And Arthur Mitchell had just crashed it with a hammer."

The only relief was in the clarity of her decision. She vowed that from that day on she would never again call him Mr. Mitchell.

KARLYA

I'D BEEN DANCING SINCE I WAS FOUR YEARS OLD. AND I *didn't get all the dancing out of me at the company of my dreams. I was lost. But when you live in New York City, you've got to do something quick. I auditioned for Alvin Ailey. Mr. Ailey was there and said he liked me, but I had very, very little modern training. I joined a contemporary company that was just starting up. Mel Tomlinson and Charles De Rose came to see me dance there. Afterward Charles said, "You shouldn't be here. You're much too good for this company." Well, what am I supposed to do, then? Where am I supposed to go?*

I had a job as a coat-check girl at the Fifth Avenue Grill. That gave me a little pocket money, but it wasn't sustainable. Two French girls danced at the company with me, and we would look through the New York Times *for bilingual jobs at beautiful places like fashion houses and perfumeries. There's a flow to the French language that takes you right into the world of glamour and beauty and fashion. Ballet is in French! I de-cided to go to the Berlitz School in New York. Then my aunt, who is fluent in French, convinced me to go to Paris instead to immerse myself in the language and the culture. I took my savings of a couple thousand dollars, packed up all my belong-ings, and moved there without knowing anybody. I was still so heartbroken, I knew I had to leave New York. If I could've gone to the moon, I would've.*

I was just trying to start anew. Leave it all behind. There was a point where I wouldn't even let people know I was a dancer. It was painful to talk about, and I told myself that that life was over. Now I was a student at the Alliance Française, liv-ing in the Latin Quarter. I'd been in Paris about a month when I met these cabaret entertainers. Every night I would go to this jazz club, the Hollywood Savoy, to see them perform, and that's where I met the fashion photographer Richard Allen, who was the first Black friend I made in Paris. He asked me, "Do you need a job?" There was a part-time opening at this company owned by Saudi Arabian sheikhs. The job was administration. One day the COO, Omar, suggested that the staff all go shop-ping. I thought it was going to be a group outing with everyone in the office, but when I got to the place where we were supposed to meet, it was just Omar. He had called everyone else and can-celed. He and I went all over Paris. We rode the Ferris wheel at the Tuileries. He walked me back to my apartment, and there was a protest on Boulevard St. Jacques, with a fire burning in the middle of the street. You couldn't ask for more on a first date. I quit the job once we became an item.

Marcia came to Paris for a visit when she was at Columbia Law School. Omar took us out to dinner at L'Arpège. There was a wistfulness for me in seeing her because I could tell she had really found her niche with law. I was still missing the DTH family that we had.

Learning French opened a whole other world to me. I stayed in Paris for three years, then came home to New York fluent. The story of the Central Park jogger had just hit the news, and Donald Trump was calling for the boys' deaths. First I got a temp job at Balenciaga, but the thought of being around jewels was much more inviting. I joined Van Cleef & Arpels, working upstairs in their office. One night Dance Theatre of Harlem performed at City Center, which was right around the corner from the store. How did it feel to see them dance? It was different than the old days. It hurt.

Omar was living in Los Angeles then, and we were going back and forth. One Saturday Philippe Arpels called me over and said, "I am tired of seeing your long face. I have a position that's open in the Beverly Hills store. Are you interested?" Marcia rented the truck and helped me move out of my apartment in Brooklyn.

I moved into a higher role in the Van Cleef Beverly Hills office. I was the only Black person there besides the security guards. I was the executive assistant to the vice president who ran the store. Nancy Reagan used to visit him. One day she was waiting with her Secret Service, and I told her, "I danced at the White House for you when you were the First Lady." I remember one afternoon taking jewelry to Arnold Schwarzenegger's house, and on the way over I was so nervous that I repeated the Dougla *prayer in my car.*

There's a closeness of people in New York, but everything in LA was so spread out. It was harder to make friends. Everyone's first question is, "What do you do? How can you help me?" I didn't have very many friends. I missed my Dance Theatre of Harlem family. I felt lost.

When Lydia Abarca opened up to the Legacy Council about her struggles with alcoholism, Shelton had a visceral reaction. She cried silently through Abarca's initial confession, and then called her friend afterward to tell her how grateful she was to her for once more leading the way.

During the next Legacy Council meeting, Shelton took a shaky breath and released herself from her own secret shame. "It got ugly there for a minute," she began.

She'd always liked to drink socially. Champagne after performances, wine in Paris. In Los Angeles, she'd turned to vodka. She started a Friday tradition of having one-hundred-proof martinis at the Grill in Beverly Hills, around the corner from the Van Cleef & Arpels store. Her habit escalated to the point that she'd need a drink first thing in the morning so she could function. Eventually she went to rehab. She tried going to AA meetings, but sharing her lowest moments there only left her feeling more isolated. She waited a year to get pregnant with her son. The family moved to Oakland. It was a good life, and a full one.

Then, in 2019, her beloved father, Lloyd Shelton, died. *To this day, I'll just be in the car and memories of him will cause me to burst into tears.* She and her husband, Omar, moved to Denver to be closer to her mother, staying with Jean in the family home until they found a place of their own. *Being in the house was so strange without my dad there. There were so many memories and smells.* Her parents had a fully stocked bar in the basement, and she started sneaking glasses of vodka. One January afternoon Omar came downstairs and saw her tipping the whole bottle into her mouth. She ended up having to go to the hospital, she was so dehydrated. When the Legacy Council gathered for the very first time just five months later, she never thought she'd tell any of the women that she was an alcoholic, or that the pain of losing her father had caused her to relapse. *It takes time to let go of the shame. Society has always told you to be ashamed of addiction. That it's a weakness. I had shame from when my son saw me at my worst. When I apologized, he told me, "You should have no shame. It's a part of what made you who you are—strong."*

"My mother has always trusted me to figure out my own life," says her twenty-five-year-old musican son, Chè Benjamin. "When my mom was growing up, my grandma saw her discipline and her determination for excellence. I like to think my mom sees that in me too. She knows that the path of an artist is never linear and straightforward, but she trusts and believes in the process. There might be heartbreak, but you have to let people do what they feel called to do."

I'm an artist. That's who I am. Music. Jewelry. Photography.

But I was always missing dance. A few years ago I snapped at my husband about something, and he said to me, "Hey, I'm not Arthur Mitchell. You're driving yourself crazy, and you're going to drive me crazy. Please do something, or you're just going to stay unhappy."

So in 2011, Shelton sent Mitchell a one-page typed letter in which she expressed a desire to "let go of baggage." *Sitting down to write it was hard. But what did I have to lose? I had to get right with me and let him go. I just couldn't carry him around anymore. I wrote him a letter and said that I'd been angry at him for a long time, but that I could never know how hard it was to be him. Starting a Black ballet company at the end of the civil rights era. I didn't know what he went through, but I thanked him for creating the company and giving us a place to dance. "I want you to know that I honor you for the person that you are and thank you for your role in shaping me into the artist and the woman that I am."*

He called me and said, "I really liked your letter." And he started to tell me about how hard it had been to be both the artistic and the executive director. He talked about going down-town to try to raise money from donors, and they'd all say yes, yes, yes, but then they'd have changed their minds by the time he got back uptown. He said, "A lot of times I would come into the studio, and I would just see an arabesque. I wouldn't even see a person. I would just start yelling at a body." We talked for about an hour and a half. Well, he did most of the talking. You don't really talk that much with Arthur Mitchell. I did tell him I'd been angry at him for all these years. I don't think he ever said, "I'm sorry." But it allowed me to let my anger go and be at peace. It was like shedding a heavy coat. Finally I've set this baggage down.

She'd gained the knowledge that artistry comes from within. It has nothing to do with ego or audience or approval. It is a person's most authentic expression of self, and thus it can never be taken away.

Act Three

16

IN 2004, DANCE THEATRE OF HARLEM DISBANDED ITS forty-four-member company for what was originally supposed to be the remainder of its season. The company went on hiatus in order to pay down a $2.3 million deficit, incurred because the fundraising couldn't keep pace with Arthur Mitchell's grandiose artistic vision. But what was supposed to be a temporary hiatus stretched on for a devastating eight years. Most of the dancers failed to get jobs in other companies, or when they did, they were brought in at positions beneath their experience and talent level. Virginia Johnson returned to the company in 2010 following Mitchell's personal request that she take over his role as artistic director. "It was a bitter pill for him," says Charles De Rose. "Very difficult. He was eating pounds of ice cream, which eventually killed him."

During the void left by Dance Theatre of Harlem's absence in the landscape, the legend of Misty Copeland was born, and the culture at large embraced her as the first Black ballerina. Her anointing was pushed by American Ballet Theatre, whose ticket sales soared. "Misty is an extraordinarily beautiful dancer and deserves everything that she's gotten," says Johnson. "But she also had a machine behind her that very carefully strategized that moment and that position. I felt like Misty went out of her way to bring up DTH when she could. But the thing that hurts me more when I hear that statement about her being the first is that in 2004 the DTH touring company closed. And for all those years, we stopped being a presence in the dance world and in the world at large. The human mind is very fickle. Not having the constant reminder that we are in this art form, and we have made magic here, we were forgotten. Yes, it did get forgotten. That's where the tragedy is."

Under Johnson's direction, Dance Theatre of Harlem began auditioning dancers for a revived troupe in 2011, then embarked on a string of performances with its new training ensemble the following year. In 2013 a lean company of eighteen members performed at the Rose Theater at Lincoln Center.

In the spring of 2016, Johnson extended an invitation to all the women who'd graced the company throughout history, as well other Black women who'd made their mark on ballet, to join in a celebration of "Black Ballerina Magic." All that talent who'd worked so hard to make ballet more beautiful and expansive so that a woman like Misty Copeland could rise. Together they would gather onstage, during the intermission of DTH's final season performance at New York's City Center, for the first time in history.

We were there. We were there. We were there.

The Black Ballerina Magic event was a rare opportunity to gather en masse and remind an audience of living history. Gayle McKinney-Griffith originally wasn't planning on attending. She felt weak, tired, and overwhelmed. Though it wouldn't be diagnosed for a couple of months, the cancer was already growing. "I wasn't doing well at all," she says of the time. "I was taking care of my mother, which was nonstop twenty-four seven. That was a stress. But then I went anyway because I wanted to see Karlya, and Lydia, and Marcia, and Sheila."

The ballerinas gathered backstage before intermission. Debra Austin was there. Joan Myers Brown. Lauren Anderson. Delores Browne. Carmen de Lavallade, who was also there on behalf of her cousin, the ballerina Janet Collins, who broke the color line with the Metropolitan Opera in 1951 and died in 2003. Rohan introduced herself to Raven Wilkinson, who would die just two years later at the age of eighty-three. "I only knew about Raven from reading about her in books," says Sheila Rohan. "We embraced. I felt like I was meeting one of my idols."

Johnson and DTH's rehearsal director Kellye A. Saunders began calling the dancers to the stage, in rows from youngest to oldest. All that power and legacy, the breathtaking visual of community. "Then one by one they read each person's name, and we each had an opportunity to take a bow," says Sells. "Row by row, we would go off into the wings. The next generation would then come out to the middle and bow. By the end it was Raven Wilkinson and Delores Browne."

The following day the women who are indeed Black Ballerina Magic reunited in Studio 3 for brunch. The fire escape was gone. The large industrial fans that used to whir in the corners had been replaced by central air. Rohan couldn't attend, but Karlya Shelton sat next to Lydia Abarca. McKinney-Griffith sat at a table next to Marcia Sells. "Debbie Austin brought us all to tears," says Marcia Sells. "She spoke about her time at the School of American Ballet and then in City Ballet."

"I don't personally know why anybody would want to stay somewhere that's not going to boost you up," says Abarca. "This is a short career. And you're just hanging in there, wasting your professional years, hoping someone takes you seriously."

Lauren Anderson, the first Black principal ballerina with Houston Ballet and the first Black woman to perform the lead in a full production of *Swan Lake,* also gave a stirring speech. "She spoke about seeing Dance Theatre of Harlem perform when she was a girl," says Shelton. "How much we impacted her."

The final speaker of the afternoon was Dr. Joselli Audain Deans, a dance scholar and educator who'd prepared a speech celebrating all that Dance Theatre of Harlem had done for the art form. "I grew up at DTH hearing about how it was the first permanent Black ballet company," she says. "I never questioned what that meant. I didn't realize there were other Black ballet companies that existed before DTH until I went and did the research."

Deans had started taking classes at the DTH school when

she was ten years old. She'd sit on the little step at the entrance of Studio 3, taking in the beauty of the older dancers. Her parents took her to all the company's performances. She'd been in the audience when McKinney-Griffith did the iconic sit lift in *Forces of Rhythm*. When Rohan commanded the stage as the Bride in *Dougla*. When Abarca premiered ballets like *Carmen, Combat,* and *Afternoon of a Faun.* Deans watched Shelton's debut showing in the corps in *Bugaku.* And when Shelton had the opportunity to go on in a principal role in Dublin in *Serenade,* it was Deans who stepped into her position in the corps.

"I grew up watching these women and witnessing not just their incredible talent," says Deans, "but their devotion to each other. Their camaraderie. The way they took care of the younger dancers." When Deans was little, Abarca taught some of her classes. "She was so intimidating to me," she says. "Like as much as Arthur Mitchell, that's how much I admired her. But oh my God, she was a wonderful teacher. Patient, gentle, and of course, gorgeous to look at. Everybody wanted to dance like Lydia." Then when Deans joined the company as an apprentice, it was Shelton who would take her under her wing. The Brooklyn girl didn't have a clue when it came to stage makeup. "Karlya took me aside one day and said, 'Okay, let me show you how to do this,'" says Deans. Which is exactly what McKinney-Griffith had done for Shelton when she first joined the company.

Deans stood up to speak at brunch that day back in Studio 3, and Christina Johnson, who during her thirteen years at DTH danced in the principal roles in everything from *Swan Lake* to *Giselle,* called out to her friend proudly: "Dr. Deans!"

"And I sort of did what I always do," says Deans. "I said, nah, nah, nah, you know, downplaying my title. And then something overtook me. I'm a very spiritual person, so I say it was probably the Holy Spirit. My speech went in another direction. I said, 'You know, I was just about to say, let's not talk about me being a doctor. But we Black women have to stop doing that. We have to stop downplaying all that we have done.' I told them that I knew the stories of most everyone in the room. Women in general in ballet suffer because it's a man's world. The danseurs are coddled. But Black women? And then dark Black women? And I just went on from there."

"I remember her telling us we need to be proud of all we had done and to start speaking up about it," says Abarca. "But we were always taught to be humble. I'm guilty of always downplaying what I've done." The other women nod. "I think we all were," says Shelton.

Back in Denver, Shelton sent Deans a letter thanking her for her urgent plea. "I wrote to her that I had known Joselli for a long time. But this was the first time I saw Dr. Deans." Deans saved Shelton's letter, even bringing it with her when she left the East Coast for a faculty job in the dance department at the University of Utah, where she's continuing her research. "I look at Karlya's card for inspiration when I'm feeling tired," she says. "Delving back into history as a Black person is draining."

Before she started taking classes at Dance Theatre of Harlem, Deans used to go to the library to search through dance books for anybody who looked like her. Then when she began at the school, she used to do class projects centered on the feats of the company. She still has a report she wrote in markers about Arthur Mitchell. She has a seventh-grade art project about the importance of seeing oneself, in which she cut out the back of a child looking in the mirror. In the reflection of the glass, she pasted a picture of Gayle McKinney-Griffith and Derek Williams from the pas de trois in *Forces of Rhythm*. "What do you want to be when you grow up?" a young Deans wrote at the top of the page in cursive script. "A dancer."

The vanished legacy of Dance Theatre of Harlem astounds. "The little girl in me is really, really angry at a world that wants to deny and destroy my incredible experiences growing up admiring all these women," says Deans. "The dancer in me who danced with all these incredible people says, *How dare you forget what we did?* I danced in twenty some odd countries, okay? Then there's me the historian. And that's the one that is truly outraged."

It's not just Black women who get forgotten in ballet, though, as in most matters of justice and parity, they fare the worst. "It's the nature sadly of this art form, too," says Sells. "Singers and musicians get to perform farther in their lives. The Met just celebrated a woman who's been sixty years in the orchestra. There's no ballerina who is sixty years old anywhere, unless she's teaching or working in a school. It ends so quickly. If you make it to your forties, you have another half of your life to live. We don't do enough to remember our history. I used to have this conversation with Arthur Mitchell over and over. He spent so much time trying to rev up and keep viable Dance Theatre of Harlem that he could forget about preserving its legacy."

Looking around Studio 3 that morning at all the women who had done so much for ballet, Shelton remembers feeling the stirring of power. *We just can't let this die,* she told herself in the most important room of her life. *There's too many of us. Everybody deserves their flowers.*

17

I N 2018, ARTHUR MITCHELL DIED FROM COMPLICATIONS OF heart failure in a New York hospital. A few weeks before his passing, Tania León visited him in his apartment. He'd agreed to speak with Alejandro J. Madrid, the author of her 2022 biography *Tania León's Stride: A Polyrhythmic Life,* on the condition that she be present for the conversation. In his apartment, he told Madrid about his great affection for his Taniacita. She couldn't believe her ears. "Arthur was always very reserved," says León. "He would let you know that he loved you because of his gestures. Flying Lydia's brother, Julio, over to Italy. Giving Sheila a raise because she had children. My grandmother died four years after my arrival in this country, and when Arthur found out, he left his office and sat with me for an entire day. He wouldn't tell you that he loved you. He would show it. We were his family. We were his artistic family and the ones who realized his dream. He drove everybody crazy. I'm telling you! I don't know when he slept! He had the energy of someone who was always in a hurry."

Mitchell later called León to let her know he was on his way to the hospital. "And of course, he likes to boss me around, to boss everyone around, so he told me, 'But don't come visit me!'" she says. "He liked to think that he was very strong, and he didn't need anybody. A few days after, I get this call that he's dead."

A pall fell over the dance world at the loss of such a giant. Sheila Rohan called Gayle McKinney-Griffith with the news. "I was speechless, it hit me so hard," says McKinney-Griffith. "It was like losing a parent. You just felt so lost."

Karlya Shelton was driving when she first heard the news. She had to pull over her car to catch her breath on the shoulder of the road.

Lydia Abarca happened to be on hold with Dance Theatre of Harlem, trying to get information about discounted tickets for the Fiftieth Anniversary Gala, when a cousin texted her: *Arthur Mitchell is dead.* Right then DTH's director of individual giving, Sharon Duncan, came on the line. "And she said, 'I want to be the first person to tell you that Mr. Mitchell has passed,' I remember saying to her, 'This can't be. He doesn't have our permission to go.'"

Marcia Sells was in her office at Harvard Law School when the news alert came up on her cell phone. She Googled for details. She called Dance Theatre of Harlem. Friends reached out to her, saying they wanted to tell her the news themselves. "And then I just wept in my office," she says. "I couldn't work.

I had to leave. Like Gayle said, it was like a parent going. My father died in 2005. My mom died in 1992. At this point, Arthur was one of the few people of that generation who'd seen me as a little ballet student trying to be a dancer. Now this person who knew I had been a ballerina and that I'd had skill and talent was gone."

Says Sells, "Nobody knew how ill he was. The hip surgery and his kidneys and dialysis."

Until the very end, he remained a force as complicated as he was pure, as maddening as he was noble. As a young man, he'd forced the world to bend to meet him, and he never stopped.

What icons like Arthur Mitchell must have encountered on their willful rise to the top, the women muse. "I was talking with some of my older friends who came up through the theater," says Rohan. "We were talking about how people must have spoken to this group of men—Arthur, Alvin Ailey, Louis Johnson, and them. They must have been treated really badly coming up as they found a way to stay onstage and have a career. So maybe it was unconscious that they all did the same thing to us, you see. Arthur made history. And he probably took whatever they gave him."

"He birthed all of us," says Abarca. "From the ground up. He was our chaperone. He was our spokesperson. He was our protector. He was who made us feel worthy of the big stage."

"We adored him because of his stature," says McKinney-Griffith. "What he taught us. The opportunity he gave us to be the best in the world. We were encompassed into his life, and he didn't let us go."

Shelton has a picture of Mitchell she took in San Francisco. The company was out on a sightseeing tour, which Mitchell liked to organize at every major destination. Shelton was snapping pictures for her personal collection, as she always did, when Mitchell started striking poses. She captured a moment of him being beautiful, which he always was, and silly, which he didn't always have the luxury to be. He's standing in front of the Golden Gate Bridge in fourth position croisé relevé. His arms are extended, the left stretching high toward the sun, the right behind him in noble counterbalance. His fingers are long and elegant, suspended in the flirtatious flick of ballet dancers. His whole body is reaching, reaching toward something unattainable and out of view. The sunlight catches the sharp planes of his exquisite profile, bouncing off his forehead and cheekbones, the white of his teeth. He's shot from the hips up, giving him the appearance of a phoenix in a silk-blend shirt with a wide collar, rising from waters pulled in from the Pacific Ocean. "I loved him and what he did for us," says Shelton, studying the photo. "I did. I really did. I know he loved me too. He loved all of us."

The 152nd Street Black Ballet Legacy Council exists in part because of Mitchell's passing. Some stories can be shared only when the giant living in them is gone. "I do believe that he would've tried to control us," says Rohan. *"What are you doing now? Why are you doing that? Let me suggest this."* It would have become the Arthur Mitchell story. Or the story of Dance

Theatre of Harlem. The women would have remained in the background, interchangeable, replaceable.

On December 3, 2018, mourners gathered for Mitchell's memorial service at Harlem's Riverside Church. The founding dancers—or the Grandparents, as they called themselves—gathered in a room before the service, minus Sheila Rohan, who was still recovering from hip surgery. There was a comfort in that private time beforehand, just for those who were there first.

During the grand service, one of Mitchell's younger relatives stood up to thank the overflow crowd of over 2,500 mourners for gathering to honor "Uncle Junior . . . who loved Thanksgiving and made sure that there was enough ham and turkey." Remy Martin sang Frank Sinatra's "My Way." Alicia Graf Mack, orphaned after Dance Theatre of Harlem's 2004 shuttering, unable to find work in another classical dance company, performed Mitchell's solo "Balm in Gilead." Cicely Tyson delivered a twenty-three-minute eulogy to her best friend, recalling the days of their youth, when Mitchell used to walk her home at night from the subway station.

Marcia Sells, sitting in the church she'd belonged to since 1984, mourned an essential member of her childhood. She cried and laughed at the wonder of Mitchell's life, comforted by the knowledge that his archives were in good hands at Columbia University's Rare Book and Manuscript Library, and that his legacy would endure.

It was an evening of song and dance and the balm of

remembrance. But for the founding dancers, there was also injury. They had been told that the first three pews of the church would be reserved for alumni. The organizers had them enter in a processional behind percussionist Baba Don Eaton Babatunde and his band, and once they got to the altar, the founders were supposed to peel off into their reserved seats. "They started playing the drums," says Gayle McKinney-Griffith. "But when we came in, there were people already in our reserved pews. Misty Copeland was up there sitting in our seats! There was no space for us. Lydia and I were looking at each other like, *What is this?* And she said, 'Come with me; we'll walk down together.' We just walked in a circle around the church looking stupid, saying, 'Excuse me, excuse me,' as we tried to find whatever seat we could."

The men and women who built Dance Theatre of Harlem belonged in those front few pews together, mourning the man who had brought them all together in the first place. "That was our daddy that we lost," says Lydia Abarca. Blame it on the chaos of grief, but during the service, the organizers of the event failed to acknowledge them. McKinney-Griffith sat in the back between strangers. Abarca found a seat next to Shelton. Before the reception that followed, Abarca tugged on Shelton's arms, as she would throughout the rest of the evening, saying, "Don't leave me. Don't leave me." She felt unmoored, not just from this great father figure in her life, but from her younger self, who had given everything to make his vision real. If her friend abandoned her now, she worried she might evaporate, and nobody would even notice.

Throughout the evening, the women kept finding each other in the sea of mourners, grounding each other with the salve of touch and shared memory. The tender circle of them, bound by a poignant truth.

We were there too.

18

ON DECEMBER 1, 2021, SIX MONTHS AFTER THE *NEW York Times* article about the 152nd Street Black Ballet Legacy Council, it's almost showtime in Boston. A young person dressed in stage blacks tells the women they have thirty minutes to go before they will join Misty Copeland onstage at a sold-out WBUR CitySpace event.

Copeland is promoting *Black Ballerinas: My Journey to Our Legacy,* her latest nonfiction book for kids, which offers brief windows into the lives of twenty-seven dancers who came before her. None of the Legacy Council members are in the book, because she never heard of them before reading the *Times* article. She first heard the name Lydia Abarca reading the Sunday paper on a park bench in Oakland, where she was filming a project about intergenerational equity told through dance.

The women pass the thirty minutes in a spartan conference room, with a table full of unwrapped catered food.

They'd had their hair and makeup done in a shared hotel room that afternoon. Everybody wears sparkly new outfits from T.J. Maxx and Nordstrom. They look beautiful and nervous, unsure what to expect from an evening they've long hoped for but never truly expected. They form a circle together, clasping hands and bowing their heads, thanking God for all that has brought them to this moment. "Our ancestors are rejoicing," says Abarca.

When Copeland enters the room, dressed in an oversize black sweatshirt and black sweatpants from her train ride up from New York, it takes the women a second to recognize her. Sheila Rohan is the first to stand, holding herself erect as she gazes on the younger dancer. Whatever hesitation hangs between the generations evaporates immediately as Copeland bursts into tears.

"Thank you all so much for being here," she says to the older women, and they all rise to their feet. "I can't wait. It's so important to tell your story." She envelops Rohan in a warm hug, then goes down the line embracing each of the others.

"And I thought I was the crybaby!" laughs Abarca.

Before Copeland changes out of her traveling clothes into a black blazer and crisp white blouse over a pair of tight black jeans and heels, she reveals to the women that she is five and half months pregnant with her first child. The room rejoices.

When the audience lights dim for WBUR's first in-person CitySpace event since the start of the pandemic, Lydia Abarca is introduced as the world's first Black prima ballerina. Copeland claps the loudest of all for her and angles her chair so that she can face the other women more directly. She knows who the real stars of the evening are and seems grateful just to be in their presence.

"We've wanted to meet Misty for the longest time," Abarca tells the crowd, who's seated next to Copeland onstage. The first Black prima ballerina sitting next to the world's most famous Black ballerina. Their feet still arch to the gods, though tonight they're both wearing four-inch heels. ("Between the two of us, I don't know whose foot was pointed harder," Abarca laughs later to her friends.)

"It's long overdue," says Karlya Shelton. "Long overdue."

"It's so emotional," says Copeland. "We've already cried."

The audience audibly sighs at the beauty of black-and-white photographs blown up on the screen behind the women during the conversation. A young Gayle McKinney-Griffith looks every bit the Disney princess in a black leotard and skirt, tiara resting atop her ballet bun. A joyful Shelton kicks her leg to the heavens while dancing the principal role of *Introducing . . .* Copeland pauses at a shot of Rohan, Yvonne Hall, Melva Murray-White, and McKinney-Griffith in Walter Raines's ballet *Haiku*. She says she can't tell from the black-and-white photo if they're wearing pink shoes. She asks the women to tell the audience how they started dyeing their own tights and shoes to match their skin tones.

Given McKinney-Griffith's poise onstage, nobody in the

audience would ever have guessed how nervous she was beforehand. Only her sisters see the twitching beneath her eye. But whatever stage fright she has vanishes as soon as she starts speaking. When the evening's moderator asks the members of the Legacy Council to discuss the importance of telling their stories now at this moment in history, McKinney-Griffith responds with terrific gravity. "Because we all have a voice," she says, looking intently around the room. "And we all need to project that out into the world. Otherwise someone else is going to write our history. Or not."

Shelton nods somberly, before acknowledging a cultural landscape finally reckoning with the idea that Black Lives Matter: "People are listening. People are hearing. We have to take this moment to preserve our history."

For all the warmth onstage that evening, there is a nod at the inciting elephant in the room. Copeland is asked how it could possibly be that she'd only just learned of the women up onstage with her. A cloud of regret passes over the younger dancer's face. The book she is here to sell, about Black ballerinas throughout history, stays largely tucked beneath her seat. "It's just—it's so frustrating," she says. "In writing this book, I felt so proud with being able to share so many stories of women that we should know about, but we don't. And then hearing about your stories and legacies . . ." She looks crestfallen as she makes eye contact with each woman. "It just keeps coming. Every day I learn about an incredible new part of our legacy. You've all contributed to getting me to where I am. I wouldn't be a principal dancer with ABT without all of your efforts. They deserve to be told and acknowledged."

Rohan interrupts Copeland, her voice full of authority. "But you should also know how proud we are of you. Not just us. The whole dance community."

"And we're always here for you," says McKinney-Griffith. "We're always here for you."

Copeland clasps her hands over her heart as she takes in the power of her community expanding in real time. "Thank you, thank you," she says, before turning to Abarca. "I wish I would've seen that *Dance Magazine* cover."

Abarca smiles graciously, with a modest little shrug.

"The first person of color I saw on a *Dance Magazine* cover was Lauren Anderson, and I was stunned," says Copeland. "I couldn't identify or recognize what it was that hit me to my core, because I was so young still at the time. But it was that recognition of yourself. *Oh, I do belong here.*"

Abarca reminds the younger woman about the value of sisterhood in their lives. "We had to have each other," she says, smiling at her friends onstage before shining her light on Copeland. "It was too hard to do it by yourself. And we're here for you. We have to be here for each other. You've got people who love you."

It's Sheila Rohan's eightieth birthday. The audience erupts into a spontaneous round of "Happy Birthday," which makes

Rohan cover her face in shy delight. "Oh no," she laughs, bowing her forehead in gratitude to her prayer hands.

At the end of the event, the audience rises in a standing ovation. "Would you all take a bow?" the moderator says to the ballerinas. Copeland stands up first and grabs ahold of Abarca's hand. Then all the women rise and join hands at the front of the stage. As the audience claps, the generations hold on to each other, bowing in unison. At the end of the row, Shelton's loose arm raises gracefully. Her ballet fingers are exquisite, from her gently tucked thumb to her slightly lowered middle finger.

After a flurry of hugs and photos and goodbyes, the older women pile into a shuttle bus back to the hotel. The mood is boisterous. As the women replay their favorite moments of the evening, laughing and complimenting one another, they pass a roll of candy from the front to back seats. Back when they were girls, there were hundreds of bus rides just like it after jobs well done.

Meanwhile Copeland is on a train back to New York City with her longtime friend and manager for company. She was the only Black woman at American Ballet Theatre for the first ten years of her career. These women on the bus never had to experience being in a company without a sense of community. They always had the gift of each other, onstage, in the wings, in the dressing room, in the studio, out in a world that didn't always know how to love them or take care of them. They danced with the core knowledge that no matter what, they were not alone.

Back at the hotel, they decide to keep the celebration going. After wiping off their makeup and changing out of their sparkly outfits, they reunite in Shelton's room in their pajamas and bathrobes. There are complaints of cramping ankles and arches and toes from an evening in high heels. McKinney-Griffith sighs that when she removed her false eyelashes, she lost some of her own, which she'd been so patiently growing back since her cancer. Shelton examines her face. "No, you still have lashes left; I can see them," she assures her friend.

They are already fielding calls from family. Everyone is so proud of them. *It's a Wonderful Life* is playing on the television. Shelton passes around pieces of Rohan's birthday cake.

The 152nd Street Black Ballet Legacy Council came together to write themselves back into history. In doing so, they've written themselves back into each other's lives. It's remarkable how intimacy builds when given the constancy of time and routine. "We're still learning from each other, still growing," says McKinney-Griffith. "Our sisterhood is present. It's active. It's a blessing."

"Well, that's our third act, isn't it?" says Shelton. "A proper teaching of history seems to be a problem in this country. There's a stubbornness there. Or an unwillingness. There's been so much African American history that's been denied its proper place in the annals of our country. It's really important that while we have the opportunity and a platform, we set the record straight. There have been Black ballerinas for a long time, and the fact of that takes away from no one."

That evening in Boston offered a chance to examine the real problem of the narrative of Misty Copeland's singularity. It tries to keep her isolated in a way she never asked to be, and it leaves all those who came before her stranded on the outside of history, feeling suspicious and neglected. The enemy has never been Copeland's success or her popularity. It's a culture whose narrow, cloudy, distractible eyes refused to see beyond her.

When the women first reunited, so much of what they hoped to accomplish was linking the generations as they did that night with Copeland. The visual of them onstage together called to mind Copeland's 2015 debut in *Swan Lake*, when she was presented with bouquets from Raven Wilkinson and Lauren Anderson during her final bows, the latter hoisting the younger dancer onto her toes in a fierce embrace.

"To me, we're just the tip of the iceberg," says Abarca. "I think everyone from Dance Theatre of Harlem deserves a chance to tell their story." They want to pass the microphone to all the other dancers who blew past the gatekeepers. Who expanded the definition of "flesh tone" tights and ballet shoes. Who thrived not just because of their fearless leader but also because of the sturdy scaffolding of backstage departments whose lifework enabled and enhanced their art. We need all our heroes, and they in turn deserve our humility and curiosity and respect.

If Arthur Mitchell was once a lighthouse, may new generations of dancers look to the women in the Legacy Council as lanterns. The path is long and uncertain, but it has been traveled before. Trust in the light and the promise of a long table up ahead. A Black child twirling in front of a mirror deserves to know that being the only one in the room doesn't mean that they're alone. The elders, even the ones who have passed on, wait with arms outstretched.

Révérence

DURING BLACK HISTORY MONTH IN 2022, THE 152ND Street Black Ballet Legacy Council members were the honored guests at a benefit gala for Philadelphia Ballet. The five women spent the afternoon together getting their hair and makeup done upstairs at the venue in a hotel suite. Lydia Abarca wondered if the slit in her floor-length cranberry sequin gown was too much. (It was perfect.) Sheila Rohan pleaded affectionately with the makeup artist to be able to recognize herself in the mirror at the end of her time in the chair. Karlya Shelton regaled the hair stylist with the story of how she and her husband, Omar, first fell in love during a shopping trip while living in Paris. Marcia Sells arrived late because of Met obligations but entered the suite with a flurry of stories of people she'd run into recently. As her daughter Alix attests, Marcia is somehow connected to just about every person in New York City. The room was awash with laughter and excitement and sequins and the smells of lotions and perfumes. Gayle McKinney-Griffith sat quietly and gracefully on the sofa, her legs crossed delicately at the ankles, holding on to her bottle of water. She was tired but insisted that the pleasure of being reunited in one space with her sisters overrode any discomfort.

Later, after the VIP cocktail reception and dinner, and after the women change out of their formal wear into bathrobes and soft pajamas, they comment on the *Swan Lake* pas de deux that was performed as part of the evening's entertainment. "I was doing the choreography with her in my head," says Shelton. "Wasn't everybody?" The women all raise their hands, with dreamy looks in their eyes.

The body remembers. "Music will come on, and parts of the steps or whole sections of the ballet will come up for you," says Sells. "When I hear *Holberg* on the radio, and they play the Grieg suite all the time on WQXR, I'll start moving and doing the combination, and my daughter will roll her eyes."

"Wait a minute, what about the *Concerto Barocco*?" asks Abarca. "It came on the radio the other day, and I had to jump up even though every bone in my body was cracking."

"*Barocco* and *Serenade*," offers Shelton.

"You know what else?" says Rohan. "Gayle in *Forces of Rhythm*. That pas de trois to 'He Ain't Heavy.' Whenever I hear that, wherever I am, I go straight to Gayle and that lift."

"If you put on any music that we've ever danced to, we're definitely going to move," says Shelton. "It may not look the same, but we'll stand up."

"And you know what?" says Sells with a laugh. "You can do *Serenade* sitting in a chair."

The next morning Sells returns to New York City, back to Lincoln Center, where she greets everyone from the general manager to the security guards with the same level of familiarity and interest. "Well, yeah, I'm interested in them as human beings. Some of the people of color who've worked around here have felt like, *There's nobody here for me. There's nobody who'll understand. I would never go to HR. I don't trust HR.* I think we have begun to move that needle. If that is a piece of what I can do, then okay, I'll be happy."

The remaining women pile into a van, bound for Philadelphia Ballet, where they're scheduled to lead a company class. Dressed in dance shoes and leggings and gray long-sleeve T-shirts bearing the 152nd Street Black Ballet Legacy Council's logo, they seem slightly tired from the night before, a little anxious about whether they still have the chops and energy for the task ahead.

When they enter the studio, forty-two dancers stop in midconversation and immediately start applauding. All these young people, their bodies strung like tight ropes, not a line on their faces. Their still-cold muscles are swathed in layers of thin, brightly colored fabrics, leg warmers on top of tights. Some wear booties over their ballet shoes and have wrapped their pining ankles and calves in tape.

McKinney-Griffith, her voice somewhat tremulous at first, introduces herself to the dancers. As soon as she begins leading the class through barre exercises, her soft power casts a spell over the room. Everything in the busy, noisy, tedious outside world melts away. There is just the quiet firmness of her directions and the pianist's melodies.

After running the dancers through their first series of ronds de jambe, McKinney-Griffith trades off with one of her sisters. Now Abarca demonstrates a series of barre combinations to get the dancers on their legs and centered, her limbs endless and graceful.

The dancers start shedding their layers. Hairlines dampen. An air of humidity rises in the room, released by bodies at work.

Shelton takes over from Abarca, guiding the dancers through center combinations of adagio movements, phrases of pliés and tendus and battements, finishing with small warm-up jumps. She demonstrates her requested foot and leg work mostly using her hands and arms. The elegance of her fingers and wrists is almost startling. A ballerina's grace forever flows throughout her body, a little Zah! beaming out of a sixty-six-year-old's extended pinkie.

She tags off again with Abarca, who leads the dancers through their petit allegros to their grand allegros across the floor on a diagonal. The piano melds with the steady alighting of dancers' feet on the floor, the whuffs of their breath, the rhythmic call of Abarca's voice as she urges them higher and stronger. The other women observe from their folding chairs at the front of the room, admiring the movements with an occasional sigh of empathy or affection.

Every ballet class ends the same way: with a révérence, a brief combination in the center of class, offered up as a thank-you. Much like a bow at the end of a performance, this final section is an expression of gratitude—for the pianist, for the teacher, for each other. It also allows for a structured moment of personal exhale, a chance to go inward and honor one's own effort and exertion.

Sheila Rohan takes her place in the center of the room. "So now we're doing révérence," she says. "Very simple, old school. We'll start in fifth position." She asks the pianist to play something slow. Lydia Abarca and Gayle McKinney-Griffith, whom she first met all those years ago in a church basement, flank her. Rohan floats both of her arms into demi-second position, a bird gently flexing her wings, then lifts them in tandem toward the sky, as the dancers behind her follow along. There is something almost spiritual about the generational energies during these sacred final minutes. At the front of the room is a line of calm majesty, women who know their own value, no longer fighting for the attention and respect of their teachers or critics. Behind them are rows and rows of dancers in leotards soaked with sweat, their faces flush with vigor and ambition, all their sinew and muscle, their striving and hunger. How vulnerable it is to be young. How easy it is to get lost in the tunnel of self.

After Rohan guides the dancers to a final bow, the room takes a few beats to emerge from her sacred spell. Jermel Johnson, Philadelphia Ballet's first Black male principal danseur, and one of a handful of dancers of color in class that day, approaches the women with tears in his eyes. "Thank you, thank you, thank you," he murmurs, holding his hand over his heart.

Later, he'll try to explain the power of being in the Legacy Council's presence in the studio that morning. "I still can't really put the experience of them into words," he says. "It was more of a feeling. I don't get starstruck often, usually because people are so full of themselves. These women weren't about that. It was like they brought this soft, regal, sincere feeling into the room. They were there for us. They had achieved something great in their lives, and now we're getting to see that it wasn't the end of what they had to offer."

"My mother's flame has been reignited," says Lydia Abarca's daughter, Daniella. "I see that she finally understands that it's okay for her light to shine, and she doesn't have to stay hidden."

A few months have passed since Philadelphia. The Legacy Council gathers over weak coffee and dry muffins in a hotel lobby, waiting on a van to drive them into Harlem. "Isn't this all a fairy tale?" says Abarca, who recently celebrated five years of sobriety.

"We've given each other back that connection to that piece

of our lives," says Sells. "So much of the past informs who we are today. When we first started getting together and sharing stories, it was like, 'Oh yeah, that was real. I'm not just remembering some fantasy in my head.'"

"It's been invaluable to be able to verbalize, release, reaffirm," says Shelton.

"Even if we didn't have cell phones and Instagram and tons of pictures all over the place," says Sells. "There are other people who were physically there and remember it all. It actually happened. It existed in this amazing moment in time, and now we've confirmed it to each other. We were physically together in that space, dancing and trying to achieve some perfection."

"You know how they say dancers are instruments?" says Rohan. "We didn't realize all those years that we were allowing Arthur to use us. He used us to build that wonderful place."

"We worked so hard," says Abarca.

"Otherwise, we would have been fired," says McKinney-Griffith. "Remember, he was always saying, 'You're replaceable!'"

"He didn't realize himself what he had in us," says Rohan. "That first group. Those first ten years. We were like disciples. Not of him, but of the mission."

"Of each other," says Abarca.

Shelton pulls a manila folder out of her bag, stuffed with archival research. "I have something that I wanted to show you all," she says. "I found another Black ballerina in an old magazine that I'd never heard of before." She passes around the August 1968 issue of *Sepia*, a national photojournalistic magazine dedicated to the celebration of Black excellence that went out of circulation in 1983. The issue is from the same month when four members of the future Dance Theatre of Harlem company performed in an upstate New York library. The article inside, "Girl on Her Toes," features photos of an elegant woman wearing what looks like the Swan Queen's costume of an ornate white leotard, tutu, and pale pink tights and shoes.

"Oh yeah," says Rohan, studying the picture. "I know Cleo Quitman. Oh, sure. Oh, yay!"

The story describes how a seventeen-year-old modern-dance student came under ballet's spell after watching the Russian ballerina Alexandra Danilova perform on a Detroit stage. "I was perfectly unaware of this incredibly gracious, light, and beautiful art form—ballet—with that soft, dream-like quality," Quitman told the interviewer. "I was just sitting there with my heart throbbing in my throat and tears of joy running down my cheeks!" Rejected from the School of American Ballet, she'd go on to train for two years at the Metropolitan School of Ballet alongside four other Black students, including Thelma Hill. Quitman joined Hill as one of the six founding members of the New York Negro Ballet Company, touring extensively in Europe in the late 1950s. After the company ran out of money, Quitman eventually returned to the States and started Dance General, an eight-member group that toured the South in two station wagons crammed with tape recorders, theatrical props, and costumes. In 1965, Quitman appeared as a guest artist in American Ballet Theatre's staging of Agnes de Mille's *The Four Marys* alongside Judith Jamison, Glory Van Scott, and Carmen de Lavallade. The four women were cast as maids, dancing on a set that included five white columns representing the antebellum South of de Mille's vision.

At the end of the article, the writer projects an airy optimism onto the dancer. "Miss Quitman feels that the world of ballet and dance is now open to the Black man and woman." Even though on the very same page, Quitman describes how she and her dancer husband couldn't book work when they returned from Europe to America because nightclubs didn't think a "Negro dance-couple" was good for business.

Don't tell a woman a problem is fixed when the mess of it all is still staring her in the face.

"Remember, Cleo was married to that eccentric dancer and costume designer," says Rohan.

"Bernard Johnson!" says Abarca.

"Oh my God, really?" says Sells. "Louis Johnson choreographed for her too."

Shelton shakes her head in frustration. "Now, see, I don't know why I'd never seen or heard of her before. You all knew of Cleo Quitman, but somehow, I didn't. It's a reminder that history isn't a one-person thing, or a one-group thing. It's going to take all of us."

People will forget a Black woman's work. Strip it of its magnitude and joy. Deny she was ever there in the first place. Rob the next generation of her example. The women order more coffee, their suitcases at their feet. There are so many stories still to tell.

Bis, bis, bis!

Acknowledgments

When you are the mother of a Black child, you look for representation in every room, on every screen, in every book, on every stage. You want your daughter to be so surrounded by the power of example that when she looks in the mirror at her own beautiful self, she can imagine herself as anyone and anything. It has been the gift of my professional life to be let into the worlds of Lydia Abarca, Sheila Rohan, Gayle McKinney-Griffith, Karlya Shelton-Benjamin, and Marcia Sells. I thank them for their substance, their vulnerability, their generosity, and their courage. My daughters are so lucky to have more lanterns in their lives.

Thank you to the Swans' families, who always made me feel at home. Al Mitchell. Daniella Mitchell Hampton, whose powerful prayer is at the heart of this book. Hannah Daniella Hampton. Eric Mitchell. Katie Mitchell. Delores Rohan. J. Ellsworth Mitchell. Gary Mitchell. Charlene Muhammad. Sheila Mitchell (aka Little Sheila; aka Freshie). Hope Clarke. Don Griffith. Khadija "Tariyan" Griffith. Katy Griffith. Emmit Griffith, whose beauty and goodness lightened his grandmother's spirit. Maxine Hunter. Victoria Hale. Todd Hunter. Kevin Hunter. Luanne Benshimol. Omar Benjamin. Chè Benjamin. Jean Shelton. Kyle Shelton. Alix Kruta. I wasn't lucky enough to meet Mamie Earl Sells, but the elegance of her archives, including copies of handwritten thank-you notes from P.S. 161 students, made me feel in some way as if I'd had the pleasure.

I am grateful for the conversations with Dance Theatre of Harlem family who helped widen my window into the early years of the company. Tania León. Charles De Rose. Virginia Johnson. Aminah Ahmad. Nena Gilreath. Pamela Jones. Dr. Joselli Audain Deans, who repeatedly asked me to call her Joselli but will always be "Dr. Deans!" to me.

And thank you to Misty Copeland. Gabri Christa. Nejla Yatkin. Angela Watson. Nardia Boodoo. Jermel Johnson. It was my luck to witness them falling in love with the Swans, or to hear how the women had brought grace into their lives.

All my love to Barbara Jones, the formidable captain of our large and hopeful ship. And to my agent, Betsy Lerner, who's been the wind at my back for well over a decade now. We all had the luck to work with Naomi Gibbs, who is brilliant and devoted and kind and also a fantastic walking partner on the beach. (Hi, Bina!) Thank you to Natalia Berry, Julianne Clancy, Michiko Clark, Cat Courtade, Altie Karper, Lisa Lucas, and the rest of the team at Pantheon Books who have rallied around us with so much enthusiasm. Thank you as well to Rachel Saltz, who first green-lit this story at the *New York Times*, Chloe Knapp, Ali Lefkowitz, Soleil McGhee, Howie Sanders, Nina Shaw, Nancy Utley, and everyone else who's had the best and purest interest of this project at heart from start to finish.

So many kind friends gave me a quiet room in which to work along the way. Thank you to my beloved Kalimba

Tuck. Sallie Patrick. Lizzie Dulien. Amber Williard and Tim Merrifield. Anna Krachey, Jen Cavner, Becky Tenney, and my favorite lover of words, Katy Chrisler, who doesn't dance but wants to.

I'm grateful for the love and support of my family, especially my dad, Gary Valby, who I know is looking forward to asking each of the Swans for a little dance; my stepmother, Kathy Awkard; and my aunt and godmother, Elaine Valby.

I forever am trying to make my daughters proud. Ava, when you walk into a room, the lights turn on, and, Zinnia, you are the precious breeze. Maybe you girls will grow up to be dancers, or Broadway stars, or painters, or community activists, or musicians, or lawyers, or social justice warriors, or teachers. Whatever your callings, may you meet them with a sense of possibility and passion. Trust in your sisterhood.

My family wouldn't be as healthy and whole as it is without the love and support of China Smith in our lives, and the vision she fights so hard to manifest at Ballet Afrique Contemporary Dance. Thank you, China, for your commitment to all of Austin's Black girls and boys looking at themelves in the mirror.

Writing is hard, tedious, lucky work. So is mothering. This book wouldn't have been possible without the constancy of my husband, Tim Dallesandro. He packed the school lunches, drove the kids to dance and gymnastics and soccer, read all the drafts, and turned down jobs so that I could do mine. Oh, Tim! Look what we made.

Acknowledgments from the Swans of Harlem

Lydia Abarca,
Gayle McKinney-Griffith,
Sheila Rohan,
Marcia Sells, and
Karlya Shelton

We offer our deepest, heartfelt gratitude to our families for their never-ending love and support.

We are forever indebted to Arthur Mitchell for his creation of Dance Theatre of Harlem, which initiated the sisterhood of the 152nd Street Black Ballet Legacy. We'd like to acknowledge Karel Shook, Cicely Tyson, Brock Peters, and Charles De Rose for laying the foundation of DTH; Zelda Wynn, our wardrobe mistress; Tania León, our first musical director, conductor, and composer; and *each and every dancer*, along with stage crew, musicians, teachers, choreographers, and administrative staff, whose blood, sweat, and tears transformed Mr. Mitchell's ambitious vision of a Black ballet company into reality. You are loved and not forgotten.

We owe tremendous debts of gratitude to Barbara Jones,

our literary agent, who introduced Karen Valby to us and was instrumental in getting our stories published; Karen Valby, our author, whose *New York Times* article about the Legacy Council ignited the spark of public interest that resulted in the creation of this book; and Nina Shaw, our lawyer, who has looked out for us from the day we met. These ladies have all shown genuine interest in our well-being and have become good friends and invaluable assets in our lives.

We wish to thank Lisa Lucas and Naomi Gibbs of Pantheon Books for their outstanding dedication and professionalism in producing this awesome publication, and we acknowledge the Lenape and Wappinger peoples and their ancestral lands, which include Harlem, where so much of our story took place. Thank you to our readers!

We are blessed and eternally grateful for this publication, which is only the beginning of our Act Three. Act One brought us together as pioneers in the world of ballet, and Act Two was going our separate ways to explore what else life had to offer. Throughout it all, our sisterhood stayed very much alive. Thank you all, and thank you, Heavenly Spirit and Creator.

Index

About the Author

Karen Valby is the author of two books of nonfiction: *The Swans of Harlem* and *Welcome to Utopia: Notes from a Small Town*. A contributing editor for *Vanity Fair*, she also writes for the *New York Times*, *O Magazine*, *Glamour*, *Fast Company*, and *EW*, where she spent fifteen years writing about culture. She and her family live in Austin, Texas, where her daughters study dance at Ballet Afrique.

KARENVALBY.COM

𝕏 ⦾